Praise for Rachel Fordham

Beyond Ivy Walls

"Reading *Beyond Ivy Walls*, I was immersed in the hustle and bustle of Monticello in the early 1900s and the smells and noises of the factory. But what about the outside world and the lives of the girls working there? Set against this backdrop, Fordham weaves a masterful tale of romance, innuendos, love found and love lost. Intrigue and mysterious twists in this historical fiction will take you back to life in a simpler time . . . or was it?"

—Jan M. Hoag, second great-granddaughter of Hoag Duster Company founder William Elam Hoag

"I am a longtime fan of Rachel Fordham, having read all of her books, and anxiously awaiting the latest! I love Rachel's easy-reading and mysteriously written novels, always ending with a profound message. What a joy and honor to read an early draft of *Beyond Ivy Walls*. I couldn't stop reading this delightful story that reminded me of "Beauty and the Beast," and the value of inner characteristics over outer appearance. It is a testimony of true sacrificial love, from the beginning to the end of this special book. The setting in Monticello, Iowa, my own personal birthplace, touched my heart. The story of my great-grandfather Elmer Hoag's Feather Duster Factory was brought back to life. Thank you, Rachel!"

—Cathy Hershberger, great-grand daughter of Elmer and [illegible] Hoag

The Letter Tree

"*The Letter Tree* is a sweet, heartfelt romance that contains all the things I love best in historical romance, including a beautiful epistolary element. Rachel Fordham writes with warmth and grace, crafting a winning love story that's sure to please. I thoroughly enjoyed it!"

—Mimi Matthews, *USA TODAY* bestselling author of *The Belle of Belgrave Square*

"Combining charming hints of *You've Got Mail* with the poignancy of *Romeo and Juliet*, *The Letter Tree* is a journey of forgiveness and reconciliation and overcoming differences. Rachel Fordham's characters are quirky and relatable, and fascinating bits of 1920s culture color the story. An enjoyable and romantic read!"

—Sarah Sundin, bestselling and Christy Award–winning author of *The Sound of Light* and *Until Leaves Fall in Paris*

"Another tender, emotionally satisfying book from Rachel Fordham. Rachel's masterful writing style and cleverly crafted storyline bring a lovely and heartfelt romance to life. Highly recommended."

—Jennifer Beckstrand, *USA TODAY* bestselling author of *Second Chances on Huckleberry Hill*

"Skillfully layered and engaging from the start, this dashing tale of secret pen pals and forbidden romance set in the 1920s is sure to win the hearts of readers everywhere. An absolutely delightful read!"

—Nicole Deese, Christy Award–winning author

"*The Letter Tree* is a little bit *You've Got Mail* and a little bit of Hallmark's *Signed, Sealed, Delivered* and all sweet, immersive romance. Using delightful and beloved tropes to spin her own unique historical tapestry, Fordham's latest character-driven historical novel is destined to enthrall readers of Robin Lee Hatcher and Gabrielle Meyer."

—Rachel McMillan, author of *The London Restoration* and *The Mozart Code*

"Once again author Rachel Fordham weaves her magic in this story of enduring love and the importance of a long and lasting friendship—not only to withstand the heartache of hatred and misunderstanding but to allow romance the chance to take root slowly, gently, steadily, becoming as strong and resilient as the mightiest oak. A tale both tender and endearing, *The Letter Tree* is sure to delight anyone who believes in true love."

—Kate Breslin, award-winning author of *In Love's Time*

"Old family secrets form the backdrop of *The Letter Tree*, a compelling tale set in twentieth-century New York. A feud that made bitter rivals of two families comes to a head when a romance ignites between their son and daughter. With a deft touch, Fordham weaves themes of freedom and forgiveness into this enchanting story. The sweet romance and multi-layered mystery keep the pages turning!"

—Denise Hunter, bestselling author of the Riverbend Romance series

"Love transcends all in *The Letter Tree*. A sweet love story rife with tension that will keep readers guessing from start to finish."

—Megan Walker, award-winning author of *Lakeshire Park*

"Penned with engaging prose, *The Letter Tree* offers a fresh approach to the forbidden romance trope. Throw in a riveting plot, a cast of layered characters, plus the vivid backdrop of the Roaring '20s, and you have an enthralling novel that is sure to captivate readers' hearts. This story is not to be missed!"

—Rachel Scott McDaniel, award-winning author of *The Starlet Spy*

"In *The Letter Tree*, Rachel Fordham spins two classic romances—*Romeo and Juliet* and *You've Got Mail*—into an engaging story sure to charm readers. Exploring familial themes of loyalty versus truth, this is a poignant book meant for the true romantics out there who believe love triumphs and hope is never wasted, as well as those who may doubt. I challenge anyone to finish reading it and not feel uplifted. Perfect for fans of Karen Witemeyer and Jennifer Deibel."

—Kimberly Duffy, author of *The Weight of Air*

"'Two houses' is how Shakespeare's *Romeo and Juliet* begins and Rachel Fordham has captured the essence of that classic in *The Letter Tree*—but oh so much more. With wit and imagination, Ms. Fordham brings us a refreshing view of family mysteries, misunderstandings, and the hope of forgiveness in even the most dire circumstances. I loved this story that is an inventively told and deeply considered romance. It is a joy to read and remember. Best of all, *The Letter Tree* has a much happier ending than that other work of 'Two houses.'"

—Jane Kirkpatrick, award-winning author of *Beneath the Bending Skies*

"What a true delight! I couldn't wait to return to this gem of a novel and see what the next page held. I've never read anything quite like it, so I never knew what was coming next. The charming premise drew me in, and then I was hooked, and couldn't wait to see what would come of these letter writers stuck in an impossible situation, and how they would each find out the true identity of the other. This is the sort of timeless love story that charms you immediately and remains with you for a long time."

—Joanna Davidson Politano, award-winning author of *The Lost Melody* and other historical fiction

"*The Letter Tree* transported me to a place where characters feel real, dreams come true, and happily ever after is actually possible. It's everything I love in a book."

—Shelley Shepard Gray, *New York Times* and *USA TODAY* bestselling author

"*The Letter Tree* is a charming and captivating romance that reminds us of the transformative power of love, hope, and the written word. Palpable chemistry, complex familial relationships, and shared dreams that transcend barriers blend beautifully in this ambitious offering from Fordham. It was worth every emotional second from start to finish."

—Rhonda McKnight, award-winning author of *The Thing About Home*

Beyond Ivy Walls

ALSO BY RACHEL FORDHAM

The Letter Tree
Where the Road Bends
A Lady in Attendance
A Life Once Dreamed
Yours Truly, Thomas
The Hope of Azure Springs

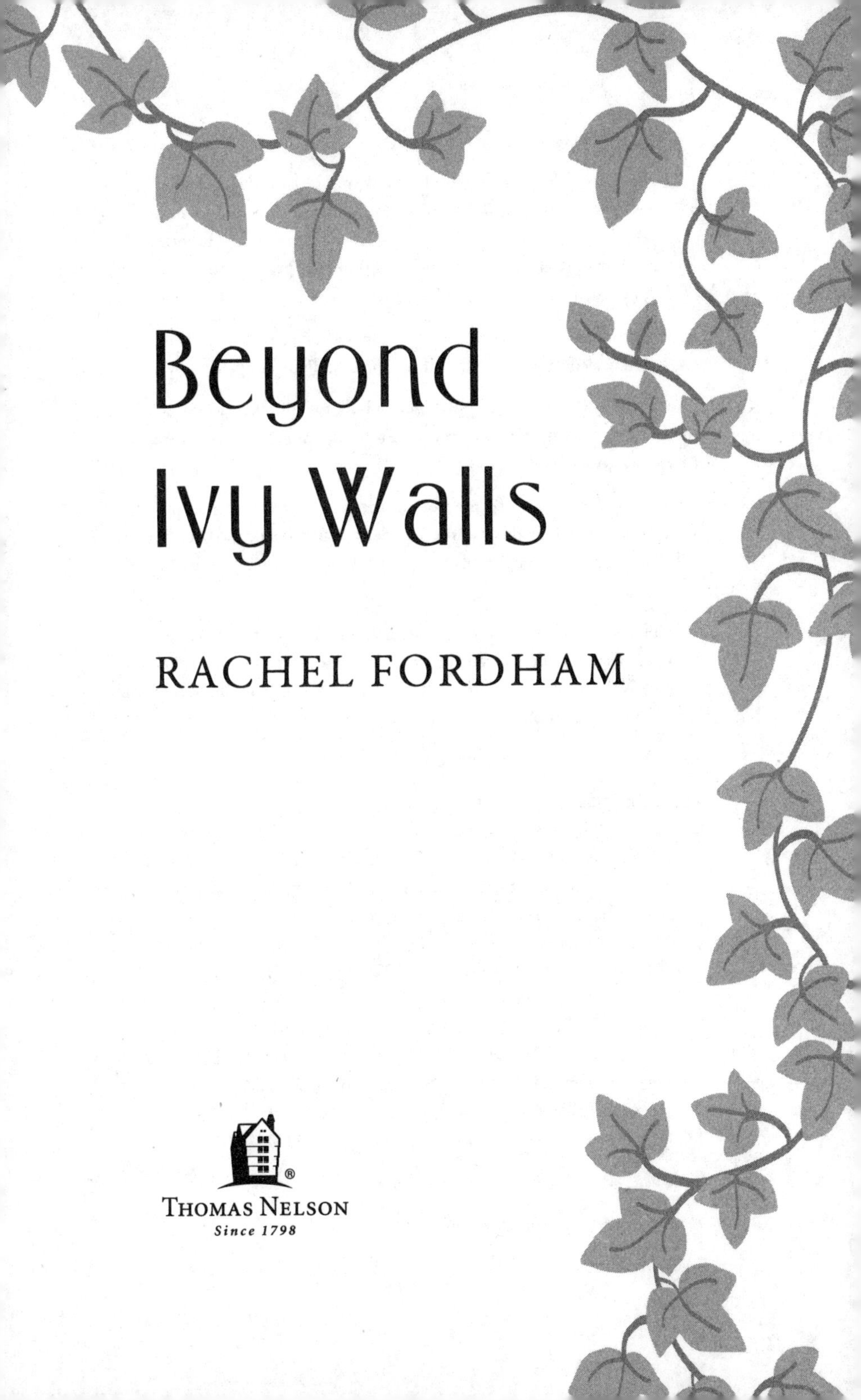

Beyond Ivy Walls

RACHEL FORDHAM

THOMAS NELSON
Since 1798

Beyond Ivy Walls

Published in Nashville, Tennessee, by Thomas Nelson. Thomas Nelson is a registered trademark of HarperCollins Christian Publishing, Inc.

Thomas Nelson titles may be purchased in bulk for educational, business, fundraising, or sales promotional use. For information, please email Special-Markets@ThomasNelson.com.

Library of Congress Cataloging-in-Publication Data

Names: Fordham, Rachel, 1984- author.
Title: Beyond ivy walls / Rachel Fordham.
Description: Nashville, Tennessee : Thomas Nelson, 2024. | Summary: "Rem iniscent of Beauty and the Beast, a recluse and a young woman discover that the scars of life are no match against an act of love"—Provided by publisher.
Identifiers: LCCN 2024007569 (print) | LCCN 2024007570 (ebook) | ISBN 9780840718808 (paperback) | ISBN 9780840718815 (epub) | ISBN 9780840718846
Subjects: LCGFT: Christian fiction. | Romance fiction. | Novels.
Classification: LCC PS3606.O747335 B49 2024 (print) | LCC PS3606. O747335 (ebook) | DDC 813/.6—dc23/eng/20240223
LC record available at https://lccn.loc.gov/2024007569
LC ebook record available at https://lccn.loc.gov/2024007570

Title page art by Tanarch from Adobe Stock

Printed in the United States of America

24 25 26 27 28 LBC 5 4 3 2 1

For my sisters: Anna, Stephanie, Leah, Heather, and Tia,

I treasure our time together, your advice, the nights we stay up way too late talking, the memories we've shared, and the ones we are yet to make.

I have for the first time found what I can truly love—I have found *you*.

—Charlotte Brontë, *Jane Eyre*

Chapter 1

Monticello, Iowa
SPRING 1903

Mama always said eavesdropping was the surest way to stir up trouble and make enemies out of perfectly good neighbors. For the first twenty-three years of Sadie West's life, she'd adhered to her mother's counsel and turned away from any gossip within earshot. But when she left home and found employment at the Hoag feather duster factory as a sorter, the only way to pass the time was to lean closer to the chin-waggers and glean what she could from their conversations. Under the circumstances, she rationalized that even her pious mother would understand.

Her father's riding accident had forced her to leave the farm a month ago and come to the city for work. In that time Sadie had overheard conversations about courtships gone awry for scandalous reasons, bar fights that required police intervention, and upcoming socials that made her long for Marvin Bennett's company. The chatter kept her mind occupied as she tossed feathers into their designated bins. It was mindless work that left her legs aching and her body covered in a fine layer of turkey dander. Hardly a romantic job.

But the bits and pieces of Monti gossip made the long days pass quicker, keeping her imagination fed and giving her titillating tidbits to work into her letters to her younger sisters, who remained at home doing what they could to plow the fields without the help of their bedridden pa. The thought of her family's situation made her shiver, but she shoved down the worries that threatened to surface. Circumstances were bleak, but things would become only more dire if she gave in to the heavy feelings.

"I thought Otis Taylor would have come back by now," Alta, a sorter stationed to Sadie's immediate right, said to Sylvia at the end of the line. Sadie's ears perked up at the mention of the elusive gentleman. His name and story intrigued her and had provided hours of entertainment as she took the fragments she knew about him and filled in the rest however she felt inclined. Otis Taylor, the handsome son of Monti elite, who'd left due to his musical genius a decade ago, was now expected to return. And the women of the town could not wait to bat their eyes and compete for his attention.

She looked at the mountain of feathers before her and buried a smile that crept to her lips. Someday she, too, would go back home and rush into the arms of her loved ones. She'd tell her sisters every detail of her time away and make it all sound thrilling. And someday, Lord willing, she would see Marvin strolling up her long walkway, back from school and finally ready to proclaim himself smitten. Gone would be his tentative smile; he'd grin at her and take her in his arms. She shook her head, chiding herself for allowing her musings to have too much rein.

"I heard he's too busy performing." Sylvia's lips stuck out in a pout as she continued her conversation with Alta. "It's not fair.

The rest of the world gets to hear Otis play, and we don't. It'd be so exciting if he came home. And he must—the house is his now."

Sadie inched closer, preferring talk of Otis, who was as good as fictional to her, over the heavier thoughts that weighed on her mind. Old worries over her father's abysmally slow recovery and her family's desperate financial situation, as well as new worries about her room and board, were ever pressing. But she had a job, and although her sacrifice had not solved all her problems, she'd managed to keep the bank at bay for this long already—that was something to be proud of. She stood a little taller. She'd sort feathers forever if that was what her situation required.

The Hoag duster factory had once been a broom factory. But as the story went, or perhaps it was the truth, the senior Mr. Hoag was approached one day by a man with turkey feathers. He insisted on a broom made of the plumage, but their stiff, brittle nature was not conducive to broom making. Rather than abandon the idea entirely, Mr. Hoag removed the pith from the feathers and attached them to a shorter handle, creating a novel duster that was soon in high demand. Such high demand that when Sadie's father's horse lost its footing and fell on him, breaking bones in his back and legs that forced the never-idle man into bed with a dismal prognosis, she'd easily been able to find a job at the factory. She'd left home in a hurry, promising the predatorial bank that she'd send money and that they had no reason to call in the family's debt. Her sisters had also rallied, promising to turn the soil over themselves and plant as many fields as they could. Though all their efforts might prove futile, they were fighters, and Sadie would keep fighting.

She grabbed a handful of feathers and began tossing them in with renewed gusto. Her sisters had often called her the General because of her tendency to take charge. As General, she'd persevere, even if doing so meant long days of tedious work and, she cringed, even longer nights spent in squalor.

When the current owner of the duster factory, Mr. Elmer Hoag, asked Sylvia to go to a different station and help remove pith, the conversation that had kept Sadie's imagination engaged died, replaced by only the whir of the lathe turning handles. Sadie sucked in her bottom lip, debating striking up her own conversation with Alta.

She cleared her throat. "I've been meaning to ask, have you always lived in Monticello?"

Alta pursed her lips before answering. "I was born in Des Moines. I came to Monti when I was seven."

"Must be nice knowing everyone," she muttered. The pinched expression on Alta's face had her regretting that she'd said anything. Alta didn't want to be her friend—that much was obvious. She'd been short with Sadie from the start, always sharing sideways glances with the other sorters and making snide comments about Sadie's clothes being out of fashion.

Alta's hands stilled. She turned and faced Sadie, a too-sweet smile on her face. "I know you're new here, and I can tell you really want to fit in—"

"I wasn't trying—"

"No need to explain yourself. I'll give you some advice. In the city people bathe often. We pride ourselves on our appearance. Your frame isn't so bad; you're dainty and you've a long neck." Sadie tried not to shy away from Alta's appraisal. "Cleaned up, you wouldn't be stunning, but you'd be tolerable. If you want to be noticed here, you've really got to try harder. The turkey dander is an inch thick on you. It's appalling. And it makes you look terribly out of place."

Sadie ducked her head and focused on the banded feathers in her hands. Did Cinderella ever want to cry out that it wasn't her fault she was covered in soot? Sadie certainly wanted to lash out at Alta and tell her how she'd been kicked out of Mrs. Smith's house because a new boarder could pay more than she'd been able to offer. She wanted to scream and tell her that if she went to the boardinghouse, she would not have enough money to make the monthly payment to the bank, and her family could lose everything. Nor was going home an option—they needed her meager wages.

Angry words rose in her throat, but she swallowed them in one uncomfortable gulp. No one could know that she'd taken up residence in an abandoned building. If her family found out, they would worry and call her home, but then they'd be in worse straits and could all end up without a place to live. Only harm would come from telling, and so she offered no defense.

"You're right," Sadie said, managing to keep her voice steady. "I've been preoccupied. Thank you for the advice."

She made no further attempts at conversation with Alta. With only the voice in her own head for company, the hands on the clock moved slowly. At last the bell rang and she was able to slink away from the bustling feather duster factory, back to the ruins she currently called home.

Dear Sisters,

She wrote huddled against the wall in the dusty, abandoned factory, her thin coat pulled tightly around her shoulders in a weak attempt to ward off the evening chill. Molly, Violette, and Flora expected her to write, and normally she treasured the opportunity to share her news and offer what encouragement she could. It helped her feel close to them despite the physical distance. Today she felt less inclined to write, but their neighbor and friend Peter Tippins, who delivered goods between the rural community and the city, would be waiting tomorrow for her letter. If she didn't write, her family would worry. If she wrote the truth about her circumstances, they would also worry.

She tilted her head to the side and looked out the broken window at the hazy sky that was just beginning to shift from day to night. Dallying would not do. When the sunlight faded, all would be dark.

> I'm now residing in a room much larger than I need. It's not grand, but it is big, and when the rain pours I am dry. It's a good place to sit and think and dream of what life will be like when all of this is over.

She'd written regularly for years, happy stories with beautiful endings, and stopped only when Marvin went off to college, leaving her with nothing but a sinking feeling in the pit of her stomach. The urge to write hadn't come back, not even when she convinced herself that Marvin did care and that he'd simply wanted to wait to make his feelings known until they could act on their love. She would have to be creative now, because the truth of her circumstances was more than her sisters could bear. A little fiction, a little embellishment, and one could almost believe this hovel was a castle and the future was full of promise.

Movement in the corner of the abandoned factory caught her eye. A fat rat scurried across the floor. She pulled her legs in close to her chest and forced herself to think only of the words on the page.

Sadie wrote until the night sky grew too dark to see by, telling her sisters what she could while leaving out the truth about the draft, the broken glass, and her heavy heart. These she would bear alone.

Dust and spiders filled her new home, causing her to sneeze, and during the darkest hours of the night, she often heard the hoot of the owls or the yap of a distant coyote. In the far corner, where the draft was less noticeable, she curled on her side. With her eyes closed, the strange sounds were louder. The wind whirred and whistled.

Once when she was a child, Pa had taken her roller-skating. He'd seen the desire in her eyes, and though they never had extra money, he paid to rent skates and smiled as she toddled around on unsteady legs. Ever since, she'd longed to go back and feel the excitement of the crowd. The whir of the wind brought the memory back, and soon she felt her breathing come softer and easier. She had lived many beautiful days, and with the memory fresh in her heart, she could believe there were more to come.

A sliver of moon, with a smattering of clouds dancing in front of it, offered a bit of light to the otherwise murky night. Otis glared. A moonless sky would have been better. He'd planned his late-night return with care, but he had no way of dimming the moon's light.

His long and tiresome journey ended in front of the mansion of his boyhood. There it was, looming before him, as large as he remembered. Stiff and gabled, with tall chimneys, sculptures, and fountains. A masterpiece, declaring to the world: "The Taylors live here!" Or at least they had. He was the last Taylor left, and he did *not* intend to live here. He was merely coming back so he could sell the place and be done with it forever. His father was dead. His brother was dead. He was free to rid himself of it all.

"Shall I put your luggage inside?" the driver asked.

"On the veranda will do." He wanted the man gone so he could face the memories alone, free from spectating eyes. Feelings long suppressed were already fighting inside, pressing against his chest, determined to surface after so many years dormant. He patted his dog, Wolf, pretending to comfort the animal, when in fact he was the one seeking reassurance. "It's late. I'm sure you have places to be."

"I am eager to get home and to my wife." In a hurried voice, the man added, "But I won't be telling her you are returned."

"See to it you don't." Otis had paid the man a sizable sum to keep his return quiet.

"I ain't no flap jaw."

"Good." Otis tugged at his hat, lowering it farther on his head. He didn't like the prospect of becoming the subject of gossip, and he certainly didn't want callers. "I have matters to settle and wish to do so in private."

"You told me." The man looked skeptical but didn't argue. He picked up Otis's luggage and carried it to the veranda. Otis's belongings were sparse. It took little time to unload everything.

"Do you need anything else, sir?"

Otis shook his head. "No, go on home—you've been paid."

"Good night to you, Mr. Taylor."

Otis flinched. The title was his father's, not his. His hands tingled as he waited for the snap of the reins, the creak of the carriage, and the sound of wheels growing faint in the distance to confirm he was alone. Just him and Wolf and the walls of ivy.

Alone.

He stood as stiff as the statues in the yard, free to face the house and its ill-begotten memories. He'd been a boy here—there had even been a time when he had been happy in this mansion. Days of racing his brother, Reginald, across the yard, playing marbles, and dreaming of a future in this very town. It had all been short-lived. Those blissful memories now buried beneath the thick and heavy happenings that followed.

He sighed. Reginald was gone. As were his parents. And now he was here, no longer a boy but a man. How strange a twist it was, to be returned, but only because he was the last.

Chapter 2

Sadie crept away from her makeshift bed early in the morning, determined to bathe in the creek before going to work. Her hair would be wet, but at least it would be free of its oily sheen. She needed to hurry so she would have time to wash her extra clothes and lay them out to dry. Staying clean while living in filth had proved difficult, but she was resolute. Alta's words stung more than she wanted to acknowledge, and from now on she would go to whatever lengths necessary to maintain at least a moderate level of cleanliness. Not for Alta, of course, but because her own pride demanded it.

The sun was not yet up, and fading stars still twinkled in the sky as she pulled herself through the broken window, soap and soiled clothes in hand. The abandoned factory sat near the road. Behind it was a magnificent house, taller and finer than any other in Monticello, and past that was a creek.

With a gentle step she began her procession toward the creek, mindful of twigs that might snap from her weight. Hanging laundry and chimney smoke had told her someone lived in the magnificent house, but from her careful watching she knew the schedule they kept. No one would be up now. She was safe to bathe and wash her clothes so long as she didn't dally.

The soft babbling of the water met her ears, alerting her that she'd made it past the house. Its pleasant sound was a welcome change from the scratching feet she heard at night. The rustle of the leaves in the wind, the water, and the dew-laden grasses elicited a sigh. She savored the calm of it all.

One more glance in every direction assured her that she was alone. Covered by darkness, she undressed down to her undergarments and slid into the knee-high, frigid water of the creek. Bending lower, she splashed water on her arms and onto her shoulders. The duster factory—with its feathers and dander floating in the air, mixed with sawdust from the lathe that spun the hubs and handles—was not an easy place to keep clean in. Her brow often grew sweaty in the hot room and every particle that floated in the air raced for her damp flesh, sticking to her with vengeance.

She worked the soap against her skin, scrubbing until at last her arms were clean and the freckles that sprinkled her skin were visible once again. She was about to begin her face and hair when she heard steps coming closer. An animal? Though she looked up and saw nothing, she sank deeper into the water, holding herself still despite the cold.

Everything went quiet except her breath, which seemed to come louder with each passing second.

After a few more moments passed, she lifted one foot through the water, then the other. Like a silent catfish she moved closer to the shore, praying that whatever caused the noise was gone. If being caught squatting was bad, being caught bathing in the creek in thin, wet underthings was surely worse.

A rustle in the brush near the bank caused her to flinch. Fleeing to the far side of the water was tempting, but her clothes were waiting for her on the factory side. Her numb and tingling legs begged her to decide quickly. Flee, hide, or fight. She had to do something.

She could curse herself for caring so much about her appearance. Never again would vanity get the better of her. Let Alta mock her—let them all mock her.

When she heard another noise, she chose to act. She crept closer, ready to glance over the bank, hoping to see a deer, racoon, or opossum. The beady night eyes of any animal were sure to make her skin crawl, but she would face them. If necessary, she'd fight off the creature. With no weapon, she prepared herself to appear large and intimidating. One more deep breath, one more silent prayer, and then she poked her head up just high enough to see beyond the bank.

Coming face-to-face with the wet nose of a panting dog, she relaxed—only to tense again when she saw it pick up one of her shoes.

"Give me my shoe," she said in a firm whisper. "Come on."

Obediently, it dropped her shoe. She smiled, proud of her commanding voice. But her moment of smugness was instantly dashed when the dog arched its back, lifted its head toward the sky, and howled.

There was no time to think. She flew from the water, wet and still dirty except for her clean arms. In one swift motion she grabbed her sparse, filthy belongings and raced past the ornate home, bound for the old factory. Giving no thought to modesty, she flew across the yard as she made her escape. She didn't look left or right—she kept her eyes on the broken window, running for it like a mouse fleeing a cat, only it was a dog at her heels.

Only once she was inside did she stop to catch her breath. The dog continued to howl, bellowing over and over, a hunter announcing to the world that it had treed an old ringtail.

She wasn't about to be caught dripping wet, shaking from cold and fear. Quick as she could, she pulled her dry skirt and shirtwaist over her wet underthings, brushed and braided her still-grimy hair, and then peered out the window, ready to make her second escape, this time to the Hoag factory.

The dog let a final howl ring through the air before quieting. It paced back and forth in front of her window entrance. She looked over her shoulder, trying to think of a way to get past it. Every couple of days, she bought a loaf of bread and rationed it as long as she could. Her loaf was down to a dry crust. She wrapped it in a handkerchief and peered out the window. Her stomach rumbled as she looked again at her crust, but she could forgo a meal if it meant escape.

Where had this dog come from? She could now see that the dog wore a collar, which—drat—made it far less likely the animal was a stray. Someone owned it and took it for walks. Perhaps it was lost and its owner was searching all of Monticello for it. That would be the best scenario. Once it was found, she could go back to her quiet existence, sneaking in and out unnoticed.

The possibly lost dog continued its nearby marching, and she could wait no longer for it to go away. She had to meet Peter and then get to work. Losing her job would make this entire endeavor for naught, which was an outcome she could not accept.

"Hello there," she said in a soft voice as she crept out the window. She'd been raised with animals. Surely this dog only wanted attention. "What's your name?"

It cocked its head to the right and then to the left, its dark ears flopping over with each tilt. Its coat was mottled and spotted, appeared almost blue, and its expression was friendly. Sadie stepped closer, held her hand out, and continued speaking softly. "Don't bark. I'm leaving. You can have the run of the place."

For one moment she believed her crisis averted. Then it leaned back on its haunches and tilted its head to the sky. Obstinate, stubborn animal!

"Here!" She meant to throw the bread only, but her handkerchief went with it. No time to fret that loss, she ran for the Hoag factory while the dog went for its prize.

Otis's heart pounded against his chest in the most uncomfortable way as he surveyed the parlor of his childhood home. He'd tried sleeping when he arrived but had found rest unattainable. When Wolf cried, begging to go out before the sun had even risen, he obliged. Wolf, crazy old coon dog, ran for the creek as soon as the door was open. Otis shrugged. Wolf might be excited about Monticello, but that didn't mean *he* had to be.

So he stood in the parlor, waiting for his dog to come back, all the while fighting the memories he saw when he looked around the room. Years of trying to forget proved ineffective as the flood of remembrances crashed against him with storm-like force. With gritted teeth he crossed the carpeted floor to the corner seat where his mother had preferred to sit in the dim evenings. He let his hand run across the tall wingback chair and tried to remember her face, but a mere outline was all he could invoke.

His father had often sat on the other side of the room. When Otis's gaze went there, he instantly saw the man he'd once looked up to, the man who let him down, hurting both his body and soul. His father had been narrow-shouldered and wiry, a driven man always reaching higher, never satisfied. Otis shook his head, trying to get the image to fade, but it lingered like a foul odor.

Wolf bawled like he always did when he caught the scent of a coon or even a squirrel. Fool dog wasn't overly particular about what he chased.

Otis went to the window, pulled back the drapes, and peered out, spying a flash of white. A person?

When he lost sight of the figure, he went to the door and opened it, trying for a better look. But whatever he thought he'd seen was gone. He shook his head. Being back at the Taylor mansion was already affecting his mind. Returning was foolhardy—he never should have agreed to come. Someone else should have managed the sale and he should have stayed hidden away.

Why had he come back? He'd asked himself many times. And every time he rationalized, convincing himself that his return would make the sale of the property easier. But in the pit of his stomach, he knew there was more to it than that. For years he'd waited to be beckoned home, and it had never happened. If he was being honest, he would admit that he'd returned so he could step into the house of his childhood and attempt to settle the tumult of the past. If he faced it, would he find peace?

Foolish. Here he was staring at his father's chair, feeling no liberation. Only the tightening of chains.

"Otis?" Leon Dawson's voice echoed through the hall. The man and his wife, Mildred, had faithfully worked for the Taylor family since Otis was a lad. It was Leon who had sent word calling Otis back to Monticello after his brother's death. Six letters later, he'd finally agreed to return.

"I'm in here." He tugged at his vest, as though clothing free of wrinkles would somehow make him less of an oddity. There was no hiding the uneasy feeling that had overtaken him since the carriage rolled into Monticello. "I didn't mean to wake you. Wolf wanted out."

"Mildred heard you. She shoved me and told me to come and see if you were in need of anything."

"No . . . N-nothing." Otis stumbled over his words. He'd lived isolated so long and conversed so rarely that his tongue caught in his mouth. "I thought . . . I thought I saw Wolf chasing after . . . something."

"We've coons out there."

At the risk of sounding out of his head, he said, "I thought it was a person. A woman, perhaps, but not in a dress." Heat raced to his face. "She was clothed, but—"

The dog bawled again. Otis sprang to the door, throwing it open. He saw nothing but Wolf.

"Come here, boy." Otis whistled several times until at last Wolf came running, carrying something in his mouth. "What have you got there?"

Wolf dropped his treasure for Otis to scoop up. "A handkerchief. It's got stitching on it."

Leon stepped closer. "I don't know where he found that. Must be something that was lying around awhile."

"It's got breadcrumbs in it, and"—he brought it closer to his nose—"it smells like birds."

"Birds?"

"Yes, how peculiar." Otis pointed to the hearth where the dog's favorite blanket lay. "Go on. You've been up long enough, as have I."

Wolf looked back toward the door before lying down.

"Is the old dog run still in working order? If he's going to find things to steal, I might not be able to let him roam."

"It's not had dogs in it since your brother died." Leon rubbed his wrinkled forehead. "I haven't inspected it for some time. I believe the winter storms did damage, but we could work on making repairs."

"I should have come sooner. Then all this would have been sold and done with long before any storms." Or maybe he should not have come at all, but he kept that thought to himself. Leon couldn't understand, at least not fully, the many memories that haunted him.

"I did write you as soon as your brother died." Leon sat, looking nearly as comfortable in the house as Wolf.

"I wasn't sure . . ." Otis's mouth went dry, so he let his words trail off. He'd not come with the first letter because he hadn't wanted to accept his brother's death. And he'd not come after the other letters because this was not how he wanted his homecoming to go.

"You're here now and we can talk about the sell. Or I can wait until you are settled in more—"

"Settle in? I've come to sell the place and be off. I'll linger a month, maybe two, while it's settled, then I'll go." Otis looked around the dark room that had once been home. There was no warmth, no swelling in his chest, no feelings of homecoming. He wasn't going to spend his life hiding in Monticello, tormented by the past.

"Very well. We still need to discuss the financial situation your brother left you with and decide how you want to go about the sell."

"Go about it? I want to find a buyer and exchange all this for money. How difficult can that be?"

"Do you want to try to sell all of it together or separately? Do you wish to keep any of it? Do you want to sell the furniture, your brother's rifles, your mother's dishes—"

"Dishes . . ." His mother had special ordered them. They'd arrived packed in crates with straw tucked carefully around each dish. Flowers, small and hand-painted, along each edge. Material things meant little to him, so why did he suddenly have the urge to find the long-forgotten dishes? "I don't know what I'd do with them." He looked away, alarmed by the lump that so quickly formed in his throat. "As for the businesses, my father never included me in his financial affairs. I'll take most any reasonable offer." The room was full of portraits, chairs, trinkets. "What am I to do with it all? Pack it into the woods?"

"The woods?"

"Or wherever I go next."

He'd inherited the house, the businesses, and every worldly possession his family had left behind, and he felt no inkling of interest in making them his own. The thought of his mother stirred a fondness, yes, but the rest could all go. It could burn to nothing more than hot coal and he would not care. "If you called me back to try to convince me to keep it all running, yours is a fool's errand. Monticello will never be home. I won't stay here. I don't know why I even came."

"It doesn't have to be home. I know . . . I am sure it is difficult." Leon's face filled with a sadness so intense that Otis had to look away. "I suggest we put off the sell."

"Put it off? Don't play games with me. I told you—this is not my home. I don't want it."

"I did not mean to suggest putting it off forever, only until we have thoroughly gone through the estate's books and talked to the bank. You may not want these properties, but there is money in them, and you don't want to sell them off cheaply and then discover your brother left you with a gambling debt you overlooked. We've had several letters from debtors saying that Reginald owed them. Thus far we've been able to stave them off by telling them that Reginald's finances are still being settled."

"Hardly seems fair that the cast-off son has to come home and settle the dealings of his reckless brother," Otis mumbled, crossing his arms.

"Life is rarely fair." Leon smiled sadly. "I'm not sure what the word even means."

Otis had no comment. He'd wrestled with the notion for years, never satisfied with the answers he found. In this moment, sleep-deprived and assaulted by the memories he'd fought so hard to tuck away, he felt utterly incapable of grappling with questions that would never have answers.

"It's good to have you back, even if it's only a temporary arrangement," Leon said, changing the subject. "Though I do wish it were under different circumstances."

"Yes, well . . ." Otis looked around, his gaze landing on his dog. "Wolf seems to like it. We'll work together to settle matters, then I'll be off."

The bluetick coonhound who rarely held still lay contently by the fireplace, his head across his paws. Otis envied him. With no memories of this place, Wolf was free to see the grandeur of the mansion, hear the singing of the creek, and stretch his legs on the grounds. Otis let out a shaky laugh. What an odd recluse he had become, believing his dog's life more appealing than his own.

"It wasn't right of your brother to take over your father's businesses without consulting you."

Otis nodded. He'd not wanted the bicycle business or his father's investments, but when he'd received no word from his brother after his father's passing, the sting of rejection pierced him again. Where once they'd dreamed of lives interwoven, in the end, they had shared little.

"But your brother . . . he lost his way. I wish the two of you . . . Well, it's done now. No use dwelling on what can never be. The town never knew of your brother's shortcomings, and they don't know about your condition. They hold the Taylor family in high regard, believing the facade they've been presented with."

"Why have you been so loyal through it all? You knew the Taylor family's secrets. You could have left."

Leon paused before speaking. His features softened. "Your mother loved both her boys. Your father . . . he did care. But—"

"He loved his business and reputation and money." Otis didn't want to be patronized. He could still remember the look on his father's face when he'd sent him away.

"Perhaps he did, but he still worried over you."

"He had an odd way of showing me his concern. An occasional letter tucked between tonics. And all his cures . . . you know what they did to me."

Leon ran his hand over the arm of the chair, and once again Otis was taken back. It was in this room that his father had told Otis that he'd be sent away. The events of so long ago should not cause such a visceral reaction, yet they did. He rubbed at his forehead, trying to keep his strong feelings at bay, but holding back a stampede would have been easier.

"Your mother asked Mildred and I to look out for you and your brother. We had no power to bring you home as long as your father was alive, and your brother . . . I believe he wanted you home but didn't know how to ask you back. He may have hoped to reform himself first, but"—his voice grew quieter—"you know how that ended."

Otis shifted his weight from his right foot to his left and back again. This conversation—all conversation—felt awkward. He could blame his father for his reclusive nature, which had been practically forced on him when he was sent to live in the woods of Massachusetts with only an aged pianist for company and guidance. It was his turn to talk; he knew that, but no words would form on his tongue.

"It's all yours to do with as you like," Leon said. "I asked you back so you could be here and choose for yourself how it was handled. But there is more . . ."

With an audible huff, Otis sank into the chair his father had once occupied and readied himself to hear whatever it was Leon was trying so hard not to say. Instinctively, he ran a hand over his wide-brimmed hat, a habit he'd acquired a decade ago.

"Tell me. I don't have all day," Otis said, then let out a cynical laugh at his own words. How ridiculous. He had no other demands on his time, nowhere to be, nowhere to go, and certainly no one to see. There was no reason he couldn't listen to Leon for hours on end, other than the fact that he did not want to. "Tell me what other mischief my brother has left in his wake. Pandora's box is open. I may as well face it all."

"Your mother loved Greek mythology. I remember her reading to you in this very room. Pandora, Zeus, Hades . . ."

Otis stopped short at the wave of warmth that rushed over him. He had been happy when he'd been by her side. As quickly as the feeling came, it left again, and in its place came a cold emptiness and the reminder that he'd not been truly happy in a long time. "Well," he said, fighting to keep his voice level. "If there's something that needs saying, say it."

"Very well. I believe your brother left behind a . . . a mistress."

Chapter 3

"A mistress?" Otis stood, unable to remain still with such news ringing in his ears like a bugle announcing a change in course. "My brother had a kept woman." He ran his hand over the brim of his hat. "I never would have suspected—but what does that have to do with me?"

Father's letters had been brief, simple descriptions of Monticello happenings and excuses for why Otis couldn't come back. Not once was there mention of his brother courting or . . . or cavorting about like a cad.

"When you didn't rush home right away," Leon said, "I took the liberty of looking through the account books to learn how crucial it was for you to settle the finances here. I wanted to protect your assets the best I could. That's when I discovered your brother's affinity for gambling, as well as how disorderly his books were and . . ." The older man paused, his face reddening. "And that your brother was spending money on other tarnished pursuits."

"Wasteful," Otis muttered.

"Most alarming are the monthly entries marked *Elisabeth*. I thought perhaps she was doing some domestic service, but Mildred handles the house affairs. I can think of no other explanation than that your brother was paying a woman an allowance for her . . . services."

"The matter is disturbing, but whoever this Elisabeth is, she must know he is dead. I don't owe her anything."

"That is what logic tells me as well." Leon opened his mouth and quickly closed it again.

"But?"

Leon's chair creaked as he shifted uneasily. "But what if my assumptions are wrong and Elisabeth is someone else? What if she is someone who depends on the monthly income? Reginald's books are a horrid—I've never seen such a mess. The only consistent entry is the 'Elisabeth' entry. Which leads me to believe she meant something to him."

"Perhaps Elisabeth is a favorite horse that he bet on monthly or the name of a widow he cared for." This game of guessing was a waste of time. If they had Elisabeth's scent, Wolf might be able to track her down, but as it was, she was simply a name. Another piece of his family's past that he would never understand.

"Well, I don't know of any racehorses named Elisabeth, and I never saw your brother keep company with widows." Leon's brow furrowed into deep rows, like a field ready for planting. "You're right, it could be anyone. I simply wanted to voice my concern so you could do with it what you wanted. Perhaps when we look over the books together, something will turn up. There are stacks of unopened correspondence, unpaid bills. We'll do what we can with what we have, and if we learn nothing about Elisabeth, then we may assume that whoever she is, she is well. Now, tell me, does anyone know you've returned?"

"I paid the driver to keep my return to himself. He seemed honest, but only time will tell if he is the nefarious sort."

"How long do you plan to keep your return a secret?" Leon asked slowly.

"I'll spend the entirety of my time here unannounced, if possible. Father loved a big show—he was always getting attention for everything he did. I don't want that. The citizens of Monticello can go on believing that I left home for career pursuits, for all I care. They don't deserve an explanation, and I don't need an audience."

"Ah, a humble Taylor man is an oddity, but in a good way."

"I am an oddity, but I'm not humble." Otis shook his head, uncomfortable with the praise. "I am private, a hermit, if you will."

Leon rubbed at his large nose, scratching an invisible itch. "I respect your desire for discretion, though I fear it may prove difficult. You may have to make yourself known when you handle the finances with the banks and the property sells."

Otis covered a yawn. The night of no sleep was catching up to him. Though, in actuality, he'd had many nights of little sleep, tossing and turning as he anticipated his return to Monticello. Banking, property transfers, a mistress . . . his tired brain struggled to make sense of it.

His own finances had been simple. When Otis was a youth, his father had paid his teacher for his care and vow of secrecy. As an adult, he'd composed music while living in an old gardener's house on the very property he'd been exiled to. His old teacher handled the music requests, he wrote the compositions, and then he was paid. He had food delivered, and on occasion he'd order a new suit, but other than paying for necessities, he had little need for money. And all transactions had been handled quietly, giving him little experience with large expenditures or complicated bookkeeping. His name was lauded and known among his pianist peers, but fame had not been enough to pull him from the shadows.

Leon stood and patted him on the shoulder. "All of that can wait. Go and rest."

Otis nodded, tempted to say something more, to tell the old man that—though he hated being back in Monticello—he was glad to see a friendly face. Instead, he nodded again. His uneasiness served as a reminder that it was best to keep to himself. If he couldn't talk easily with a welcoming old man, he would be an abysmal failure if he were to attempt a social endeavor.

"It's good having you home," Leon said. "Mildred will send you up a meal when you're rested. She's been looking forward to your return ever since you sent word you were coming. She's so eager to see you that she's ready to kill the fatted calf."

Otis turned away, surprised by the tears that stung his eyes. He cleared his throat. "Tell her that I am grateful for her kindness."

Otis returned to the guest room he'd declared his refuge for now, refusing to step foot in the room he'd slept in as a boy. He was too afraid to find it the same and equally afraid to find it altered. This room was smaller, but he didn't care. It met his needs and was furnished with pieces he had no memories of. There were no family portraits, no family heirlooms, and no belongings he'd left behind when he was a boy. It was a safe room, or so he thought.

He lay down and closed his eyes, expecting the heaviness of sleep to win at last. Instead, he saw his father the night he shared that Otis was to leave.

"I've made arrangements," his father said all those years ago. "A family outside Boston takes in music students. The man is very old and has decided to stop boarding and tutoring. I've reached out to him, and for a fee he has agreed to take you on as his only student. Their home is far out in the country, away from gawking eyes. You can play your music and enjoy peace while you recover. No one will ever know about your condition."

His father smiled as though he were making a great sacrifice by sending Otis away. Pleased with himself, he'd even sat back and begun lighting his pipe.

"I don't understand. When will I return?" Otis's still-changing voice cracked. He'd argued with his father many times, insisting that his life go on as before, but this time he was too shaken to fight. "Will I come back for Christmas?"

His father refused to meet his gaze. He looked at his feet, at the drawn drapes, at the pipe in his hands . . . anywhere but at Otis. It was then Otis knew for certain that his father's *gift* of music was only given to ease his own conscience and rid himself of his disappointing son. "When you're recovered you can come back, and things in Monticello will be as before. Until then it is best for you to focus on your music and continue with the tonics and the plasters."

Two weeks later Otis left with no return date and without so much as a goodbye to his friends. Tears filled his eyes as he was driven away from the only home he'd ever known. For years he waited, clinging to hope that one day he would be beckoned home, that old relationships could be rekindled. But he was never summoned. There had been no reconciliation. There was never another carefree day spent with his chums—Dan, Wilbur, and Andrew grew up without him. There was no sitting beside his father's bedside when he passed, no fatherly advice, and certainly no rekindling of familial feelings. Like a shoe that rubbed the wrong way, he was cast off.

"Why?" he whispered into the early morning light.

Wolf walked over and sat beside the bed. He propped his jaw up beside Otis's face and whimpered. From the start, Otis had been convinced Wolf understood more than he could say.

Otis put his hand on the dog's head. "It's all right. Just bad memories. We'll get out of this place quick as we can."

Sadie was more cautious than ever as she snuck back across the road to the old factory at the end of her workday. She had a new loaf of bread, a knapsack full of feathers, and a stick in hand. Every dog she'd ever owned knew how to fetch a stick. Half the canines that had walked the West land had been unable to control their excitement at the thought of chasing a flying object. She could only hope this blue dog found as much sport in it.

The dark sky made it difficult to pick her path as stealthily as she wished, but she'd been too fearful to come earlier. She looked past the factory to the mansion. A sliver of light shone between the drapes—someone was there. Other nights she'd seen light, too, only now she feared whoever lived inside the ominous house had recently acquired a dog.

She hefted herself through the factory window and, quick as she could, went to her corner and sat near a window that faced the moon. The light was dim, but it would have to do. At work she'd asked Mr. Hoag if she could have feathers from the discard bin. He'd given her a curious look but agreed.

Now back in her makeshift home, she sat on the floor with her knapsack full of mangled feathers and set to work stitching a ragged curtain into a pillow. She laughed softly to herself. What would Marvin think of her, sitting on the floor, legs crossed in an unladylike fashion, sewing rags together so she could lay her dirty head upon it as she shivered through the night? Rag pillows, running from the creek in her underclothes—what an unexpected life she was leading.

She picked up one of the small feathers and brushed it across her palm.

A dog bawled. She threw the feather to the ground and listened. It howled, like a sick wolf, yelling up at the moon. The sound grew louder . . . closer. Sadie sprang from her spot and rushed to the corner, ready to hide in the darkest of shadows, before changing course and heading to the window.

"Stop that," she commanded. To this, the animal only tilted his head back and readied to bawl again. "No, no, no."

She climbed out of the window and patted the crate she used for a stool. There was no one in sight, but still she worried. "Quiet down and you can come inside. Climb up."

The dog's head came down. For a moment its perpetual frown seemed to be replaced with a smirk. Sadie rolled her eyes. Outsmarted by a dog. She could add that to her list of indignities. He climbed up, turned, and looked at her. She patted his head and paused her worrying long enough to get a good look at the animal. He was a male, medium-sized. The floppy-eared rascal.

"Where have you come from?" she asked after they were settled beside each other in her bedroom corner. "You have a collar with no name on it. You ought to tell your owner that a collar is for more than walking a dog. Your stomach appears more rounded than mine, so I am sure that you do have an owner. Where is he?"

The dog lifted a leg and scratched at the collar around his neck. How quickly he'd made himself at home.

"Do you mind if I give you a name?" She stroked his head, feeling less alone, thanks to the dog's company. "I suppose you already have one, but I don't know it . . ."

She studied him a moment before yawning. "I'm too tired," she said and then yawned again. "I'll call you Blue. You can stay if you like, but I don't have much to feed you. And I smell awful. And I can't promise to be good company."

He sat beside her and rested his head on her lap, unaffected by her decree of poverty. For no reason at all a powerful urge to cry swept over her, but she fought off the tears. He was a dog. Of course he cared nothing for her financial status or the state of her attire. Still, she felt comforted, grateful for his large, accepting eyes.

"My mama never let the dogs sleep with us. But it's cold. You can stay if you want."

Blue, her new friend, her only friend in Monticello, didn't leave her the entire night.

. . . I've made a friend and feel far less lonely now. . . .

Chapter 4

Otis paced back and forth with his arms folded across his chest. Where was that dog? For six years Wolfgang, named after Mozart and shortened to Wolf, had rarely left his side, and he'd never run off at night.

But now, six nights in a row, Wolf had been let out and high-tailed it away from the mansion. He'd come back hungry the next day but unremorseful, prancing inside as though he'd done nothing wrong. Otis had done his best not to care that the dog was deserting him, but he did. Wolf, though a dog, was his friend—his only true friend. Were raccoons so enticing that he'd run off to chase them *every* night?

Traitorous animal.

He had other matters to worry about though. His brother's account books were not exactly books—they were stacks of banknotes, promissory notes, threatening letters demanding payment, and receipts. Unopened mail, water-damaged records (how they had become water damaged, he would never know), and of course the consistent entries in simple line form marked *Elisabeth*. The ever-mysterious Elisabeth, the name that had called to Leon and, if he was being honest, the name that also drew his attention time and again.

Otis groaned, annoyed with his deceased brother. How dare he die and leave an aftermath of trouble behind him? Begrudgingly he sat, determined to make some progress on the mountain of neglect.

"I've brought you a cup of tea." Mildred stepped into the study, her round cheeks sagged with age, but when she smiled, they brightened, making her look more like the woman he'd known in his childhood. "I will never tire of walking through this house and seeing you."

"You flatter me." He offered her a forced smile. "Thank you for the tea."

"I saw your dog go out." Mildred moved a stack of warped papers and sat in a wooden chair across from him.

"The dog run is in disrepair. I should keep him in, but he howls at the door until I open it. I am not firm enough with him."

"Did he wander when you lived with the Crawfords in Massachusetts?"

"He'd run, but he always returned."

"Home has a way of calling us back."

Otis only grunted. He shuffled aimlessly through the papers nearest him. Receipts, bills, a badly torn letter. He picked that up, expecting to find another request for money or an invitation to a social gathering.

Dear Mr. Reginald Taylor,

I have been caring for Elisabeth for some time now, and I find that her needs are increasing. Last month

> she needed the doctor called twice. If I am to continue caring for the baby, I will require an additional five dollars a month. If I do not hear from you within the week, I will bring her to your residence. I know you want discretion, but if you don't respond, I'll have no choice. I am not a charitable organization.
>
> Sincerely,
> Mary Stevens

Otis stared, and then he read the letter again. Still shocked, he read it aloud in hopes that Mildred would help the words make sense.

"Oh dear." Mildred's eyes grew large.

"Elisabeth . . . is a child." Otis pushed away from the desk and stood, too overwhelmed by the revelation to sit, only to find his legs weak and shaking beneath him. He leaned against the desk, but his head continued to spin. "She's a child."

"It can't be." Mildred picked up the note. "Oh my."

"She is out there, somewhere. My brother . . . he must have been the child's . . . guardian?"

"Could be he was the child's father," Mildred said without looking up from the page. "He wasn't an overly virtuous man . . . but I never expected this."

"He can't be her father." Otis balked. "He wasn't married. I am sure my father would have told me if he was."

"He was *not* married. I am certain of that." She spoke in a gentle tone, but still the accusation hit him like a lightning bolt, forcing him to sit again.

"Are you suggesting that my brother left me more than an enormous financial riddle? He left behind a daughter?"

"This letter leads me to believe that."

"And you believe it possible?" A new pain pierced his side. There had been a time when he and Reginald were inseparable. Now here he sat, realizing he knew little of the man his brother became.

"Reginald was not one to be benevolent without a motive. If he was supporting a child financially, he had a reason for it." Mildred's voice carried no doubt. "Does the letter have a return address?"

"Yes. Springhole."

"That's not far. We can find Mary and ask questions."

His finger tapped nervously on the desk. Mildred put a motherly hand on his shoulder. "Don't worry. We'll sort this out. This letter can't be older than the entries in the book—most likely she's still there. Perhaps this can all be explained away."

"How can I not worry? I can't even make sense of Reginald's finances, and now I find out that my brother may have had a child—out of wedlock, no less. And she's been hidden away somewhere?"

"He may have worried about your father's reaction, or he may have been ashamed."

Shame.

The word pinged around inside, colliding against his conscience in an uncomfortable way, and then the discomfort grew to pain. Shame, embarrassment, disgrace . . . he knew them all too well. Such feelings had been the catalyst to his own neglect. He pressed a hand to his pounding forehead. An unexpected seed of compassion sprouted, not for his brother but for Elisabeth, a child, perhaps his niece, who hadn't been wanted. The pursuit to avoid public ridicule had already instigated too much secrecy in the Taylor family, where decisions had been made based on ignominy and fear rather than heart and wisdom.

"I want this resolved." He wrung his hands together in his lap. "Would Leon go? Could he inquire after Elisabeth for me?"

"Yes, of course," she answered for her husband. "Or we could write?"

"No—if she's there, we need to know now. It cannot wait." A driving force made him wish they could go that very day. If only he were better spoken and not so marked, he would go himself. But Leon would go in his stead, and surely they would find Elisabeth. "If she is my kin, we have to find her. My brother and father might be comfortable hiding the unwanted branches of the family tree away, but I am not. I will not . . ." His voice faltered. "We'll find her."

Mildred's face puckered. "You're a good boy. Always were."

"I was cast off," he said, more to himself than to Mildred. "I could never . . ." He shook his head. "I *will* never do that to family. If she is my responsibility, then I will find her and I will not abandon her."

"There could be a reason—"

"There could not! There could be *no* reason to hide a child away. Circumstances of her birth, scars—no reason!" The power behind his words scared even him. But he stood by them.

There would never again be a discarded Taylor.

"Wolf," Otis called in a low voice for his dog. He wanted to shout, to call the animal all sorts of names and even throw empty threats into the air, but he feared some distant neighbor would hear him, and the last thing he wanted was for the whole of Monticello to learn of his return. All he wanted was his dog beside him.

"Wolf," he called again, voice still low but more demanding. "Wolf."

In the woods of Massachusetts, Wolf had always come when called. He would run full speed over brambles to get to Otis. What in blazes had gotten into him since coming here?

Otis looked in every direction before stepping out of the house. He was alone. The clear sky was dark, save the twinkling stars and partial moon. The air, warm and humid, was damp just as it had been when he and Reginald played in this very yard.

"Wolf," he called again, then whistled and waited.

Sadie wrapped her arms around Blue and cooed soothing words into his ear, hoping they would keep him from barking.

"Hush, don't worry. Whoever is out there, they'll go away soon enough."

Blue sat up straighter, his floppy ears turned toward the sound. Someone—a man—was calling out for *Wolf* and whistling. Blue, or Wolf, clearly recognized the voice. He looked at her and then back at the sound. She should send him on his way—after all, Blue was not her dog. But she'd slept much better since he'd joined her, and she hated to lose the one friend she'd found. When he continued to look toward the sharp whistling, she took her arm off him.

"Go on, if you must," she said. It would be better if he jumped out the window and was discovered outside than if he barked and brought this stranger into her hideaway. "Go," she said, nudging his side.

Blue moved slowly, and for a moment she thought he would stay. But then he stretched back on his haunches and let out three sharp barks.

"No!" She pushed his side. "Go, get out of here!"

He looked back at her, his eyes full of confusion. He'd been there beside her keeping her company and now she was sending him away. He couldn't understand, and she had no way to explain it to him, so she shoved again.

"I'm sorry," she said, "but you have to go. You can't bring anyone here."

"Wolf," the man's voice called again, this time sounding closer to the factory.

Her heart beat faster, harder. She gathered her few belongings and pushed them behind a pile of old crates, glared at the dog who refused to leave, and then crept into the shadows, pressing herself against the wall.

"Come here, boy!" The man's voice came from the window. "Don't make me come in there after you."

Go! Sadie silently tried to will the dog away. But instead, she watched Blue open his mouth, yawn, and then sit himself down. She'd labeled him friend, but in this moment he looked the part of a turncoat.

Moments later she heard the man climbing through the window. Every fear she'd harbored since declaring the old factory her home surfaced. What would her family think if they knew she'd been living in squalor? No West girl had ever gotten into trouble, and now here she was, about to humiliate the family. She could die of shame. And worse yet, where would she go?

Her stomach clenched as a new fear came forth. Who was this man? What would he do if he found her? She grabbed her lunch tin—arming herself—and crouched down. It wasn't much of a weapon, but with enough force it would leave a mark.

"I remember this place from when I was boy," the man said to the dog. His voice did not sound like the voice of a villain, although she had no idea what a villain sounded like. "That was a long time ago. Back then this place was crowded with machines and people. When I left, they were making wheels and bicycles."

There was a far-off sound in his voice, a mix of wistfulness and despondency that made her want to see his face so she might read it better.

"I'm too tired tonight," he said, continuing to speak to the dog. He did sound tired. The deep-down, weary-to-the-soul sort of tired. "Let's go. Some other time we can explore."

Blue barked, and from her corner she saw him resisting as the man urged him toward the window. A sneeze tickled her nose. Blast this dust! Her eyes stung, burning as she fought to keep her sneeze inside.

Go! she nearly shouted, wanting to hurry their departure. Blue broke free from the man's grasp and came right for her, panting and barking as he went.

"What is it?" The man followed, and though she tried to make herself melt into the wall, she knew she'd be discovered.

There was no escaping, no way to make a run for it. If he didn't leave soon, she would have to face him.

She sneezed, and all hopes of going unnoticed vanquished.

Tin pail in hand, she stepped from the shadows, ready to launch an attack on the intruder.

"What—"

"Leave!" she shouted, then held up her pail, threatening him.

The man stepped backward, tripped over his own feet, then scrambled across the floor as he struggled to find his footing. "Who? What?" he growled as he wrestled with the floorboards, all marks of wistfulness gone from his voice.

She rushed for him, ready to strike. An instinct to protect herself flooded her veins. Blue got between them, barking first at her and then at him. The man had come with no light, and she possessed none, so the three stared at one another in near darkness.

"Quiet, Blue," she said when she could take his barking no longer.

"Blue?" the man said, finally uttering a coherent word. "His name's Wolfgang . . . his name's Wolf."

Wolfgang? Did villains name their dogs after brilliant musicians? "He didn't tell me his name, so I gave him one."

The man gawked, and she covered her mouth—this was no time to be making conversation. She stood taller, making herself as big as she could, which was no easy task for a woman with a slight build.

"Well . . . his name is Wolf."

"And you are?" In the dark, shadow-riddled room, she could make out only his outline, but it told her he was a large man with broad shoulders and a hat atop his head. Despite her efforts, she could not see his eyes nor tell whether he smiled or scowled.

"My name isn't your concern. I've simply come for *my* dog."

"You won't tell me your name?" She moved away from him, speaking as she went, only because she felt safer talking than standing in silence. "I will just have to name you as well."

"Name me? Like you did my dog?"

"Yes. I can't very well write my sisters and tell them I met a stranger—they'd be worried. I will tell them I met"—she tapped her lip—"Edward Rochester."

"Rochester . . . from *Jane Eyre*?"

"You've read *Jane Eyre*? Well, now I do know something about you." She took another half step backward and stopped. More to herself than to him, she said, "I wouldn't want to be in company with a vagrant, but a man who has read Charlotte Brontë cannot be all bad."

"Don't you think bad men read when they are desperate to fill the long winter months?"

"I hadn't ever thought so, but you could be right. Does that mean you *are* a bad man?"

She saw him shrug. "I am just a man."

"Rochester suits you. He had secrets too."

He humphed and the tension in her shoulders relaxed some. This man may not be a friend, but he didn't seem eager to assault her or run for the authorities.

Wolf—it would take her a while to get used to his *new* name—waffled between them, running to her and then back to him, unsure who to stay beside.

"What are you doing in here?" the man asked, still not giving her his real name.

"I could ask you the same question."

"I am fetching my dog. You on the other hand cannot offer that as an excuse." His voice wasn't harsh, but it wasn't friendly either. Oh, how she wished she could see his face and read his expression. "You need to leave. This factory is not yours."

"I have come to *think* of it as mine. Besides, no one was using it and I needed a roof over my head. I'm sure if the owner were here, he'd understand my predicament."

"You presume . . . That is how you justify your squatting?" His tone had grown harsher, and even without seeing him she knew he scowled.

It should not have hurt, having a stranger judge her actions, but it did. And though she was determined to persevere, doing whatever she must for her family, guilt nagged at her. Honor had driven her from home to the city. To have her indiscretion called out stung.

"I'm sorry," she whispered, feeling sheepish like she so often did when Alta looked at her with disdain, seeing only the dirt on her skin and not the motives of her heart. "I work at the duster factory. My pa is injured and we needed money, so I came to work in Monticello." She spoke the words quickly. "The bank has threatened to take our land. Last season was so bad, we borrowed money. And now I've got to find a way to pay it."

"None of that tells me why you are here, in *this* factory."

"I had a place to live, but I lost it. I couldn't tell my family," she said, her voice cracking on the last word. That wouldn't do. In times of battle, a general could not appear weak. She rallied, and this time she spoke with a firm voice. "You may think me selfish, and I admit, staying here goes against my principles, but . . ." She glared into the darkness. She didn't have to explain herself to him. This wasn't his factory any more than it was hers. He was simply a stranger looking for his lost dog. "I was desperate. Judge all you like, but I had nowhere else to go and people depending on me. Someday I will find the owner and I'll pay him back."

"Indeed. And what if he doesn't accept?"

"I'll grovel."

"Hmm," he said, then motioned for Wolf to follow and started for the window. She stepped closer, wanting to see his face, but he kept going, putting more distance between them.

"Are you going to tell anyone that I'm here?" She scolded herself for letting fear creep back into her voice. "You won't, will you? You have your dog. That's what you came for."

He stood near the window, saying nothing.

With each moment that passed her worry increased, growing wider and deeper, until she feared it would consume her. In two giant strides she crossed the floor and put her hand on his arm. "Please."

He brushed her off, and in an instant he was gone through the window with Wolf behind him.

Chapter 5

It's my factory, Otis rationalized as he turned his back on the unlawful tenant and walked to the house. He had every right to throw her out. He could even fetch the police and punish her for living in his building without his permission. And she'd threatened to attack him—albeit with a tin pail, but still it showed she was out of her head, did it not?

What sort of woman moved into a factory anyway? It was dark, cold, and dusty. She'd be better off somewhere else. Somewhere with a stove to cook on and a bed to sleep in. Some place with electric lights, a telephone, and other modern niceties. Sending her off was for the best. Had her proximity not caught him so off guard, he would have sent her away himself right then and there. He stomped his feet as he walked, fighting the niggle of curiosity that threatened to beset him and his resolve. It was better to go on believing her mad. Safer. Curiosity, pity—he didn't have time for such feelings. He had Reginald's affairs to settle and a house to sell.

"Leon!" he shouted the moment the door was open. He shouted again, feeling only a small bit of remorse for waking the man. Leon did not come right away. When he did, he stumbled in. "I have discovered where Wolf has been spending his nights."

"Coons?" Leon said. "Have you gotten me up to tell me that Wolf has been chasing coons?"

"No," Otis said, shaking his head. "That would be expected, but this . . ." He could hardly believe what he was about to say. "There is a woman living in the factory."

"Ah, I meant to tell you."

"What?"

"I've seen her from the window. She leaves early in the morning and comes back late in the evening. Poor thing, she's thin as a rail. I've considered introducing myself, but she's so careful, coming and going when it's dark, always looking around, so I've just let her be."

"You knew and you haven't sent her off?" He pressed his palm to his forehead. "You have to. I can't have her living there. She'll tell the entire town I'm back. And I can't sell the factory with a woman living in it. She has to go."

Leon rubbed at the scruff on his chin. "Do you suppose she is more likely to keep quiet if I send her off?"

"The factory is not for living in." His jaw flexed. "It's got broken glass and cobwebs. There isn't even a bed."

"That's good of you to think of her comfort. She must have a reason for being there." Leon scratched his head. "We should discover that, don't you think, before we clank pans together and drive her to who knows where?"

"Clank pans? That's absurd. It's no great mystery. She's working in town to help her family." The pounding in his head grew stronger. He had enough worries—he didn't need this one. His chest hurt. He couldn't breathe in this house, not properly. "She's a grown woman. She will have to sort it out. The factory is not a charity home."

"You sound like Reginald." Leon let his words hover in the air. "I'll go and speak with her in the morning, unless she's gone already. Does she know who you are?"

"No, I don't think so. She made it quite clear that she believed me looking for a lost dog," he said, trying with little success to ignore Leon's remark about Reginald. Was he like his unruly brother? Like his father? Had he grown not just awkward but cold?

"She must not be very bright. Everyone is always talking about your family and about you. Perhaps she's lacking in—"

"I don't think she's daft. There were moments when I thought that . . . well, she looks the part of a squatter, but she's spry enough."

"You've formed a rather extensive opinion of the girl."

Otis scowled. "She called me Edward Rochester. Perhaps she is daft."

"If she is gone tomorrow, we needn't worry. We will simply hope she's not prone to idle chatter. If she is, you will have to brace yourself for callers."

He gnawed on his bottom lip. "I can't have her living in a building I aim to sell, nor can I have her spreading word that I am back. She's put me in an awful predicament." Wolf walked beside him as he continued his mumbling. "I'll think on it. There's nothing to be done until morning. Come, Wolf."

"Until tomorrow," Leon said before retreating to his room.

From the window of the guest room, Otis could see the factory. He sat for a long time, watching the broken window so he could see if the uninvited resident snuck out in the night. He could not pry his sleep-heavy eyes away, nor silence the questions that rumbled like thunder inside him.

Wolf whined every few minutes. "Your fickle loyalties won't earn you a bone. She's a trespasser."

He whined again.

"You like her." He patted Wolf's head while keeping his gaze on the factory. "You've been hiding in the woods too long, same as me. But she's not the sort of woman a Taylor man associates with."

His hand stilled. The words tasted vile in his mouth. He'd been away from the family's pomp and haughtiness for so long, he'd believed himself rid of it all, but there he was, sounding exactly like his father. His father would have thrown her out and washed his hands of the matter.

Otis wasn't his father. He'd promised himself that no matter how odd and out of place he became, he would never become callous and heartless like his father. *Stop thinking like him*, he rebuked himself, wishing he could spit out the bitter taste.

"What am I to do?" he asked Wolf, who gave him no answer. Otis was left to decide his own course of action.

And decide he did.

In the early morning hours, long before the sun lit the sky, he made a choice, one that had him surprised by himself.

Running in the night had crossed Sadie's mind, but where would she go? A different abandoned building? Finding a place in the dark would be near impossible, so she stayed, prepared to accept whatever fate came at dawn.

A fitful sleep followed, until at last a few rays of light roused her.

No one had come for her—but they may yet be coming. Darkness could no longer be her excuse for staying. It was time to act. She would leave this rat-infested ruin and try again.

She shoved her spare clothes, hairbrush, soap, and bread into her small carpetbag. She even packed her prickly pillow that smelled heavily of turkey. It took only a minute for her to pack the entirety of her belongings, but the time was long enough for her palms to grow sweaty and her heart to beat frantically.

"Goodbye," she said to no one as she stepped near the window. Then she stuttered to a stop. A folded sheet of paper stuck to the window frame gave her pause. She looked around, but no one was there. This note was for her—it had to be. A flutter raced through her. She'd so rarely received mail from anyone other than her sisters. A few brief notes from Marvin over the last two years had been exciting, though they'd lacked any real heart. But she understood. He was so busy with school he didn't have time to write lengthy epistles.

She tore the note from the shard of glass and reminded herself that her life was not a novel and this note was not from a suitor. It was most likely a formal request for her to remove herself from the premises. *Go on, be off.*

There was no need for a note. She was going anyway—the stranger had won. She almost wadded the paper up and threw it on the ground, but curiosity got the better of her. How would he send her off? What words would he use? She unfolded the note.

> Dear Jane Squatter,

She rolled her eyes. Rude, but clever.

> I realize that I do not know your name and so I have given you one. Do you find it fitting? The Jane, in case you wonder, is for Miss Jane Eyre, and Squatter, well, that is because you are . . . a squatter.

> I need to speak to you. When you are able, come to the mansion house. Don't be spooked; I have a proposition for you. Until we speak, I ask that you do not discuss our encounter with anyone. It's important, for reasons I will explain later.
>
> Blue-Wolf says hello. He's a traitorous animal and has been whining since our encounter. I fear he misses his trespassing friend.
>
> No need to bring your pail. I assure you, I mean you no harm.
>
> Edward Rochester
>
> (PS: I find it worth mentioning that I do not have a wife hidden away in the attic.)

She laughed at the letter's absurdity. How unexpected, how intriguing and crafty. Aliases, pails. After so many dreary days of nothing but labor and judgmental words, her chance meeting with this mysterious man she knew only by alias enlivened her. Did she dare meet him?

Sadie tucked her bag back into her corner and climbed through the window. She had no idea what his letter meant, but she'd been in need of a miracle, and if it happened to come in an unusual form, she'd accept it.

For today, she would choose to believe that Edward Rochester had decent motives and that whatever he proposed was worth listening to. If that was foolhardy, so be it. She had no better solutions.

She stuck her hand into her skirt pocket for the sole purpose of hearing the paper crinkle beneath her touch. How strange that in the two years since Marvin left for school, he had never written a letter that had brought such intrigue. His words were always so serious, a recap of his studies and a wish for her well-being.

"I'll be back soon. I intend to do my schooling in two years rather than three," Marvin had said as he took her hand the last time she saw him while they walked through the back pasture. She'd felt ready to burst with happiness. "When I do, I hope you'll still be here."

She squeezed her fingers around his and waited, knowing he would follow his sentiments with a promise. For years she'd known she would wait forever for Marvin Bennett, and in that instant, she felt certain her long-dreamed-of moment was coming. Waiting for him to finish his schooling would be so much easier with a promise between them. And oh, how she longed to tell the world of their commitment to each other. To shout it to anyone who would listen. Her happy ending was there beside her. Someday she would be Mrs. Marvin Bennett, wife to a striking man who had always been well dressed, well mannered, and everything she ever wanted.

"I'll be here," she whispered, her voice laced with emotion. "I will *always* be here."

"It's nice thinking that things back here will be the same, even when so much is different for me. Well, I'd better be off," he said as he let go of her hand, leaving an emptiness where his touch had been. He was off, but where was his promise? "I catch a train first thing tomorrow. I'm so eager, I can hardly wait. All I ever think about is going off to school and coming back with a law degree."

"Two years," she murmured. Two years was fast for such a degree but an eternity to wait with no promise.

"Think of all the people I'll meet and what I'll learn." He paused and looked at her, his gaze holding hers for a long moment. Earthy-brown eyes framed with perfect brows bore into her soul. "Someday I'll buy a big house and have my own office."

She opened her mouth to speak, but in the end, she only nodded and blinked, trying to hold back her disappointed tears.

He left then, his gait and the swing of his arms exactly as they had always been. Where she felt a great loss coming, he seemed unaffected. One more wave, a smile, and then he mounted his horse and rode away. No promise, no kisses or talk of their future.

At first she'd been hurt, but with time she'd come to see his departure as an act of good faith. He was off having adventures of his own, and rather than strap her down, he'd given her freedom, knowing that their love was strong enough to endure. How many characters in novels waited patiently for their love to return? Surely their feelings were stronger than those of a fictional couple.

It'd been nearly two years. Marvin and all her dreams could wait—they'd waited this long already. And someday they'd have tales to tell. What mattered now was ensuring that the man behind the note did not lose his temper and tell the police she'd been living in the old building.

Jane Squatter, she mused and laughed aloud. Edward Rochester had not written her a romantic letter, but his words left her curious and a little hopeful. She stopped, pivoted, and hurried back to the jagged glass. On a whim, she wrote a note and left it on the broken windowpane.

Dear Edward,

Is it all right if I call you Edward? Mr. Rochester seems far too formal. After all, we already share the loyalty of a dog. I've heard dogs are very good judges

of character, and he seems to find us both tolerable—
even, dare I say, good company.

As for your request, I will come to the mansion after I finish work. I'll consider whatever it is you are proposing, and for the time being I will keep quiet. If it eases your mind, know that I have very few connections in Monticello, and though I listen to a great deal of gossip, I rarely have anything to add.

Besides, if I were to tell everyone that I was acquainted with Mr. Edward Rochester, they may think me mad, at least if they are well read.

Until this evening,
Jane Squatter

PS: Jane is fitting enough, but Squatter? I would have expected more creativity from you. A man who names his dog Wolfgang surely has some imagination.

She grinned as she walked away, knowing it was a risky endeavor to correspond with a stranger, but her spirits were soaring. The police had not arrested her, and the monotony of her days had been rattled. Even if there was no good gossip at the factory today, she had plenty to think about, and that alone was reason to smile.

Outside the general store she met Peter and his young daughter, Bessy.

"You look happy this morning," he said, making no mention of her filthy appearance. He was tall and thin as a rail, with a wide smile that she'd known for years. Peter and his wife were the Wests' nearest neighbors and dear friends. Just seeing him was a taste of home.

"I woke up feeling grateful this morning," she said and then smiled at Bessy. "Did you get up early so you could go for a ride with your papa?"

Bessy nodded her head and grinned up at Peter. "I said, 'Please, please, please!'"

"Who could say no to that?" She grinned. "The weather is beautiful. It was a good day for you to go for a ride."

"Papa said we could go in the store."

Peter shrugged his narrow shoulders. The man shamelessly adored his daughter. "She said please three times—I couldn't say no. I might even buy her a piece of penny candy if she says four pleases."

Bessy laughed. "I'll say ten pleases and give you a hug."

"I remember coming into town with my papa. Sometimes he'd buy me penny candy, and once he even let me go skating."

"Really?" Bessy's eyes lit up. "What's that?"

"When you're a bit bigger, I'll take you," Peter said. "I've got a lot of deliveries to make today. I best get going."

"Before you do, how did my pa look?"

Peter rubbed the back of his neck. "Well, he's managing to keep his spirits up, but the doctor's worried he might not walk again. They said something about the surgery not going well and the bones not being set right. The doctor says rest is the best medicine for now. Your pa is real thankful for you. They all are."

"I always dreamed of leaving the farm and having an adventure. But I didn't ever imagine it being quite like this." Sadie gave Peter her letter and smiled again at Bessy. "Be sure and say a lot of pleases. Maybe your papa will buy you two pieces of penny candy."

Bessy grinned at her father as Sadie walked away, quickening her step so as not to be late to the factory. The bell was just ringing as she hung her thin coat on a hook.

"Mr. Hoag was looking for you," Alta said shortly after she arrived. "He needs someone to help remove the pith today. Francis isn't coming because of a bicycle accident. We suggested you."

Sadie glanced heavenward. The assignment was a godsend. She had dreaded spending the day beside Alta and Sylvia, afraid they would sense how distracted she was and pry secrets from her.

"I don't mind working on the pith," she said, already moving deeper into the factory toward the back corner where three stools stood beside a large square table.

Turkey tail feathers could be a foot long, and inside the shaft, they contained a soft, spongy fill known as the pith. To make a proper duster, the pith was removed—a tedious but necessary job. It wasn't a task employees coveted, and she herself had often dreaded it, but today she didn't mind being nominated by her fellow sorters.

Her companions for the day were two older men who preferred to work in silence. They made no remarks about her faded dress or lack of hygiene and spoke only when there was something worth saying.

Sadie's hands moved mechanically, one feather after another. Her mind was not as rhythmic. Safe at the factory, with no gossip to distract her, her questions grew louder. Who was Edward? A salesman? A friend of the caretakers? Someone passing through?

Midway through the day, the obvious answer, the one so close she almost missed it, shouted at her. Every story, every whisper about the famed Taylor family came rushing back at her. *Gone ten years but expected back someday . . . older couple managed his house.* Could it be? What a fool she was not to guess his identity sooner. She bit her lip. To think she'd almost *hit* the man! And she'd told him he had no right to the factory—she could die of shame. Though, she rationalized, it might not be him. If it was, the whole town would know, wouldn't they?

"Do you know the Taylor family?" Sadie sliced the feather in front of her with a quivering hand and did her best to appear only halfway interested in the response.

"'Course, everyone does. We all thought they'd be running the town for years to come, but they've mostly died off."

"But not all of them," she prodded, hoping they'd tell her everything. This time the gossip mattered. She needed details. Like an investigator in one of the many novels she'd read, she needed a clue to put the pieces together.

"The old factory and mansion house are waiting for Otis to return. Word is he made a name for himself playing his music." The old man shrugged and went right on cutting the feathers. "They're a high-nosed lot. Always a rung above the rest of us. I suspect Otis is the same as his father and brother were. Probably thinks he's too big for his britches and little old Monti."

She wanted to know more, but it seemed that Otis Taylor and his whereabouts were not known, and her questions were bound to be answered only with speculation. Edward Rochester could very well be the elusive Otis Taylor, and today she had an appointment with him.

Chapter 6

Otis found her note at midday while walking Wolf, and he'd since read it more times than he cared to admit. Now he patrolled the parlor, peering out the windows, waiting for the letter writer to arrive.

"You look nervous," Leon said as he stepped into the room. "You intend to offer her a job. That makes you the employer. You've no reason to be nervous. Relax—look the part."

"The part? If I were playing the part my father played, I would have sent her off last night."

"I did not say *be* your father, only to remember you've no reason to be nervous."

Otis shook his head, his black hat shifting with the movement. "You forget, I do have reasons to be nervous."

"You're offering her room and board, not matrimony. It makes no difference what you look like."

Otis chose not to argue with him, but he was not convinced. His looks did matter. They always had, and they likely always would. While traveling from the Crawfords' to Monticello, he had met the eyes of a young boy. Those small blue eyes had locked on his, but then his mother had looked up, seen Otis, and tucked the child behind her. Leon, with his old eyes and blurred vision, may not care, but others would. His own father had.

Leon stepped outside, gardening shears in hand. From Otis's spot near the window, he watched as the elderly employee trimmed bushes near the front of the house. Pruning back one branch and then another, he gave the shrubs a uniform shape.

Otis remained frozen, waiting for Jane Squatter, regretting his impulsivity. When she arrived, she stopped and talked to Leon first. Otis could see her brown skirt and birdlike arm, but the rest was hidden behind the bush Leon trimmed. It was poor manners to watch and even worse to eavesdrop, but it *was* his property. Without giving it another thought he cracked the window and leaned closer.

"No need to apologize for your appearance," Leon said.

"I did try to bathe in the creek . . ." Her voice trailed off.

"That's right. The master of the house said he saw you."

She gasped and Otis groaned. Leon made it sound as though he were a Peeping Tom, when in fact he'd been trying to find his dog and seen only the faintest glimpse of white.

"No need to worry," Leon said.

"Is . . . um . . . I was asked to come here today. I have a meeting."

"He's here. I'll show you in."

Otis kept his ear turned toward the window. Though their voices drifted as they made their way to the front entrance, he heard enough to know she was telling Leon about her father's health and her job at the Hoag factory.

"Come along." Leon's voice was in the entrance. "You've an appointment to keep. And have no fear, there is nothing to worry about. These ivy walls might seem a bit intimidating, but it's not such a bad place."

Otis stepped away from the window. He backed himself against the wall, regretting their ridiculous letters and his invitation for her to come. But his regrets came too late—there was nowhere to go, nothing to do but face her. The door creaked open. He tugged at his hat, lowering it further on his head, and braced himself.

❦

"What name can I give him?" Leon asked as he led Sadie through the foyer of the portentous house. When she had time, she would write to her sisters and tell them of the magnificent inlaid floor, high ceilings, and stained glass.

"Tell him that Jane Squatter is here," she said, earning her a sideways glance and a smirk. She found Leon a welcoming sort and could only hope he had a sense of humor that matched the twinkle in his eye.

"Very well," he said as he opened the door to his right and motioned for her to enter. She left the grand entryway with its wide staircase and gold-painted trim. "This way."

"It's beautiful," she said. The parlor's splendor exceeded the entryway's, leaving her awestruck and extremely aware of how out of place she must look.

"The late Mr. Taylor spared no expense."

Sofas with carved legs, wingback chairs, lights with dangling crystals, and rich papered walls affirmed that he certainly hadn't. Wolf ran to her with a wagging tail. She crouched and petted him behind the ears. "Hello, Blue."

"Wolf." A voice from the corner startled her. She bolted upright and faced him. She'd not seen him when she first entered, but there he was, her mysterious man from the night before. Tall and broad with a hat on his head, which created shadows that covered his face, leaving her in want of a better view.

"Mr. Taylor, a Miss Jane Squatter." Leon's voice was laced with laughter. "I'll leave you two."

There was no longer a need for a clue. This *was* the much-talked-about bachelor, the famed Otis Taylor. She stepped farther into the room. "If you prefer Jane Squatter, I will do my best to grow accustomed to it. But most everyone calls me Sadie West."

"Most everyone?"

"My father often calls me his little bird, and my sisters call me Captain or General when they feel I am bossing them unjustly."

"I will keep that in mind." He nodded but still looked ill at ease. "I am Otis Taylor."

"It'll take some adjusting to think of you as Otis Taylor and not Mr. Rochester."

"I pitied Rochester, even if I did not agree with his choices."

"If nothing else, he teaches us to be thoughtful when choosing a life companion. He may have led an entirely different life if he'd been a bit more cautious." She wrung her hands together. "I am rambling. I apologize, and I will do my best to remember that you are Otis Taylor."

"Does Otis Taylor not fit me?"

"I'm not sure. It seems everyone in town has an opinion of the Taylor family, but I am not from here and so I cannot say if you are anything like your late father or brother." She looked closer at him, wishing he would take off his hat so she could see his face better. "As for Otis, I find it a good-natured name. Would you say that you are good-natured?"

"No," he said without even a moment's pause. "My manners are . . . well, they are out of practice. Ask Leon. He'll tell you. I am ill-tempered, especially being back in this house."

"The house is very grand. I suppose one could feel lost in it. But it's not as though you have to stay here all the time."

"It has nothing to do with its size, though it is gaudy." He spoke through gritted teeth. "You wouldn't understand. No frivolous girl could. What I've endured within these ivy walls . . ."

Sadie looked at her threadbare dress, a testament to all that she'd endured. It was true she had many frivolous dreams, but at present she wasn't living them. His words and assumptions hurt like a slap in the face after her many weeks of sacrifice and hardship.

"I may dream of trivial things." She steadied herself, refusing to be bullied by a stranger. The rest of the town may have romanticized Otis Taylor, but she hadn't. Quite the opposite, each word he spoke put more distance between him and the pedestal. "I long to have a night of respite from the life I am leading, I admit that. I would love to go to the socials and the skating rink, but you can't claim to know me or what my life has been like."

"I don't claim to. I know very little about you other than your propensity for bathing in the creek and claiming abandoned buildings as your own," he muttered before running his hand over his chin. "I told you, I'm not a good-natured man. And this house, it has me . . ." He shook his head. "You wouldn't understand."

"Why don't you tell me why you've summoned me here. Tell me, and then I will be on my way."

He stepped out of the corner and motioned toward the chairs. "Will you sit?"

"Yes," she said, though she hated thinking that the chair would now smell like the factory. There was something unusual about Otis's appearance, but she could not decide what it was. His clothes were tidy, his hands clean—far cleaner than her own—but his face . . . Something was different. Was that why he hid beneath his hat?

"Your note mentioned a proposition?" she said, breaking the silence. The sooner they concluded this conversation, the sooner she could find a new place for herself. She'd have an easier time finding a place to lay her head when it was still light, and daylight was already fading. "If you've changed your mind, I can go now—no need to drag this on."

He rapped his fingers against his knee. "I . . . I was led to believe your situation was dire, and though you are not my responsibility, I thought . . ." He stood and his features grew tense. His lips pulled into a firm line. "Forget it."

"Forget what?" She, too, stood, utterly confused by this man. "I *am* in a dire situation. I owe the bank money again next week. If you won't let me stay at the factory, I have nowhere to go, and people are depending on me. I don't care about my own security. Look at me, I am dirty and desperate, but for them—"

"You said you would pay the owner back. I am the owner."

"I said I would grovel too." Her voice rose an octave. "What are you saying? You want payment for the nights I spent there? Is that why you wanted me to come? So you could ask me for money? Or did you have some other payment in mind?"

"No," he barked. "I don't want you to grovel or pay. I am botching this." He exhaled and she held her breath, waiting. Wolf pushed his nose against Sadie's hand. She responded by scratching behind his ears. Otis focused on her hand and his dog. "Even my dog is abandoning me."

"What?"

"I'll have Leon talk to you."

"Leon? Can you not tell me?"

He shook his head, then left without looking back. Stunned, Sadie remained in the parlor, unsure what had just transpired. Leon did not come, nor did Otis return. Like a dunce, she waited. Just as she was about to see herself out, an older woman stepped into the room. She introduced herself as Mildred, Leon's wife.

"My dear," she said as though they were already well acquainted.

"Did I do something wrong? He was cordial enough, and then he wasn't . . . and then he just left. I don't understand."

"That's our Otis." Mildred's lips raised in an affectionate smile, reminding Sadie of the smile her mother so often wore. "Poor boy, he tries, but . . . well, it's hard."

"Is he angry with me? I didn't mean to cause a problem. It was an empty building."

"No, his anger doesn't have anything to do with you. He's been through a lot, that's all. He has matters that keep him in town, but he doesn't wish for anyone else to know he's here. He's a solitary man."

"I won't tell anyone that he is here." She looked toward the door that Otis had gone through. "I would have told him that. I can respect a man's desire to be left alone."

"He'll be glad to hear it."

"Should I go?"

Mildred shook her head. "No, please stay. He wants to offer you a job, if you're willing."

"A job?" Her hand went to her heart. Was she hearing correctly? Time slowed as her mind tried to understand this turn of fortune.

"I'm getting older and Otis plans to sell the house. We intend to go through all the belongings, clean every room, and of course there will be daily maintenance until a buyer is found."

The thrill of the offer was tempered by reality. "I would like to help, but I work at the duster factory."

"I know."

"You do?"

The creases near Mildred's eyes deepened. "You smell an awful lot like turkey."

Heat raced up Sadie's neck, all the way to her ears. "I would have bathed, but—"

"No explanation needed. What do you say? Do you agree? You work in the evenings, and in exchange you can stay in the staff quarters, eat with us, and you'll earn a decent wage. Our accommodations are nothing fancy, but they're better than the floor of the factory, and from the sound of it, a little extra money would be helpful."

It was too good to be true. To live here and to have additional income . . . But she'd heard the distrust in his voice.

"Are you certain Mr. Taylor wants me here?"

"I don't know if he knows what he wants." She laughed, the sound jolly like the ringing of bells. "Don't worry about Otis. We'll get you settled, but you've got to promise not to tell anyone he's here. It's his one demand."

"Demand?"

"Request."

"Of course, I promise." Relief—sweet, blessed relief—sent Sadie's heart dancing, and a few tears of pure joy ran down her face. "I'm sorry," she said as she wiped her eyes. "I've been praying for a miracle. This is . . . unexpected. I'm so grateful."

"Oh dear, we're the ones who are grateful. Both Leon and I have been hoping for a way to help Otis. And now you are here, and you may be exactly what this house needs."

Sadie had no idea what she meant, but she smiled as she wiped at her face. "I'll work as hard as I can."

"I'm sure you will. Now tell me about yourself."

Sadie told Mildred about her father, her sisters, and their plan to save their farm. More tears came with the telling, but not regret, not even when she talked about her cold nights in the factory.

Mildred patted her on the cheek. "You have endured a great deal."

"He's my father. We've got bank debt and doctor bills. They need me."

Mildred took her hand. "You sweet girl. I am quite certain you are exactly the miracle we need. Come along, let's fill your belly and get you cleaned up."

... I have now set foot in the finest house I have ever seen. It's as breathtaking as it is mysterious. The type of place an author would use for the setting of a novel. There must be a story here....

Chapter 7

"You look tired," Alta remarked the next morning when Sadie stepped into the factory. "But cleaner."

"Amazing what a bath will do," she said, allowing the sarcastic lilt to frost her words. Sleep had evaded her, despite the fact she'd slept in an actual bed. She'd been too preoccupied trying to piece together the mystery of Otis Taylor. The town believed him a famed musician. Women swooned at the thought of his return. But the man she'd met didn't fit the gossip. He'd been awkward and short with her, but there had been moments of wittiness, and as to his looks, she'd been unable to properly deduce, but he did not carry himself like a man who was believed to be a fine specimen. Nonetheless, he'd hired her when he could have thrown her out, and that was a mark in his favor.

In short the man was a conundrum—there was no understanding him.

"Let's hope you don't wait so long before the next one." Alta's smile wasn't convincing. "Next thing we know you'll be at the socials, trying to draw the attention of all the men."

"Do you think it possible? I don't have much experience with men." She would have to go to bed earlier tonight. Biting her tongue proved more difficult when she was tired. "I had a late night. I don't plan to seek attention from anyone."

"Shush." Alta grabbed Sadie's arm and pulled her toward the center of the main floor. "Look, Mr. Hoag's gathering everyone together."

Sadie quickened her pace. Soon the nearly forty employees were all standing shoulder to shoulder, squeezed in the center of the large workroom. Mr. Hoag spoke quickly, reminding everyone of production goals and congratulating them on their hard work.

"I'm pleased to tell you all that the orders are still coming in as strong as ever. We're shipping all over the world to cities as large as London and as small as Azure Springs, Iowa.

"We produce more feather dusters than anyone else in the world. We can't shirk, not with so much demand. Not only are the orders coming in, but there is also high demand for the dyed dusters and custom orders. Another lathe is going to be added to the main floor and perhaps another winding machine." He pulled a piece of paper from his pocket and unfolded it. "Just today a Mrs. Lorraine Morris, the mayor of Blackwell's wife, has put in a custom order. She wrote to me directly, asking that we make her a duster different from all others."

Sadie had come to appreciate the production of dusters, but all this talk of shipping and numbers had little consequence on her job as a sorter when she had already committed herself to working as quickly and efficiently as possible.

Movement to her left drew her attention. She looked away from Mr. Hoag, then flinched when she saw Leon and Mildred enter the factory. "Excuse me," Leon said, nodding at the crowd. "I'm sorry to interrupt. I can wait outside until your meeting is over."

"No need. What can I do for you?" Mr. Hoag stopped giving details on the custom duster. All eyes and full attention were on the guests.

"I'm looking for one of your employees. I require only a moment of her time."

"Of course. Who are you looking for?"

"A Miss Sadie West."

Alta grabbed Sadie's arm and leaned in. "Mr. and Mrs. Dawson work at the Taylor mansion. How do you know them?"

"I-I . . ." she stammered.

"Go see what he wants. When you come back, tell me what's going on."

Sadie stumbled from the depths of the crowd, emerging in front of the Dawsons, who smiled and motioned for her to follow. They stepped out of the factory building but did not go far.

"We were passing through town, fetching supplies for the house, when we realized you hadn't taken anything to eat." Mildred smiled, making her glasses rise and fall with her cheeks. She held out a tin. "We brought this for you."

"I'm grateful," Sadie said, taking the offered gift. "But what am I to tell everyone when they ask how I know you?"

"Tell them . . ." Mildred looked at Leon, who shrugged. "Tell them you are taking an order for a duster from us."

"Do you need a duster?"

Mildred nodded. "A house that big ought to have a duster for each floor, don't you think?"

"But why ask me? If it's custom, Mr. Hoag will take the order himself."

"Because we met you recently and thought you had an honest face," Leon said. "You do have an honest face."

"I aim to be honest. But keeping Otis's secret and working here might make it difficult to remain completely honest. The women in there are all convinced that Otis will return one day and sweep them off their feet."

"Oh dear," Mildred said. "We didn't mean to cause a problem."

Leon leaned against the wall of the Hoag factory. "We have another reason for coming. Otis has asked us to apologize for his behavior yesterday."

"He was out of sorts," Mildred said.

"I hold no grudge. Though, I confess, I spent much of last night trying to understand the man. He seemed very changeable."

"May I be frank with you?" Leon asked slowly.

"Please." She looked back at the factory, duty insisting she hurry.

"Otis hasn't been home in a long time. You would think that coming home would be— Well, tell me, how would you feel if you walked into your parents' home?"

"I would smell my mama's cooking, and my sisters would be there, and we'd sneak off to the barn so we could tell one another secrets." The familiar ache formed in her chest. "It would be wonderful."

"Coming home for Otis is not the same," Mildred said.

"Oh." She bit her bottom lip. Even leading a sheltered life, she knew that not all homes were welcoming and happy like hers, or as complete. "I should have known that he was hurting, grieving his brother. His house must feel very lonely."

"It's complicated, but he is lonely," Leon said. "You're right in thinking he has a lot to grieve. Still, I don't excuse him—he was rude to leave so abruptly."

"I expect in a home so large, we will hardly ever see each other. I'll make myself scarce."

"Nonsense. We hope your presence will remind him that companionship is a good thing."

She'd not been able to get her Marvin Bennett, with whom she was well acquainted, to make promises. There was no way she could get a man like Otis Taylor to face his grief and come out of obscurity. "No, I don't think that's wise." Sadie took a step backward, as though she feared the man himself would come to greet her if she didn't flee. "He seemed adamant that he prefers his privacy."

"He doesn't know what's good for him." Mildred patted her shoulder. "We best be going. Order a duster for us and hurry back tonight. We're eager to get to know you better."

"I will." Their kindness seemed to know no bounds. She narrowed her eyes, suddenly skeptical. "You don't know me. Why have you been so kind? What if I am a thief and . . . and I steal . . . a desk?" She laughed, despite her honest question. "Or something smaller that I could actually carry away."

Leon's face was creased with gentleness and mischief. "Are you in need of a desk?"

"No," she replied, her head spinning. "I don't understand, that's all. Why be kind to me?"

"Since Reginald died the place has been lonely." Mildred sighed. "You are in need and so are we. We've no other motive."

Sadie nodded, choosing to accept their words. She thanked them again and bid them farewell for the day before going back inside, where she had to give vague answers to make it through the day without divulging secrets that were not hers to share.

. . . The mansion is so large, it makes me feel very small. . . .

Sadie sighed as she continued writing. Talking to her sisters in their presence would have been so much more satisfying.

She soon finished the letter and left her small staff room to walk the halls, admiring once again the portraits and photographs. Following one picture and then the next, she gave no thought to where she was in the house until a sound from deep in the belly of the home drifted through the air, dancing down the hall to where she stood. Fear of intruding where she was not invited kept her from drawing closer. She pressed her back to the wall and listened to the notes of the piano.

A sad song, beautiful in its hollow, desperate way, set her heart aching. The melody captured the homesickness that welled inside her. The worry for her father. Her fear that the bank would stop accepting her meager payments or that new doctor bills would come. A touch of sadness over the loveless letters Marvin sent. She put a hand to her heart. The storm of feelings twirled with the notes in the air.

The captivating song ended abruptly, and she snapped back to reality. Those notes hadn't felt like the end of a song. Where was the rest? A clatter rang out—something had been thrown, broken, and shattered—and then she heard a heart-wrenching cry, deep and agonizing.

Otis had always turned to music when life became too heavy to carry. Into the notes he played his sorrow, hope, and even his dreams. Like a prayer, he communed with God, wrestling with him as he tried to make sense of his place and his purpose.

Tonight the notes failed to soothe him. He played with passion and deep feelings, pouring everything straight from his heart to the keys, but his feelings only grew and grew, bringing with them harrowing memories.

He recalled his father looming above him, pouring hot oils onto his scalp, burning his skin despite his anguished cries.

"Hold still." His father's hand gripped his shoulder tightly. Tears ran down Otis's face as he fought, unable to free himself.

Overcome by the memory, Otis rose from the piano bench, grabbed the framed photo of his father off the wall, and threw it against the floor.

Chapter 8

Leon left before the sun was up, bound for Springhole, leaving Otis wandering the halls as he awaited Leon's return. Would Elisabeth be with him? The sooner he found her, the sooner he could leave Monticello for good. He knew he could leave now and handle matters via correspondence, and there were moments when the thought tempted him, but the finances were still being sorted, and the matter of Elisabeth was of utmost importance—he needed to be here for her.

Wolf tilted his head and looked up at him.

"I'm worried too," Otis said. He had no experience with children. He swallowed, but the lump in his throat refused to go away. If he didn't find her, he would always wonder. If she was found, he'd be responsible for her every need, which was an intimidating prospect.

Wolf yawned. He had an advantage over Otis. Everyone liked Wolf when they met him. They found him striking in looks and an agreeable companion. Neither could be said about Otis, who lacked in both areas.

"You ought to busy yourself." Mildred brought him a cup of coffee. "Time won't go any faster with you staring through the gap in the drapes."

"You're right." He turned his back to the window and looked at the endless stack of letters sent to his late brother. It held no appeal. "I think I'll search Reginald's room. I've put it off long enough, and there may be information on Elisabeth in there."

"Excellent." Mildred clapped her hands together. "Go on then, and stop fretting. We'll find her."

"I wish I were so certain."

"Your mother would have told you to cling to hope."

"Do you think . . . Would she have sent me off . . . ?" His voice failed him.

"No," Mildred said with an affirmative shake of the head. "I think she would have done everything she could have to keep you here and to convince you that your worth was not in your looks."

There was no way to know for sure. His mother had been gone from this earth for a very long time, but he wanted to believe that Mildred was right. That not everyone who mattered would have sent him away given the chance.

"I wish I could know for certain. I'll be in Reginald's room." He backed away from her and made his way to his brother's garish abode. It boasted finely crafted walnut furniture covered with burgundy blankets and pillows. Furniture fit for a king, or for a man who thought himself equal to a king. What a waste to furnish a bedroom with such luxury.

No one even sees the chamber of an unmarried man. He cringed, realizing that might not be true of his brother.

"Come, Wolf," he ordered. "Let's see if we can learn something about Elisabeth."

He began at the closet, sifting through Reginald's tailored suits. When he'd last seen Reginald, they'd been boys, just beginning to grow into men. These suits would not have fit the lad he'd butted heads with and who he'd missed every day since they'd said goodbye.

"I don't think anyone thought you were going away for good, especially Reginald." He nearly jumped at the sound of Mildred's voice. Where had she come from? "I thought I'd see if you wanted company. Some rooms are harder to go in."

"I didn't think I was going away for good either. I thought when my head healed, or when my father accepted me as I was . . . But he couldn't stand the sight of me. After his hot oils failed, nothing was the same. Not even my scalp."

"The scars . . ." Mildred shook her head. "Your father cried that night."

"And then he made arrangements to send me away." Otis grasped the foot of the bed. "I hated his miracle cures. I was a fool to believe." Even now that he was a grown man, the memories stung as much as the tonic rubbed into his once smooth scalp had. No, the memories of his father's disapproving eyes stung more than even the hottest oil.

"You were a boy—of course you believed. Your father failed you the day he sent you away, and he failed himself. I can't speak for him, but he was never the same after that. It was as though he carried a weight he couldn't free himself of."

Otis never saw his father again after that. And though his father continued to send remedies, he never asked Otis to come back. Mr. Crawford, the quiet old pianist, would hand him the parcels when they arrived, and like an innocent child, Otis believed he would find a reminder of home, a loving gift, or at least a letter full of heart. Instead, he found glass bottles that crowed their ability to cure any ailment. Bottles of lies. Bottles of rejection. Bottles of pain. In tears he would massage his scalp, his arms, his eyebrows, and take spoonful after spoonful of sour liquid that turned his stomach but did nothing for his hair.

At twenty he stopped, no longer believing he would be beckoned home nor that he would ever be cured. He looked in the mirror at his face, void of eyebrows or hair on his scalp, riddled with scars from the many failed attempts to regrow what was lost. He touched his smooth arms and blinked his eyelids that had no lashes and accepted that he would never look the part of a Taylor gentleman. He'd merely live inside the shell of a broken man. His warring emotions were poured into his music, and he captured the pain so thoroughly that his songs sold well. But even the piano could not ease the pain he carried.

Over the years the packages came with less frequency, and then his father died, and Otis grieved. He wept over a man who hadn't wanted him. No packages came after that; no tonics, no letters until Leon sent for him. He was no closer to knowing where he belonged or what to do with his life, but he did feel driven to find Elisabeth.

It made no difference that she was an illegitimate child. She could be disfigured, and he would not look away. When he found her, he would keep her safe, no matter the cost. His resolve was firm. He would love her in the deep, forever way that he had yearned for. If the feelings growing in his chest were any indication of his conviction, one could assume he loved her already.

"I do hope to find Elisabeth," he said. For himself, he no longer knew what to reach for, but he would give her the world.

Mildred nodded and began searching the room.

His brother, he discovered, cared a great deal for clothes. His dressers and armoires were filled to bursting. His pockets were mostly empty, aside from the one or two that contained sugar cubes.

"How strange that the only things I know about my grown brother are that he was obsessed with clothes and expensive furniture, that he had an abandoned offspring, and that he held an apparent affection for his horse," Otis said after finding another sugar cube. "Mother used to take sugar to the horses too."

"He kept your mother's mare until she died of old age only weeks before your brother died. Likely, those cubes were meant for her."

"Ah, now I know another fact about Reginald. He looked after mother's horse. I'm glad of it. I have many memories of her in the stable brushing that mare."

"There is talk that horses will soon be a thing of the past. Everyone says automobiles will take over the world," Mildred said with one hand on the back of the chair by the dressing table.

"Mother would rue the day."

Buried in the back of a dresser drawer, Otis discovered a few unpaid notes that made them both groan. What they found next silenced them. A handkerchief with his mother's initials embroidered in the corner was placed atop an embossed frame with cracked glass sheltering an image of Reginald and Otis's mother. He stared into her soft eyes and she looked back at him, the smile never leaving her lips. His throat tightened around words he wished he could speak to her. If only he could sit beside her and search her every gesture for acceptance. Would she smile so contently if she saw his scars? Would she run her fingers over his head in the same affectionate way she'd run her fingers through his once thick hair? If only he could take her hand and listen to her voice instructing him on life and love and faith.

He turned to Mildred. "Why do you suppose Reginald had these?"

"Even a grown man misses his mama. Life soured him, but that doesn't mean he didn't grieve."

"When she was here everything was different."

"Your mother was a loss to both of you. But Reginald grieved your departure too. When you first left, he asked your father every day when you were coming back."

"What did my father say?"

"At first he told him you would be back soon."

Otis scoffed. "Father wouldn't like knowing I'm back here now, still scarred and hairless."

"He should have gone and seen you. He would have realized that you're still you," Mildred said. "I tried to tell him to visit, but he was a stubborn man. I think he even wanted to, but—"

"You know, I used to watch for him." *But he never came.* The words didn't need to be said aloud. They both knew the truth. Otis's temper threatened to boil over. The hurt young man who still lived in him wanted to lash out, but then he saw his mother's face in the cracked frame and held on to the calming love she had always shown him. "Tell me what happened with Reginald. You said he asked about me."

"Your father grew tired of answering him. I believe the guilt nagged at him, all the lies about where you were, and the constant asking from Reginald wore him down. He slapped Reginald one night when he asked about you, and after that I never heard him speak your name again." Mildred closed the drawer they'd found the photograph in and stepped away from the dresser. A heaviness, like a thick fog, filled the air. "Your father put his energy into his businesses, and Reginald worked with him."

"Hmm." Otis set the frame aside and busied himself by shuffling through belongings. The fact that Reginald had asked after him, at least for a time, made it harder for Otis to hold on to his anger. But that was all he'd felt for his family for so long. Anger and a persistent longing to be near them—the mix forever sparring inside him. Now he wasn't sure what to feel.

Their continued search revealed more clothes and worldly possessions but little evidence of Reginald's comings and goings.

The obvious places had been thoroughly investigated, and they'd found nothing that pertained to Elisabeth. Otis shoved his hands in his pockets and looked around the room. He must have missed something.

He looked under the dresser, tapped at the floorboards—nothing. He pulled every drawer from the dresser, looked for a false bottom—nothing. His heart beat faster. There had to be more than trinkets and clothes. He ran his hand along the top of the drapes. Dust soared through the air and he sneezed, but he kept his hand moving, feeling for something. Then his fingers brushed across metal. A key. He grabbed it and held it tight.

"Mildred!" She rushed to his side. "What do you think this could be to?"

"I don't recognize it." She reached for it, and though he was remiss to let it go, he put it in her hand. She raised it close to her face and studied it.

"It must be important," he said, eager to have it back in his hand.

"I wish I knew." She returned it to him. "Keep it. Someday we might know what it goes to."

He tucked it into his pocket, relieved that their efforts had amounted to something, even if they weren't sure what it was.

When they could think of nowhere else to search, Mildred opened the bedroom door. "I best get supper ready. You ought to go and clean up—wouldn't want Sadie seeing you so disheveled."

He groaned. "I think I'll stay here."

"You stubborn man." She laughed as she walked from the room, leaving him with Wolf, a key with no lock, and thoughts of his new employee.

He'd kept to himself last evening, afraid to confront her. The last time he'd been alone with a woman his own age, he was fourteen, just a boy. Mr. Crawford ensured that he received a solid education in mathematics, Latin, and even geography. But no one had taught him how to converse with women or how to make himself feel at ease in their presence.

To Otis's great relief, Leon arrived before Sadie. "Tell me everything," Otis said, ready for a distraction and hopefully a lead.

"Elisabeth isn't there."

"She's not?"

"No. Mary sent that letter two years ago. Reginald wouldn't pay more for the child's upkeep. He came and took the child, and Mary doesn't know what happened after that. Since he didn't bring her here, she assumes he found a different home for her."

"I don't understand. Does Mary run an orphanage?"

"Not exactly. The children aren't orphans."

Otis clenched his jaw. "You're saying she takes in children whose parents don't want them?"

"They may want them," Mildred said. "But this world is harsh—"

"You can't excuse it," Otis said. He'd heard every justification, every reason why it was right to abandon one's own family. They were lies, all of them. "Did she say what Reginald's connection was to Elisabeth? Are we sure that she is his child?"

"He is the father. Mary was brought the child as an infant and paid to care for her. Elisabeth was only a few days old when the arrangement was made. Reginald said the mother left the baby with him and he could not keep her."

"*Would* not keep her, you mean."

"I don't know his reasoning," Leon said. "Mary did say he was adamant the child be kept a secret."

"And she does not know where the child is now? But his bank books continue to list Elisabeth up until his death."

"He must have found someone else willing to care for her," Mildred said. "But whoever has her hasn't been paid since his death. It's been a year . . ."

"So whoever has her could turn her out?" Otis said.

"It's possible." Leon frowned. "I don't mean to speak ill of Mary, but . . . well, she wasn't caring for those children because she felt a love for them. It appeared to be mercenary."

"Oh dear," Mildred said. "I don't like the thought of that."

"Could we discreetly ask around and see if there are known people who care for foundlings or children who have no one?" Otis tapped his foot impatiently. He had to find her. Taking her in would be frightening, he knew so little about children, but the thought of her being out there with no one was far worse.

"When I go to the next quilting night, I'll see if I can get the women talking. They love to gossip," Mildred said. "But I can't promise anyone will know anything."

"I am not keen on gossip, having been the subject of so much. But if you would ask, I'd be grateful."

> . . . I've never understood men, and the owner of the mansion is more complicated than any other. Whenever I see him, he ducks into another room and looks away. Perhaps I should write him another letter. . . .

Chapter 9

Dear Edward Rochester,

You once wrote, and so I am hopeful you will not find this letter presumptuous. I can sometimes hear you playing the piano. The sound echoes through the halls, and no matter where I am, I listen. I don't know much about you, yet I know you must feel deeply. You played a sad song last night, and I felt as though you understood the worry I have for my family and father. It was as though I had someone to commiserate with. I wonder if you are missing your family and if that loss weighs heavily on your heart. If so, I am sorry for your pain.

I thank you again for hiring me. I realize my presence makes you uneasy. When our paths cross, you pull your hat down low on your head and step away from me. If I have done something upsetting, I am willing to make it right.

Jane Squatter

PS: Perhaps we should change my name to Jane Boarder?

She tiptoed through the house, stopping at the guest room she knew he slept in. The hall was dark and silent, nothing but long shadows and creaking floorboards occupying this end of the house. A shiver raced down her spine. She shouldn't be here, not when she knew he detested her presence. Looking over her shoulder, she confirmed she was alone, then slid the letter beneath the door. There was no changing her mind now. Her words were written and delivered, and soon they would be read. They may widen the chasm between her and her employer, or perhaps, she hoped, they would prove a bridge across the expanse. When a cool draft sent her skirts dancing around her legs, she rushed from the hall and away from the mansion.

Off to work she raced, grateful to be out of the house when he received her missive. When she was away from the mansion, her days were predictable. She would say hello to Peter on her way to work, give him any letters she had for him, and accept whatever news he brought about her family. She would enjoy her moment with him, thankful that his presence felt a bit like home. And then she would sort feathers and listen to Alta and Sylvia dissect the comings and goings of everyone in Monti.

She was right, everything went as predicted, until the evening. When she arrived home, she found a note under her door.

Dear Jane Squatter (I find Squatter has a more pleasant ring than Boarder),

I have received your letter, and now I have a secret for you.

She smiled, grateful to at last be given a chance to understand the man.

> I don't know whether it is proper for us to exchange letters. I am inexperienced in the art of writing, though in many ways it is easier than speaking, and since this is not the first correspondence between Rochester and Squatter, the damage to our reputations is likely already done.

What? She paused. That could not be his secret—that he did not know if it was proper to write. She wanted more. She needed to understand him. She'd never enjoyed mysteries that had no solution, and she aimed to piece together who this man truly was. Working for a mysterious employer was fascinating in novels, but this was real life, and it felt utterly important to understand how the man in the shadows and the man on the lips of gossips coexisted.

Still, he'd written, and for a reason she could not quite pinpoint, her stomach danced with anticipation as she read on.

> I lived for many years in the country outside of Boston. My circumstances were unusual, leaving me inept socially. My father told everyone I was making a name for myself with my music, which was not entirely a lie. I have sold and composed a great deal of music, but that was not my sole purpose for being away. Needless to say, I am not the bachelor Monticello expects, nor am I grieving my lost family, at least not in the way you suggest.
>
> I will do better in the halls. I'll try to even nod my head and offer a half smile.
>
> E. R.

PS: You look much cleaner now. Mildred must have found you something better than the creek to wash in.

Sadie should have gasped, but instead she laughed. This mannerless man left her bewildered and intrigued. And since Mildred had requested she befriend Otis, she chose to write again.

Dear Edward,

A nod and a half smile—how blissful. I will look forward to this exchange with eager anticipation, and one day, if I am very clever, I will find a way to pull a full smile from you.

I don't understand your life. You speak of isolation in the woods of Massachusetts, but why were you there? I have many questions, but my mother taught me that it is rude to pry. You are a grown man, capable of divulging whatever you wish to share. Know that I will be a listening ear if you are ever in need of one.

While I await the details of your time away, I will tell you about my family.

Her letter grew long as she described in detail her parents and each sister. She told him that she had always wanted adventure but now felt guilty for ever wishing to leave, and that being away reminded her of how much she truly had. She told him how she loved writing and stories. She told him how she longed to go roller-skating again and how she hoped to one day own a home with a library. She wrote of her father's injury and her mother's worries that he would never walk again. She wrote about the bank and the doctor bills and why she came to Monticello. She told him about Peter, who delivered her mail, and how the letters from her family kept her from crumbling with homesickness. And she told him of her nights in the abandoned factory.

> I was cold and alone, but Blue (also known as Wolf) came, and then you chose to let me stay. I thank the Lord for your goodness.
>
> Jane Squatter

Her letter had grown longer than she had planned. It was more vulnerable than she had intended. But it was all true, so she delivered it.

Two days later, key in one pocket and letters folded in the other, Otis sat near the kitchen window, drumming his fingers on the table. He was hoping that Mildred, who had just left for her evening of quilting, would come back with some bit of information about children hidden away. Too much time had passed already. He needed something to help him find Elisabeth.

"I'll be very careful what I say," she had said before leaving. "No one will know you are back. Though I wish I could tell them. I'd love to tell them how much warmer the house is now that you've returned."

"You flatter me. I thought I'd brought a frigid air."

"Nonsense." She looked him in the eyes. "It's good having you back, and I'm not just saying that because every time I turn around, I find something else you've repaired for me."

"I gained a few skills living on my own. Didn't seem right keeping them to myself."

"If you wish to do your kindness quietly, I'll let you. Sadie is rather clever as well. She knows just the solution for getting the silver to sparkle. You ought to go and find her and pass the time together. Won't do you any good sitting there, drumming your fingers on the table. It could be hours before I'm back." She waved her hands in the air. "Go and find her."

"I . . . perhaps."

She left with an eagerness to her step. He watched her go before sitting at the table and peering through the gap between the drape and the window frame, unsure if he should take her advice or not.

"Mildred suggested I find you." Sadie's voice startled him. He let go of the drape and did his best to appear at ease. In reality his heartbeat quickened from a peaceful rhythm to a rapid pound. She stood in the doorway, wearing the same brown skirt she always wore, her hair loosely braided and hanging over one shoulder. He'd not really looked at her since she moved in, only sideways glances. In many ways, he knew who she was inside better than who she was on the outside, thanks to her letters. Now his gaze lingered against his will. She was not a fancy woman, but her long neck and blue eyes were not something he would soon forget.

"Mildred can be a rather conniving woman," he said, pulling his gaze away.

"I believe she worries about you." She stepped closer, and his impulse to flee surfaced. He flinched, fighting off the natural urge. This was Jane Squatter. He owed her at least a half smile.

"I suppose we should oblige her." He nearly choked on the words. "If you wish?"

"Oh, I do. Mildred told me to leave the laundry and come find you. You have saved me and my back from the scrubbing board."

"Ah, so my company is better than the wash. I'm flattered."

"I *believe* it will be better, but the jury is not settled. You could prove incredibly dull, and I may end the night wishing I had spent it with my hands in scalding water."

He laughed. How absurd his few encounters with Sadie had been. He'd spent years hating everyone in Monticello, but Sadie and the Dawsons made it difficult to cling to such a notion. "Tell me, what could I do to make your time with me more appealing than water that nearly burns?"

She pursed her lips. "Will you call my desires frivolous?"

"No."

"If I had skates and a proper dress, I would say that we should go roller-skating or to the dance hall. I would love to write my sisters and tell them that I had been out enjoying the city."

He frowned. "I can't—"

"I know. You don't want anyone knowing you are here. You want to settle matters here without any commotion. I respect that." She fiddled with the end of her braid. "We could go to the music room. You could play and I could listen."

"I don't play for an audience." He never had. He'd played for a teacher and for himself but for no one else. His teacher had handled his commissions and sold his pieces. Others played his notes onstage for huge audiences, but he never did. "Your letter said you listen in the halls. It's a compliment, but I could never play with you in the room. There must be some other way to pass the time."

"We could take Wolf outside. It's warm and pleasant."

Could she suggest something he could accommodate? He could walk the property in the dark of night or stay directly by the house, but he wasn't ready to venture. He might never be.

"Do you play chess?" he asked when no other ideas came to him.

"I have before, but not often enough to be a skilled player."

"Excellent. I am rusty myself. We will be a fair match."

The first game, she lost nearly immediately. By the third game, she'd improved but was still easy to beat. She smiled, even when she lost, and he had to remind himself not to stare. But he kept going back to her face, so alive, so bright and cheerful. Her presence surprised him. It made him want to smile in return. He'd avoided her, aware of his lack of social skills, but here they sat, and though he was not a skilled conversationalist, he was enjoying himself.

"Might I ask you a question?" she said as they set their pieces up for a fourth game.

"I don't know," he said, stalling. He feared he knew what she would ask, and he did not know how he would answer it. "Might I ask you one?"

"A question for a question." She grinned, put her elbows on the chess table, and leaned closer. "You first."

His mind went blank. Drat. For days he'd had questions piling up in his mind, but now when he had the chance, they dissipated, floating just out of reach. He fumbled, then threw out the first words that came to him. "You slide letters under my door. Is this something you do often?"

"Write letters?"

"To men?"

Her face lost its color. "No, of course not. Well, I have, but . . . not—"

"I wasn't making an accusation." Where was a rock to hide behind? Of all the questions he could have asked, why had this one come out? "Blast. I should go back to the woods."

She reached across the table and put her hand on his arm. "No."

He swallowed and fought to steady his breathing, but she was touching him. Heat rushed through all of him, setting him on fire with her gentle touch.

"I write to my sisters and my parents. I write to a friend who is off at school. And I write to Mr. Rochester, who I hope is becoming a friend."

Wolf, who sat near the hearth, lifted his head, stood, stretched, and moved closer to them. His coat caught the light, and his hair looked as blue as the moon on a crisp autumn night.

Sadie took her hand back and put it on Wolf. Otis stared at the spot where her hand had been, wishing she would put it back. When her hand was on his arm, it'd caused him to feel normal, less of an oddity.

In a singsong voice she talked to his dog. "You were my first real friend in Monti."

Wolf wagged his tail and Otis felt a stab of jealousy. Which, of course, was a ridiculous feeling. No grown man should ever be jealous of a dog, but here he was, wishing the dog would run off so Sadie would give him all her attention.

"Is it my turn to ask a question?" She kept her hand on Wolf's floppy ears.

"You want to know why I wear a hat?" he said, and at last she looked up at him.

"If you're willing to tell me. If not, you must only say so and I will think of a different question for you."

Otis did not answer right away. He feared that by giving her the truth, this new friendship, if he dared call it that, would be lost before it had truly begun. What was friendship, though, if it was not the sharing of confidences?

"The women at work, they talk of you," she said, leaning closer, and he felt certain she was trying to see deeper into the shadows of his brim. He'd never felt so exposed. If only he were a handsome man, he'd take off his hat and move closer, giving her as much time as she wanted to look at him. "When you decide to tell everyone you've returned, they will want to meet you."

"My father did me no service when he told everyone I was off making a name for myself. He let them believe I was something I am not. And now I'm the one who will have to see their faces when they realize the truth."

"I don't understand."

Otis stood. He walked to the window and looked out. It was easier, talking in letters or with his back to her. "Tell me, do your peers at work dream of a wealthy, handsome man?"

"I suppose."

"Would they want a reclusive man? One who intends to live far from the rest of the world?"

"I don't know. I imagine they dream of this house when they think of you, but I can't say for certain."

He grimaced. She would never understand. This friendship was an illusion, one bound to fade away.

Better to face it now. He turned toward her and pulled his hat from his head.

Chapter 10

Sadie gasped, then she swayed and covered her mouth, ashamed of herself for responding so openly and at the same time trying to make sense of what she was seeing. Raised scars riddled his scalp. Where hair should have been, there was none.

Otis's eyes narrowed. He stepped back quickly, putting a gulf between them. He took one more step, his fisted hands trembling at his sides. His lack of hair and his scars had shocked her, stealing her composure, but now her heart beat rapidly because of the fear and hurt she saw in his expression.

She stood. "Wait," she said, afraid he would leave. "I'm sorry. You startled me, that's all. I did not expect—"

"Sorry for what? For looking at me exactly how I knew you would?" He turned his back on her but did not leave. "Now you know."

She heard his words but couldn't comprehend them. Her eyes were rapidly exploring his bare head, searching for understanding. She had seen plenty of bald men before, but he was different. The entire surface of his scalp was riddled with uneven, discolored skin.

"Does it hurt?" she whispered, afraid she would ignite his temper or add to his anguish. Old wounds, she knew, would bleed if picked, and she had no desire to tear the scab from such painful injuries. Whatever caused such scars must have hurt not only his scalp but also his soul.

Otis ran his hand across his head, his fingers slowly moving along the rims and crests of the range of scars. An urge to reach out and let her hands feel what he felt grew inside her. Perhaps if she could touch what she saw, she could understand.

"It doesn't hurt." He mumbled. "Not anymore."

"Is this why you left Monticello? You had an accident?"

"I didn't leave. I was sent away. Exiled." His voice was terse but not in a frightening way. "This head of mine . . . it changed everything."

"Why not tell everyone what happened?" There were other injured men in town. She'd not spied another man quite like Otis, but surely, when he explained, he'd be welcomed. Injuries were a part of life. Even she had small scars from mishaps on the farm.

Otis turned and faced her again. She looked closer at him. It was the first time she'd seen him without the shadows of his hat obscuring her view. He had no eyebrows, no lashes, and though it gave him an unusual look, she still found his blue eyes fascinating. Wells of color, full of story. Frantic and enticing, unique from all others.

"It was no accident." He spoke through clenched teeth, picked up his hat, and pulled it over his head, putting himself back into darkness. "Do you think the women you work with would want to court me? These women who talk about the elusive Taylor man, would they want to be on my arm?"

She didn't answer.

"Look at me," he barked, "and tell me the truth."

Sadie swallowed as she searched for words. She began to speak, starting and stopping. His piercing eyes unnerved her. She shook her head, embarrassed by the truth, but it would have been a lie to say that Alta would set her vanity aside to court him.

"I knew it." He moved for the door, tension palpable in the air as he went. "I'm a beast, but I am free. And if I choose to stay away, so be it. Tell your friends the truth if you wish. Tell them that I ought to be in the circus, a sideshow act to be gawked at for a nickel."

"Stop," she said when he moved for the door. One word was all she could manage. He stopped, looked at her, and waited. She focused on a knot in the floor near his feet, away from the pain she'd seen written on his face. "I've never been to the circus. I don't know about gawking for nickels or sideshows. Perhaps I am naïve, but why would someone pay money to stare at a man simply because he looks different?"

"Save your duster money and go when the circus is in town next. You'll see men not so different from me. Some ailment or oddity on display for the viewing pleasure of the masses." He glared at her, the place where eyebrows should be pulled tightly together. "Or look at me and skip the show. Save your nickel."

"You're being cruel." She fumbled over her words. "Accusing me of desires I have not voiced. How can you say I would gawk when you don't know me? Not really."

"I saw your face when I pulled off my hat."

"I—"

He turned, cutting her off, and left. She pinched the bridge of her nose and fought the tears that wanted to come.

"I didn't cause those scars," she said to no one. Weak in the knees, she sat and tried to still the rapid flutter in her chest. Words she wished she'd found sooner were on the tip of her tongue. If only she'd told him that it was only hair, that Alta would not want to court him but that Alta was not all women. Someone better suited to him . . . She shook her head, berating herself. If only she'd had the right words, she could have kept him from leaving in such a dejected way.

Then again, he seemed to be a man full of angst. Her words may have done no good. Despite his anger, the heaviness of regret pressed against her chest.

She picked up a chess piece and mindlessly rolled it in her hand. There were chores she ought to do, but a sudden weariness kept her from moving. Otis had shared his secret. Since their first encounter she'd puzzled over him, but not once had she pictured what she'd seen tonight. How did it all fit together? Who was he? A beast? A man with a buried heart? Or some strange combination of both?

"It's getting late," Leon said as he entered. He crossed the floor and sat across from her. "If you're waiting for Mildred, I suggest you don't. When she goes to quilting night, she always says she'll be back in an hour or two, but then she gets to talking and doesn't come home for twice as long as she says."

"I have sisters," Sadie mumbled, still thinking about Otis and what she'd seen. "I never run out of things to say to them."

She felt his eyes on her and tried to offer a convincing smile, but he saw through it. "Something has happened?"

"Otis . . . he showed me . . . he showed me his wounds."

Leon set up straighter, then nodded his head slowly. "Mildred said she hoped he would soon. For an old gal, she's got a keen sense about things."

"Otis left angry." Her stomach twisted. He hurt because of her. "I wish I had been quicker to speak. I should have told him that hair and scars . . . they matter little."

"It's probably best you didn't say that."

"Why?"

Leon picked up a pawn and knocked a king over, only to stand it back up. "He doesn't like being lied to."

"But it is *just* hair and skin."

"No, it's not. Not to him. It's the reason his father sent him away, it'll be the reason he will struggle to find a wife, and it's what keeps him from feeling whole and confident. Everything changed when his hair fell out. It matters to him, even if it shouldn't."

"But he can't be miserable forever. What sort of a life would that be?"

"Someday I hope he knows his losses matter, but they are not what matters most." He looked around the fine room. "Monticello is a hard place for him to be happy in. I don't know how long he'll stay here."

"Couldn't he make new memories here? It's been so many years, surely he could try. He must still have some friends here."

"He did have friends here, but now there are so many years between them and so many unsaid things. He disappeared with no goodbyes to anyone. There's a lot that would have to be explained, and Otis isn't ready for that. I don't think he has any desire to start over here, but he can't leave yet. Not until he finds— Not until his affairs are settled. It could take time."

Sadie didn't press, but her intellect was quick and bright enough to know there was more going on than Leon was ready to be forthright about. Like a rain barrel during a storm, this house was overflowing with questions.

"I can't make sense of him. Or any of it." She said the last part under her breath.

"Let me ask you. What do you know about him?" Leon asked, challenging her.

"I know about his scars and his . . . baldness." Leon's brows lifted, pressing her for more. "I know that he has a temper—I've heard him break things and cry out. Only now I realize what you meant when you said his life has been . . . complicated."

"What else?"

"I . . . I know that he plays music in a way I have never heard before. When I hear him, I know that Otis Taylor is not all hurt and anger. He has a soul and a heart. No man can play like that who does not."

Leon clapped his hand against the table as though she had hit the nail on the head. "We are all a lot of things. But what you heard when he played—I believe that is the real Otis, and the anger is part of what he hides behind."

. . . When I used to write stories, I was always looking for a hardship to throw at my characters. I wanted to send them on a journey and saw pain as an efficient means to that end. The challenge and quest made a story all the more thrilling.

Real life is much more complicated. Pain does so much more than create tension between characters, and it does not always mean a happy ending is right around the corner. It can mean years of heartache.

I am missing you all tonight. I could use the comfort of your love, and I could use your wisdom. I find myself in need of it.

Somehow, I hope to convince a man who wishes to live in a cave to come out into the sunshine so he might discover whatever is around the corner. . . .

Chapter 11

Three letters written and discarded riddled Sadie's bedroom floor. Each was an attempt to tell Otis she was sorry for the way she'd reacted, but they felt trite and inadequate. The jesting and pseudonyms that had been used in their previous letters felt wrong under these circumstances, and when she tried to express herself in a serious tone, she struggled for words.

In the end, she snuck off to work at the duster factory without facing him. A coward's move, but fear was a powerful foe. Until she had the right words, she'd simply keep to herself.

❦

Mildred came in late the night before and went directly to her room before Otis could corner her and ask if she'd discovered anything about where Monti's illegitimate children might be hidden. It was for the best. His mood had been foul since his encounter with Sadie.

He'd driven Sadie away all because he feared she would run. He saw her leave for the factory, earlier than necessary, head tucked in and pace swift. Eager to turn her back on the mansion and on him, and he had no way of knowing if it was his temperament or his scars she ran from.

"Elisabeth," he said aloud. His niece. She would not run. He would go to whatever lengths necessary to convince her that he was more than he appeared. Today he would focus on her. She was what mattered.

If sleep were not medicine for the elderly, he'd have knocked on Mildred's door. Instead, he waited impatiently for her to rise. Three songs in the music room and he was back to pacing and hoping with all his might that she'd found a lead for them to follow.

"Otis," Mildred said, surprising him when she entered the parlor at seven thirty in the morning. "I'm sorry I kept you waiting."

"It's no matter. I hope you enjoyed your night out."

"There is something delightful about a room full of women, especially when it gets late. That's when the best conversation happens." She sat and leaned back, a tired smile on her face. "Your name was mentioned."

"Let me guess, a money-hungry mother wanted to know if I would ever come back and marry her daughter."

"They may have been thinking that, but they only asked if I expected you to return. They seemed eager."

He grunted. "Eager."

"Don't worry. I told them that your comings and goings were for you to decide." She studied him a moment. "Are you not a little excited to see your old chums and become reacquainted? Dan and Andrew and some of the others still live around here. They were all such nice boys."

As a child Otis's days were spent galivanting around with nearly every boy in Monti, but things were different then. He'd had a creek running through his yard and other niceties that the other lads couldn't resist. Grown men didn't feel the same urge to splash in the water. Picking up where they left off wasn't an option. Seeing Sadie's eyes when he tore off his hat had been harsh enough. An entire town turning tail and running? No thank you. "Tell me, were you able to learn anything about foundlings or orphans?"

"Not as much as I would have liked. But I would not call the night fruitless. I mentioned a different child, one with a similar background who was born in Monti a few years ago. A poor little lad who had been unwanted. I asked if anyone knew what became of him."

He cringed. *Unwanted.* It was a label no child, no person, should have.

"All the women became very quiet, and no one would look at me. I noticed a mother and daughter share a glance . . . I don't know what it meant, but I kept thinking about it. I believe it was a knowing look." Her lips drooped into a frown, and her eyes glimmered with dampness beneath furrowed brows. "It's a shame, the way we shun when we should rally around those who struggle. And no matter how others behave, in the pit of their stomachs, I think they know it too."

"That is something I know about."

She patted his knee. "You, poor dear, should have been wrapped in loving arms, not sent away."

He cleared his throat. "Don't get all weepy on me. I may have grown into a grumpy recluse even if I stayed here."

"That may be." She sniffled, pulled her handkerchief out, and blew her nose. "Enough about the past. I plan to go and pay a call on the mother and daughter. I believe they know something." She looked away, staring at nothing. "I'm not sure how I'll bring up the topic again, but I'll do what I can."

"Will you go today?"

"No, she mentioned a trip to see a sister. I will visit once I hear she's returned."

It was impossible to hide his disappointment. He didn't want to continue waiting, grasping at threads of hope that may well lead to nothing. He wanted Elisabeth here, beside him. "No one else said anything?"

"One woman mentioned an orphanage in Des Moines."

He sprang to action, grateful for something he could do. "I'll write to them and ask if they've had a young child named Elisabeth arrive in the last year. She may have been taken there when the payments stopped coming." Otis stood, ready to go for paper and pen. "It's worth a try."

"Yes, you write it and I'll mail it." Mildred's voice grew softer. "Finding Elisabeth may take time. Making your presence known might be important. There are people who might talk to you more readily than to me. Have you considered letting people know you've returned?"

"If I become convinced it will help me find her, then I'll do it. But for now, I have no desire to be a spectacle."

"There *are* some good people here," she said.

"My own father couldn't stand the sight of me. He believed my lack of hair a sign of evil spirits. Even doctors said ludicrous things. And all that was before the scars." He shook his head. The idea of having people in his life appealed, but not so much that he was ready to walk the street in broad daylight.

"We all have scars," Mildred said. Shafts of light from the rising sun twirled through the gaps in the drapes, adding a dancing brightness to the dreary room. He looked at his hands, half in the shadows and half in the light. "You don't have to hide. People with good hearts won't care. Anyone who does, let them talk. You don't need them."

If only it were so simple. Perhaps it was. He pulled his hands away from the light. "Even Sadie gasped."

"She's not perfect, nor are you. But if I have any sense of her character, and I believe I do, she will try again. You've had ten years to grow accustomed to the face in the mirror—you can hardly blame anyone for being startled or staring a moment too long."

"I'll think on it," he said, knowing he had no intention of showing his face in Monti.

❧

"I heard you were seen walking out of town last night," Sylvia said during their afternoon break. "I assumed you were staying at a boardinghouse, but I don't know of one out that way."

"I've taken a new position." She tapped her toe nervously against the floor. Mildred had instructed that if she had to tell someone where she was, she should say she worked with the Dawsons. "I'm at the Taylor mansion. The Dawsons were given permission to hire other employees. I am helping around the house in exchange for my room and board."

"You can't mean that you are going to be living with Otis Taylor if he returns." Alta's voice was a harsh whisper brined in accusation. "That's not fair. Had I known—"

"You make it sound scandalous, but it's not. I stay in the staff quarters. It's just a job."

Alta folded her arms across her chest like a spoiled child. "I should have known that a country girl like you would sneak around trying to steal the very man I've dreamed of for years. He won't pick you. Don't go setting your sights on him. Once he—"

"You can have Otis Taylor," Sadie whispered in a shaking voice. She leaned closer, trying to keep the dispute private despite the many people working near them. "I needed a job and a place to live. I can't give this up just because you have an infatuation with a man you know nothing about."

"I know enough! I grew up in this town—you didn't."

Think of Pa. She wouldn't lose sight of what was important, no matter how desperately she wanted to tell Alta that they worked at the same factory and she had no right to act superior. "We should get back to work," she said, hoping to change the subject. "There's no point to this argument. If Otis Taylor decides he wants to court a Monticello woman, you will find a way to stand out in the crowd—I have no doubt about it. I came here to work, not argue over nothing. I heard Mr. Hoag say he might move a sorter over to shipping."

"Shipping is as dull as sorting." Alta looked around the factory. "But it is near binding, and I wouldn't mind working near Lorenzo."

Sadie shook her head. Alta was always batting her eyes at someone. "I thought you were waiting for Otis Taylor."

"I am. He's the one I'm truly after, but there's no law against noticing other men while I wait."

"But you haven't even seen Otis." She bit her lip, chastising herself for letting her mouth flap. Not engaging with Alta was better. Safer. But an outspoken woman could only stay silent so long.

"I haven't, but I saw his brother." She smirked. "I don't approve of you working there, but they may have hired you because they expect him to return. You'll need to tell me right away if he's there."

"It's not my job to speak of his whereabouts."

Alta grabbed her hand as though they truly were the dearest of friends. "I won't be mad at you for working there if you promise to help me get to know him when he returns. Find out if he has a favorite food or if he has interests that I could take up or educate myself on. I want to know everything."

Sadie tore her hand away. "He's my employer. I can't work behind his back."

Alta inhaled. "Stop being selfish. I helped you fit in here at the duster factory. You can help me too."

Sadie threw herself into her work. Body. Tail. Wing. Body. Tail. Wing. She sorted feathers faster than ever before. "What you do with Otis is between you and him. I'm not working there to be your scout."

Alta humphed and turned her back on Sadie. The tension between the two women was palpable and lingered throughout the day.

Sylvia caught her arm later in the afternoon and said, "Alta is only jealous because she is used to getting her way. Can't you just tell her that you'll introduce her to Otis when he comes back? I'm sure if you did, she would let you come to the masquerade skate with us. Dr. Henry has them at least once a month. Please."

"I'm not a matchmaker."

"Will you try? It would mean so much to her. And we all have to work together here." Sylvia begged her friend's cause despite having expressed her own interest in Otis Taylor mere days ago. "Please."

Sadie did not want to agree. She wanted to stomp her foot and yell that she wouldn't. But in the end, she nodded begrudgingly, only because she needed to keep this job. "Tell her if I *can*, I will."

Upon returning from the factory, she paused in her room long enough to scribble a few lines to her sisters.

> . . . Jealous, petty women are the worst part of my life in Monticello. I only just escaped a catty woman who is all sweet and soft one minute and feral the next. . . .

Chapter 12

Sadie did not see Otis when she stepped into the kitchen after dusting the library. She did not see him after supper, and though she felt a growing urge to offer her apology, she was grateful she did not encounter him while the Dawsons were present.

Her evenings were often passed in the company of the older couple, who had quickly become her dear friends. They talked endlessly as they worked, unless Mildred fell asleep, which was a habit that in mere days already made Sadie smile. At first the three were careful, conversing only about subjects they were sure to agree on, but each night they grew bolder. Sadie opened up, expressing her longing for home and how difficult the circumstances around her move to the city had been. And they told her about their life in the mansion, painting a picture of Otis as a mischievous, delightful boy whom they had loved as though he were their own.

"Tell me," Mildred said from her old rocker in the back parlor, darning a pair of socks, "do you have a beau?"

Leon, who sat near the fire reading a book, lowered it, and Sadie felt certain he was more intrigued by the question than the adventure story in his lap.

"Not exactly." Heat burned her cheeks as she told them about Marvin and her hopes for the two of them when he returned. "He's everything I've always wanted. He's very hardworking, and he's handsome. He goes to church every Sunday. I believe we could have a very happy future together. I've simply got to be patient."

"I went away to save money," Leon said as he rose from his place near the fire. He rubbed his back as though he could remember the hard work from years ago. "I wrote whenever I could and practically begged Mildred to wait for me."

"He did." Mildred looked at Leon with dreamy eyes. "He wrote the most romantic letters. I was a widow and he'd never married. We were older than most when we began our courtship, but don't let age fool you. A woman in her thirties has a heart that beats as wildly as a young woman's."

"I knew it wasn't every day you find a woman like Mildred," Leon said with a chuckle. "I pored over those letters. The men I worked beside laughed at my words, but I didn't care. They were for Mildred, not them."

"How romantic," Sadie said, aching anew for a promise from Marvin. "My parents met as children. He was throwing a snowball at his friend, who must have seen it coming. The friend ducked and the snowball hit my mother instead."

"A snowball?" It was Mildred who chuckled this time. "You never know what will prove a romantic gesture."

"They laugh about it often. They've been inseparable since." She couldn't keep the longing from her voice. "Someday . . ." Her voice trailed off.

"How often do you write to Marvin?" Mildred asked.

"I always write back the very day I get a letter from him. He's so busy with his studies that he is often slower to respond. Sometimes there are months between letters. He's determined to finish early and with high marks."

"Seems to me he isn't a beau at all." Mildred clucked her tongue disapprovingly. "Two years is a long time to wait for a man who only writes on occasion."

"School is so important to him. I've tried to respect that." She ran her finger around the button on her sleeve. "He's always had a plan for his life. An order he was going to do everything in, that's all."

"Perhaps." Mildred did not seem convinced. "Or perhaps, he's not the man you've built him up to be. Even a timid man finds his voice when he's in love. A man in love will put his other plans aside if love requires it."

"When will he be back?" Leon asked. "If he doesn't come see you the moment he returns, we'll know he's not the man for you."

Sadie shifted uneasily in her seat. "I believe he is due to return home very soon. I'm not aware of the exact date. He hasn't mentioned it in his letters."

"We will all be watching for him." Leon leaned forward as though he were expecting him that very moment. "When he walks in he will see none but you, and we'll all know what he's feeling. A man who has been missing his love for two years shouldn't be able to keep his affections to himself. I expect the truth will be written all across his face."

"You are quite the tease. I don't expect a suitor to come walking through that door—"

"Excuse me," Otis said as he stomped into the room, interrupting their conversation and leaving them all with their jaws agape.

"Oh," Sadie said on a gasp, dropping the embroidery that had been sitting in her lap. He bent to get it for her at the same moment she leaned forward. Their heads collided, or rather, her head collided with his hat.

"I'm sorry," he said, quickly handing her what she'd dropped. His hand brushed hers, and the touch startled her. She straightened, trying to make sense of the heat that seared her veins. Her knuckles turned white as she gripped the embroidery. The awareness of him was more startling than his unexpected arrival had been. Perhaps it was her guilt for not apologizing that made her stomach flutter. "I came to find you because a woman is at the door. She claims to be your friend. She knocked incessantly despite my trying to ignore her."

"My friend?"

"I spoke to her through the door—she believed me to be Leon. I couldn't understand what she said her name was, and I wasn't interested enough to ask her to repeat herself."

"Ha!" Leon chortled. "You're a young buck. She must not be very bright if she thought your voice sounded as old and wise as mine."

"Bright or not, she is at the door waiting for Sadie."

Sadie stood, rubbed her hands on her skirt, and looked at the others. "I can only guess it's a woman from the factory." There was so much unsaid between them, but even so, the blue of his eyes lured her closer. "If it is who I think, she has her heart set on you."

"You told her I had returned?"

"No. But they suspect you will soon. She's rather sly. Most likely she's come to walk the halls of the house she hopes to call her own."

"You ought to go and meet her," Leon said with a laugh. "It'd be entertaining for the rest of us."

"No." Otis scowled. "Seeing the shock on people's faces is not funny."

The room fell silent. Her wish to apologize without an audience was not to be. "I'm sorry." She stepped closer and cocked her head, looking at him face-to-face despite his wide brim. "I was surprised, and I am sorry it showed. I haven't mastered the art of masking my feelings. But I am looking at you now, and if you will look back, you will see that I do not have contempt or disgust on my face."

Believe me, she silently pled. *Please.*

"Your guest is waiting." He looked at his feet, bowed, and then backed from the room, urging Wolf to follow.

Leon took her arm. "Come, let's go and say hello to your friend. Mildred and I will bring you tea to sip while you visit. The water is already hot—it'll take only a minute."

"I won't have her stay." Sadie shook her head. "Otis doesn't want anyone here."

"Nonsense. This is a welcoming home," Mildred said. "Don't worry over Otis. He'll come around. More rumors will start if we are unhospitable than if we are welcoming."

"It's still not right."

"You're a good woman to think of him. Go on though."

"Very well—I'll say hello," Sadie said, seeing no way around confronting her visitor. Moments later, she opened the door to find Alta standing with her hands on her hips and a look of annoyance on her face. "What took you so long? I want to see the house!" She clapped her hands together, a greedy glint in her eyes. "I've always wondered what the inside of the mansion looked like."

"I'm working, but the Dawsons have agreed to our sitting on the veranda for a moment. That will have to do. I am not free to take you through the house uninvited."

"I talk to you every day. I didn't sneak out to socialize with you." Her shoulders drooped and her lips dipped into a pout, but she sat when Sadie motioned toward the seats. "You said you would help me."

"I said I would help you if I was able, but I am an employee of this house. I could lose my job. I'm sorry you snuck out for nothing."

She leaned back on her chair and sighed. "Everyone is talking, wondering when he'll come back."

They sat in uneasy silence, waiting for Leon to bring tea so they could pretend to be friends for a moment before Sadie would shoo Alta off the porch and rid the household of her for the night. Their cordial pretense was short-lived. Alta's frown turned into a devilish look. She stood quickly, startling Sadie.

"I'll go in myself," Alta said, taking a giant step toward the door. "The Dawsons won't see me—I'll be quiet. You go distract them, and I'll take a quick look inside."

Sadie grabbed her arm with a firm grip, the way she would have grabbed Old Red, her rooster back home, if he got too feisty. Gone was the docile woman she'd become at the factory. She had to stop Alta and protect Otis's secret. "If Otis returned, and he ever found out you came into his house uninvited, what would he think of you?"

"Would you tell him?" Alta challenged her.

"It might slip out." Sadie didn't back down. "I can't promise you it wouldn't."

Alta glowered and pulled her arm away from Sadie. "Fine. But you will tell me when he returns?"

"I . . ." She wrestled with her conscience. "He's a Taylor. When he is ready, he will make a big show of his return."

"You know something, don't you?" Alta pressed. "Have the Dawsons heard from him?"

Sadie said nothing.

"They have! He is returning soon. A grand return. He's planning it, isn't he?" She clapped her hands together, her frustration replaced by excitement. "You will tell me more, won't you?"

"If I am told his plans for resurfacing, then I will tell you. But promise you won't spread rumors about him—I don't want to spoil his surprise. Besides, don't you think a grand reentry to the town is far more . . . romantic than letting anyone who wants stop by? We wouldn't want rumors ruining such an event." Her mouth went dry. What had come over her to say such things? If she could have sunk into the ground and been swallowed up in one giant gulp, she would have gladly embraced her end.

"I will keep his secret." Alta giggled. "I'd better go. I didn't tell anyone I was coming. I just got so tired of waiting." She grabbed Sadie's hands. For a moment it felt like they truly were friends. "You've given me hope. I'll see you tomorrow and we can talk all about his return."

She waved as she pranced away from the mansion.

Confused by Alta's shiftable ways, Sadie remained on the veranda. She'd never had a *friend* like Alta, one minute kind and another forceful, making it impossible to feel at ease in her presence. More shocking than Alta's changeable behavior was knowing she'd just contributed to what was likely going to be the biggest piece of gossip Monticello had heard in years. There was no chance Alta would truly keep this "secret," a truth that left Sadie's heart thumping.

"Tea?" Leon asked as he walked through the front door and held out a warm cup to her.

"Did you hear her?"

"I did. And I heard you too." He offered the cup again. She accepted it this time and took a sip.

"He doesn't want anyone to know he's here. What have I done?"

"You kept her at bay today, and the rest will sort itself out. But you'd best tell Otis."

"I suppose it's inevitable."

"Come along then."

She stalled by taking one more sip of her tea before leaving it on the table and following Leon through the house, grateful for the shield of protection his stooped back provided. The closer they got to the music room, the clearer she could hear the melody ringing out from the piano. They stood outside the door, listening. Notes—sweet, soft, and beautiful—filled the air. She closed her eyes and let the music stir her soul. She'd heard Otis play as she worked before, but she had never been this close to the source of the music. Tonight, with her hands free of labor and fewer walls muffling the sound, the beauty of it consumed her.

"It's magnificent," she whispered, pushing the door open and silently walking into the room so she could watch his hands as they moved across the keys. As though she had no control over her movements, she drew closer to him. Soon she stood just behind him, nearer than she'd ever dared to go, and became his audience. The music continued, filling the room, making her heart rise and fall with each phrase. Her troubles were all forgotten, lost to the music.

But then his hands stopped—the song ended. The brightness vanquished like a smothered fire. Without turning he said, "You didn't knock."

"I . . ." She searched for words while at the same time bracing herself, unsure what he would say next.

"I don't play for audiences."

"You should." She looked behind her for Leon, but he was gone. There was no shield to hide behind. "You compose beautifully. Everyone should hear the music from the creator himself."

"I write it knowing others will play for the crowds."

"What would you say if I asked you to play me another?" The request was bold, but she longed for more. "Please."

❦

Otis had sensed her enter the music room. She'd been quiet but not quiet enough. He'd almost stopped but instead had let his emotions travel through him and come out in the music. And now she wanted more. Old fears resurfaced, making him vulnerable. He looked down at his hands resting on the keys. She'd heard him already. Could he play one more?

When he played, he felt almost normal. He could hide behind the notes that spoke his heart better than his words ever had and pretend a little longer.

He closed his eyes and traveled back in time to another place and season of life. He let the music come. A song composed during a dark season insisted on filling the room. Melancholic, sweet, raw music saturated the air, and his own heart ached as he played, reliving years of loneliness and distress. He held nothing back—there were no placid notes, and every time his fingers connected with the keys, a feeling floated into the air for his audience of one to catch and decipher at her will.

She remained near him, close enough that he could feel her presence. The loneliness that had driven him to write this song weakened as the song went on and she remained in the room. When at last his fingers stilled, silence followed.

He waited.

"You are so much more than your scars and what happened within these walls," she whispered, her voice sounding breathless. "You have heart."

"That tune was not one of heart," he said, turning on the piano bench and facing her. "It's a sad song."

"One cannot understand sorrow if one has no heart. It was achingly beautiful. You are gifted." She paused, her eyes on his hands.

"My solace has been music—that and the remnant of faith my mother gave me." He cleared his throat. "Tell me, why have you come to the music room? Has your guest left?"

"She's gone . . . but I have to confess something. Though I would rather not. I would much rather beg you to play another song and then close my eyes and pretend nothing else exists."

He swallowed. If only it could be so. Many times he'd tried to drift away with the music, but it never worked. Reality was always there waiting to greet him the moment the last note dissipated.

"She wanted to come inside." Sadie's voice came in unsteady waves. "I kept her from it but only by leading her to believe that you intend to return to town and society."

"What?"

"I didn't tell her when." She recounted the conversation, nearing tears as she did so. "I never meant to cause a problem. It just happened."

"You told her it could be months away." He left the piano and paced the room. "I could be gone by then. If I could just . . ."

He had to find Elisabeth, and he had to sell the house and settle all of Reginald's debts. His fingers, no longer acting the part of talented musician, were now tense and fisted at his sides. All he wanted was a quiet life, and here he was fighting battles on every front.

Sadie was quiet. "I've angered you. I'm sorry. Is there any way I can convince you to call a truce so I can help?"

"Are we battling?"

"I don't know, but I am sorry."

He studied her but found nothing insincere in her features. "On what terms?"

"Excuse me?"

"You want a truce. What does that mean exactly?" His jaw flexed. He sounded idiotic. "Forget it."

"I would rather not." She walked around to the front of the piano and leaned her elbows on it. "I suppose a truce would mean . . . it would mean that I ask your forgiveness—"

"You've done nothing wrong. Other than squatting. But I've forgiven you for that and whatever else you feel guilty about."

"You made that much easier than I expected." When she smiled at him from across the piano, a desire to keep the smile on her face took root in his heart. "And now that you've forgiven me for gasping when I saw your scars and for inadvertently announcing to a woman prone to gossip your plans to return, we start over. But this time we begin as friends. Of course, I am still your employee, but you would trust me like you do Leon and Mildred—"

"I've known them for years."

"True." She tapped her fingers on the smooth piano top. "You do not have to care for me as you care for them."

"You are . . . different from them." He floundered, still thinking about the way her lips curved up so beautifully. "Very different." He hadn't meant for the words to come out that way, all airy and sincere. They were bantering, nothing more. "I can do a truce. As long as you don't bring any other designing women into this house."

"I did not *bring* her. You don't know what it's like for me."

"For you! Pity, what could be so hard about being you?"

The smile vanished, their cordial friendship and truce already hanging by a thread. "My father . . . you do remember that he is the reason I work day and night? He's made no progress. He's still bedridden. And the bank hounds us every week about payments.

I send them all my earnings, and it's barely enough. If anything goes wrong, we will lose everything."

He winced. What a buffoon he was. How cold to forget her familial woes?

"And now I work with other women who all talk about the Taylor bachelor and how they long for his return, and I do what I can to avoid the conversations because I have always strived to be honest. But someday they'll corner me, and I'm afraid I'll say the wrong thing."

"Tell them to jump into the creek and leave you be."

"I hadn't thought of that." There it was, that smile again. When it returned, some of the tension left the room. "For tonight, I will be grateful that you have forgiven me."

"That is all you plan to do?"

"No, I also plan to spend the night thinking of ways to appease Alta. But that can wait. I've more important matters to address first."

"You do?"

"Ever so much more important. I plan to beg my new ally for another song."

"I'm told that friends oblige each other." He sat, and when he searched for the right notes to play, a hopeful melody jumped from his heart to the keys.

> . . . I have heard the most beautiful music. In fact, *beautiful* doesn't seem adequate to describe it. There are no words for how it captured my soul. . . .

Chapter 13

Two weeks passed. No, *passed* was not the right word. They didn't march by like the days at the Crawfords'. Those days hidden away in the woods had been monotonous and dull. They'd been safe but lifeless—nothing like his days now.

He wrote letters to every orphanage in Iowa during the day while Sadie worked at the duster factory. He also made progress on his brother's finances, puzzling over the mess of debts, business transactions, and angry letters from men he didn't know about circumstances he did not know how to verify.

Consuming above all else was the pull he felt to Sadie. The first night after he'd played for her, he found himself wandering the halls. Hearing the Dawsons and Sadie laughing as they sorted through items in an old gardener's office, he sheepishly attempted to join them.

"I was wondering if there was . . ." he said, looking around the small room, "a watering pail."

Leon reached for the tin pail that hung on a hook near the door only inches from where Otis stood. "Are you planning on doing some gardening?"

"There's a plant just outside the back door that looks parched," he said as he took the pail. With water pail in hand, he grappled for another excuse to linger.

Mildred called his bluff, likely due to the fact he'd never been particularly interested in gardening. She winked and said, "Put the pail down. You can water later. You might not even need to—the sky looks ready to burst. Why don't you stay awhile?"

"I suppose I could." At first he sat stiff and tense, but as the night wore on, he relaxed a little more and then a little more. His eyes often found their way to Sadie. He watched her hands as she talked. They moved more when she was excited. He watched her mouth and the way her lips showed a glimpse of her white teeth when she smiled. He hung on her words. To say he was intrigued by her was an understatement.

After that first night, Mildred began inviting him to join them. At first he pretended to go reluctantly, but the ruse was short-lived and soon he needed no cajoling.

The fifth night, he looked at his idle hands and put himself to work, helping as they sorted through a guest bedroom together. Mildred smiled at the work they'd done before sending him and Sadie away, telling them that since they worked so hard, they ought to go and enjoy the evening.

"Wolf wants to go out . . ." Otis said as he tugged uneasily at his vest. "And he likes your company."

"I like his too," Sadie said. "If we stay behind the house, no one will see you."

The area behind the house and creek bed was small but secluded. The sun was low, giving everything a golden haze and magical feel. His chest felt tight the entire walk, in the most intoxicatingly full way. In the evening sun the subtle red in Sadie's hair stood out, and her smile seemed twice as bright. When she threw sticks to Wolf and laughed, he had to press a hand to his chest, afraid it would burst. He'd known that life in the woods had been lacking, but until this moment he'd been unsure what exactly he was missing. Now he knew. He'd missed the joy of sharing his life with someone, even if that someone was but a friend.

No, these days had been nothing like the days of his past. Sadie, true to her word, looked at him without gasping, staring, or any sort of gawking. There was a kindness in her gaze that unsettled him, but not because it contained malice. Her presence was a gentle nudge that slowly led him back to life, back to smiling, and back to hope. He could even feel the sprouting seed of belief that perhaps his future did not have to be as dark as his past. Conversing became easier, and the dark memories—though still present—grew quieter, muffled by these new moments. He was cautious and careful, keeping his unfamiliar feelings to himself, afraid that it could all fade away in an instant. It could all collapse. He feared it would, but for two weeks, he'd relished the taste of belonging and purpose he'd found.

"I've got it," Sadie declared when she entered the kitchen bright and early one morning, a cheeky grin spread across her face. She'd been smiling a lot lately. Living in the mansion had proved more exciting than she could have imagined. "He'll hate it, but it'll work. I'm sure it will!"

"Tell me what it is you're smiling so impishly about?" Leon's butter knife froze above his biscuit. "Go on."

"Remember when Alta stopped by and, well, you heard me tell her that Otis planned to return to Monticello in a grand way? I have since been wondering how to bring that about."

Humor lit up the old man's face. "And?"

"As you know, Otis isn't eager to go out. But he'll never like it here or realize that there are people who will not care about his appearance if he insists on staying inside this fancy, dark prison. He acts as though the entire town of Monticello is guilty and has played a hand in his injuries. Which is unfair, but understandable. My plan—I hope—will help him realize that he is wrong."

"Lately he's seemed happier, but I'm not sure he'll go out." Mildred handed her a plate of breakfast.

"Last night I couldn't sleep." She sat at the table, her body present in the room but her mind filled with Otis. She'd never known anyone like him—so talented, so complex. "I kept thinking about his injuries and about his bad memories. And then I remembered what my mama once said. She was trying to convince my younger sister Flora to go to a recitation at school. Flora was terrified. Mama told her that it would only get harder if she waited, but Flora still wouldn't go, and her fears grew and grew. It got so bad that if she heard us practicing our own recitations, she would burst into tears."

"What a dear," Mildred said as she sat beside Leon. "What did your mama say?"

"She said that sometimes we only have to go to the edge of our fear and that Flora should be proud if she could take a step toward being braver. So Mama took Flora to school and had her recite for her teacher alone. She did splendidly and has gotten braver since, though she still prefers avoiding crowds."

"The world needs both the timid and the bold," Leon said.

"Yes." Sadie smiled at Leon. How right he was. "She's walked to the edge of fear many times, an inch or two farther each time, and now, though she may not like it, she can speak in front of others."

Mildred nodded, the tight bun at the nape of her neck bobbing along with the movement. "And how do you intend to bring Otis to the edge of his fear?"

She wiped the corners of her mouth with her napkin and replaced it in her lap. "Sylvia asked me not long ago if I would go to the masquerade night at Dr. Henry's Big Rink. She didn't exactly ask me, but she did say that if I was nice to Alta I could go with them." Sadie grunted. "I had no interest. Well, I do think skating would be fun. It's something I did once with my father."

She rocked slowly in place. Mentioning her father always brought her worries to the surface. Only the day before, Peter had delivered a letter bearing news that her father was not improving. She prayed for him every night and sent money as quickly as she could, but it wasn't quick enough to keep up with the doctor bills and money owed to the bank. The situation was ever pressing, but worse was thinking of her father's suffering.

"How is your father?" Mildred asked.

"My sister Molly said she doesn't think he is healing properly." Sadie looked at her plate.

"You ought to go and see him," Leon said.

"I would, but I can't miss any work. He's not able to farm, but I don't think his life is in jeopardy." She fiddled with her fork. "Every day I worry, and then I try not to worry because I know my pa would hate knowing that his injury was keeping me from enjoying the good around me."

Leon and Mildred shared a worried look that Sadie chose not to acknowledge. She allowed herself to think of her father and her family's woes only on occasion. It took effort, but she tried to keep her focus on sending money and writing letters that would make her sisters smile and uplift their spirits. And since moving into the mansion house, she'd found herself heavily consumed with thoughts of Otis.

"I didn't mean to bring up your worries." Mildred slid into the seat beside Sadie and took her hand. "You walked in so happy this morning. Tell us about your idea."

"It might sound silly." She tucked her family's troubles away safely in her heart. "I used to read books and write stories. I still do—it's something I love. In them there were often fancy balls, sometimes masquerades. I wrote a scene in a book once where a couple danced together not knowing whose arms they were in because they were both in costume. And then I remembered Sylvia telling me about a masquerade skate coming up. It would be the perfect place for Otis to walk to the edge of fear. He could see his old friends and experience the excitement around his return without having to show his whole face. When he is ready, he can take off his mask."

Leon startled her by clapping his hands. "Well done. It would give him a chance to reconnect while he settles other matters."

With her eyes on her plate, Sadie asked, "What other matters does he have to deal with? I know it's not my place, but . . ."

"It's nothing to trouble yourself over." Leon pushed away from the table and stood. "Convince him to skate with you first and then—"

"He wouldn't be skating with me. I don't . . . I couldn't." Her pulse quickened. She shoved a large bite of biscuit in her mouth, then struggled to swallow. The thought of skating beside Otis unnerved her. They'd shared their evenings together, growing bolder and more comfortable, but he was still Otis Taylor, owner of the mansion, musical genius; and she was simply his employee. To be beside him, on his arm as they skated—a prickle of desire raced up her spine. The delightful feeling only further convinced her that skating with Otis was imprudent. Her loyalty lay elsewhere. These strange flutterings were simply the by-product of all the upheaval in her life.

"What day is the masquerade skate?" Mildred asked.

"I looked at the newspaper before coming to breakfast and there is one in two weeks. I don't know if he'll go, but I hope so. It seems a shame for him to leave without ever giving the people here a chance." Her mouth was dry and her throat tight. It was difficult to picture Monti without Otis or Wolf. The Taylor mansion could hardly be the Taylor mansion without a Taylor in it. For reasons she could not explain, she wanted Otis to stay.

"You are clever." Leon brushed crumbs from his front. "I best get to work, and you should hurry and find Otis before you head out for the day."

"I was hoping you would suggest it to him." Sadie paused, still avoiding eye contact. "He listens to you."

"I think he'll be more open to the idea if it comes from you. But I do want to hear about his reaction." Leon chuckled as he left the women alone.

"And you? Will you ask him?" Sadie asked Mildred.

Mildred put a hand on her heart. "I'm too old for such scheming. Leave your plate and go talk to Otis."

Sadie stalled.

"Run along." Mildred hurried her from the room, a smirk on her motherly face.

"Excuse me."

Otis turned at the sound of Sadie's voice. How alarming it was that every day his reaction to her presence grew stronger. The sound of her tread on the stairs, the look in her eyes when he played his music, the pitch of her laugh—without his permission, he'd become attached to it all.

"Yes," he squeaked out, then cleared his throat and tried again. "Yes?"

Sadie's expression was tentative and . . . hopeful? She was about to ask him something, he was sure of it. "Did you need something?"

"I need a great many things. Most are out of your control, but . . ." She crept directly in front of him, pulled her lips into a line, and then said, "Mr. Rochester can be terribly moody."

"Are you implying that I—"

She laughed. "I was only trying to get a look at you to make sure you were in good spirits."

"I find myself in exceptionally good spirits, but you have a twinkle in your eye that has me worried."

"My mama says that she can see mischief in my eyes. I guess she's right."

"Are you wanting to raid the kitchen? Jump in the creek? Well, you've done that already."

She swatted his arm. "Nothing like that, and I thought I told you to forget about my creek incident."

"You did tell me that, but no matter how hard I try I can still see the flash of white I saw running in front of the mansion. I thought a ghost had taken over while I was away."

"Where has the quiet, aloof man I first met gone?" She smiled.

He didn't answer right away. He paused, appreciating what she'd said. Her presence was changing him. Slowly breaking him from the bonds that had held him so tightly for such a long time.

"I suppose," he said at last, "that a person is always changing. This house and its memories make me want to run and hide, but you and the Dawsons, you're all so loud that there are times I can't hear the past at all."

"Loud." She pulled her mouth to one side. "A strange compliment, but thank you."

Fearing he'd said too much and made his feelings too visible, he shrugged. "Do you need something?"

"I have an idea. Don't say no right away." She spoke quickly, talking of skating rinks and masquerades, giving him no time to cut in and object. Twice she mentioned fear and the edge of it, and then she begged him to give living in Monti a chance. "You could become reacquainted with the town. You could find that it is a more welcoming place than you remember. You might even like it, and then you wouldn't have to go."

His head shot up. "You don't think I should leave?"

"I think you should consider staying before you run off. You could try it out here first."

What she wanted was not an easy thing to give. He opened his mouth, ready to tell her no, but then he thought of how he'd been driven away, how he'd never said goodbye to Dan or Andrew or seen his brother again. He didn't want to face Monti, but he didn't want to run either. If he left, he wanted it to be because he chose to go, not because he cowered away.

"Otis," she said. "Aren't you curious?"

Was he? Yes, of course he was. For years he'd gone to sleep dreaming of a homecoming. With Elisabeth still out there, and no word from the orphanages, he would not be leaving Monticello anytime soon. And if he were reading her expression right, Sadie was not in a hurry to see him go. But there was a problem. "I don't skate."

"You could. Or just go and sit and watch. I'm sure all the women would be eager to sit beside you. Although, you would have to . . . you would, well, you would need to be on your best behavior." She covered her mouth, but he saw the sides of her lips creep up. "I'm sorry. I'm not laughing at you, not really."

"I'm not sure if I believe you. Tell me, what is so funny?"

"I was just imagining Alta and what she would do if you were to growl at her like you did me the last time we played chess."

"You cheated. Of course I growled."

"I didn't cheat. I changed my mind about where my queen should be."

"Even I know that is called cheating."

"Innocent cheating."

"No such thing."

She held up her hands in a posture of surrender. "I concede—I cheated. But I apologized and will not rearrange the board next time. That doesn't change the fact that at the masquerade you should remain composed."

"Composed? I haven't said I am going."

"But you are thinking about it, I can tell. And it *is* a good plan. It's two weeks from now, so there would be time to polish your manners and learn to skate. You could roll down the hall." She folded her arms with exaggerated impatience. "I only hope that you decide quickly. I have to go to work—there are feathers to be sorted. If you say yes, it'll make things easier at the factory. Please."

As quick as he could, he thought through the benefits and risks. They were near equal. But what his mind grasped onto was the fact that she'd made this plan to benefit him. That was a gift, and he'd received so few. He hated the idea of rejecting it.

When he remained standing, unmoving, unspeaking, she offered him a half smile. "I best be going."

He rapped the top of the piano, pushed past the dam in his throat, and said, "I might go."

He almost gagged on the words. Roller-skating. Masquerades. Crowds. As soon as the words were out, he wished he could pull them back, but the barricade was down. He'd spoken.

"You *might* go? Is it impossible for you to fully commit?"

"Even saying I might came at a cost. I think I'll be sick all day." He put a hand on his tight throat and let out a dramatic groan. "Go to work, I don't want to keep you. Hopefully, I'll be recovered when you return."

She grinned as she moved to leave. "I'm going to tell them you're coming!"

With her hand on the doorframe, she turned back, challenging him. It was a simple look, but one he wished he could capture, hold on to, and revisit whenever he felt alone.

"If you must," he muttered.

She squealed, then pranced away.

"But I'm not taking the mask off," he said to her back. She waved a hand in the air, and he could hear laughter.

What had he done?

He went to the place she'd stood, touching the doorframe where her hand had been. The plan she'd presented made him uneasy, but Sadie West—the girl who had seen his scars, looked him in the eyes, and even witnessed his awkward ways—believed it might work. She cared. Perhaps only a little, but she cared.

"Leon!" he shouted as he walked down the hall, driven by a desire to give her something in return. A gesture of thanks, of armistice.

Chapter 14

Otis stood in the guest room staring at his reflection in the mirror above the washstand, his hat off and his face freshly washed. He ran a hand over his rough scalp and then down over his smooth jaw. His hair had fallen out before he'd ever grown enough stubble to need to shave. With no hair to style, cut, or comb, he rarely looked in the mirror, but today was different. He'd worked so hard and felt so normal, he could almost believe that in the mirror he would find an *ordinary* man.

But the man in the mirror was as scarred as ever. He leaned closer, searching his face. There was a subtle difference. He could see it in his eyes. They were the same blue, still framed by bone structure and not brows, but there was an eagerness in them that was new.

A man could look at his own reflection for only so long before growing either vain or remorseful. He turned away from the mirror and went to the window, where he peered through the gap in the curtain. At first he saw only nature and the road that led to the mansion house.

And then there she was, practically dancing on her way home. Otis could think of nothing so beautiful. He left his quarters and went to greet her.

"Sadie," he said in the foyer. "Um, how was your day?"

"For once everyone wanted to talk to me. They all wanted to know more about your return and the masquerade skate. I don't think there has ever been so much excitement at the duster factory. What about you, did you have a good day?"

Leon peeked around the corner. "He's been smiling all day. He's giddy about something." He winked, and Otis scowled at him.

"I think Mildred needs you in the kitchen," Otis said. Sadie looked between the two of them.

"Ah yes, that's right." Leon chortled as he walked away.

"Does Mildred need me too?" Sadie asked.

Otis shook his head. He'd been waiting for her return all day, and now his mouth was dry and his tongue in knots.

"Are you feeling unwell?" she asked and took a step closer.

"No, I'm well. I have something I want to say." He shifted uneasily. This was proving far more difficult than he had imagined. "Working here in Monticello," he said slowly, "you must miss your family. And now you live here with an odd man."

"You're not—"

"Please, allow me to finish. You work hard, and . . . what I am doing a terrible job of saying is that I have a gift."

"A gift? For me? You didn't need to."

His heart raced, afraid she'd reject what he so badly wanted to give to her. "I know I didn't need to. But, well, will you accept it?"

"I don't know what it is. How can I accept?"

He held out his hand, palm up. "Come with me, please?"

Time slowed. She reached out, pulled back, and wiped her hand on her skirt before putting her hand in his. With great care, he held it. Her hand was so small and trusting in his. And though he touched only her hand, his entire body reacted, screaming for more.

She took her hand away, clasping it against her chest.

"Sadie," he said, unable to mask the pleading in his voice. "I want to thank you. Taylors do not apologize or offer gratitude easily. It's a strength my family lacks. We battle our tempers and our pride."

"You are your own person," she said, staring at his hand that now swung by his side, empty without hers. "You have the power to be the sort of man you want to be."

"I want to believe you. For so long, I believed—" The intensity in his voice startled him and he abruptly stopped speaking. He was better with letters or the piano. Saying what he felt was difficult. For as long as he could remember, he'd been guarded and careful. He shifted under the weight of vulnerability, but he did not falter. "I'm sorry. I'm sorry I nearly had you run off my land. I'm sorry I don't remember how to have fine manners or that I growled over chess."

"It sounds to me like the Taylor man I am looking at knows how to apologize."

"I want to thank you for devising a plan on my behalf. More importantly, for looking at me, scars and all. You make me believe . . . You and the Dawsons are the first and only people to see me and not look away. Even mild Mr. Crawford preferred to keep his distance."

"You defy the family name again." She smiled up at him. "That was a well-delivered confession of gratitude."

"Thank you," he whispered as walls of insecurity came down. She couldn't have known how perfect her words were.

"You're welcome." She broke their gaze, easing the unexplainable tension. "Well, Otis Taylor, what shall we do now?"

"Close your eyes, and trust me." The giddiness came back. He was a boy on Christmas morning again. "I want to show you how I've spent my day."

Sadie put her hand out for him to take. Like before, an unfamiliar and altogether pleasant sensation raced through him.

She didn't pull back but instead let her hand rest in his. Otis didn't waste time wondering if she felt anything from his touch. Later he could mull over the possibilities.

"Close your eyes," he said as he began leading her through the house and toward the back door.

"I don't think it is customary to walk with one's eyes closed on an evening stroll," she said when he opened the door and they stepped outside. "Is this a Monticello tradition that I have not been informed of?"

"I didn't know you wanted to go on an evening stroll," he said before playfully squeezing her hand.

"That's not what I meant."

"I was jesting."

"Of course you were."

"Mr. Crawford didn't believe in humor. I haven't tried to make anyone laugh in years."

"You've a natural gift for it. Mildred told me you were a mischievous boy. I don't know how you survived ten years with no one to josh."

"One lonely day at time," he said as he helped her along the overgrown path toward the abandoned factory that had led her to him. With each step his spirits soared higher and higher in anticipation. His gift would be the climax. Metal met metal as he slid the key into the lock on the factory.

"Are your eyes closed?" he asked.

"Yes."

Sadie tightened her hand around his but didn't open her eyes. "Are we going in the old factory?"

"Tonight it's not a factory." He helped her over the threshold and then closed the door behind them. "Now you can look."

"Oh!" She brought her hand to her mouth and stared in wonder at the transformation. The old building with its neglected furniture and dust covering everything was now bare and clean. It was nothing like the hovel she'd once resided in. Where once the building had looked useless and forgotten, it now looked ready for a future. Otis picked up two pairs of skates and dangled them in front of her.

"You wanted to skate," he said. "It was your dream, and I called it frivolous. Forgive me and skate with me?"

"Would you think me silly if I told you this was beautiful and the kindest thing anyone has ever done for me?"

"I might." He smirked in a positively roguish way that made her toes curl. "But silly and frivolous are not such bad things."

"You must have worked all day. It was nothing but cobwebs and dust before." Her shoulders fell at the mention of work. "I don't have time to skate. I had plans to clean another guest room tonight and wash all the table linens. I don't think they've been done in months, and—"

"Table linens can wait. I have no plans for hosting house parties. As far as everyone knows, I am returning in two weeks. Until then, it's only you and me. Do you care about table linens?"

"No, I—"

He cut her off by putting the skates in her hand. "The truth is, this gift is selfish. I need to learn to skate. And I need a tutor."

"I suspect Leon can skate better than I can. I've only skated once."

He snatched the skates back and held them close, pretending to study them. "I don't think these will fit him. That leaves no one but you or Mildred, and she is always telling me that she's no longer spry. So, Miss Sadie West, will you teach this boorish, lost soul to skate? Shall I get down on my knees and plead?"

"No, of course not. If you wish me to instruct you, when I know very little about skating, so be it." She ran her hand over the dark leather strap. The skates were beautiful, the finest she'd seen. "You're so happy today and you did all this. What happened?"

"I . . ." He looked away, once again the uncertain man, sinking into the shadows without even taking a step into the dark. "You didn't run."

She made no response, hoping the silence would pull more of an explanation from him. He'd been a boat lost in a raging sea when she'd come, and now he seemed to have regained some control of his sails.

"You saw my scars and . . . and yet you still made a plan to help me. No one has done anything like that for me in a very long time."

"I knew it'd make things easier at work. It wasn't purely selfless. I'm not that perfect."

"I'm glad to hear it. I was imagining that I was the only true human in the room and you were an angel."

She laughed, delighted that he'd once again come out of the darkness. "I've never had anyone thank me for being imperfect."

"As we skate you can tell me all your many wrongs."

"Otis Taylor, the women of Monticello are in for a surprise when they meet you." She laughed, snorted, then laughed harder, embarrassed by her guffaw. Otis joined in, laughing with her—not as boisterously, but the sound of it was as mesmerizing as the music he played. "I never know what to expect from you."

"Years of loneliness left me a bit off my rocker. A recluse and a country lad. We will make an excellent pair."

Her head jerked in surprise.

"As we skate."

"Of course," she said. "I had not realized that two people should be equally odd and flawed in order to skate together." This was by far the strangest conversation she had ever shared with a man. When she'd strolled with Marvin, they had talked of farms, family, and school. Everything they'd done had been proper, predictable, and pious, nothing like this foray into the unknown. Reason said she ought to turn back and stay where it was safe, but instead she asked, "Tell me, Mr. Taylor, are you ready to skate?"

He looked around at the makeshift skating rink, at her, and toward the boarded-up windows. His attention turned to the skates he was holding, and he gazed at them as though he saw them for the first time. "I think I'd better be. Leon bought these for me today. He came home and told me everyone at the mercantile is now planning to attend the masquerade night. I think the crowd will be bigger than I would like."

"It's all anyone talked about at the factory."

He grimaced. "Let's not talk of the gossips. That may sour my mood, and then I'll have to practice apologizing again."

"That may not be all bad. We learn things by practice."

"I'd rather practice skating than apologizing."

"Very well." They sat in chairs that had been moved to the edge of the empty floor and laced the leather straps around their feet. Sadie looked at the corner she'd shivered in. During those long, cold nights, she had never imagined that something so beautiful could be born out of such neglect.

Otis stood, wobbled, and sat right back down. "People do this for fun?"

"Yes, everyone." She stood, keeping her hands out to her sides. "Give it a try. I am convinced it won't be long before you understand why Monti has held on to skating fever for so long. This town has three rinks."

"Four rinks, only no one but us knows about this one."

He stood again, slower this time. Once they were both steady, they rocked forward, slowly making their way around the room. With no furniture to hold on to, they had their arms out to their sides for balance. Their progress was slow. At first they weren't really skating but walking on their wheeled shoes. There was nothing graceful about their form, but their effort was commendable.

On her second lap around the large floor, Sadie grew more confident. She smiled, proud of her progress. With now steadier legs, she tried to go faster, only to flail, swaying back and then forward, her arms pumping as she fought to stay upright.

"Are you—"

"Ahh!" She interrupted him with a squeal as she braced herself for her pending collision with the floor. She was going down, and then she wasn't. His arms came around her, steadying her.

Up snapped her head. She was in his arms, her face near his. Her heart did a somersault in her chest. Otis's hat lay on the ground, a casualty of his heroism, allowing her to see his face fully. The cut of his jaw, the line of his nose, and the blue of his eyes—all he needed was a white horse. His hands remained at her waist even after her legs regained their balance.

"Are you all right?" he asked in a husky voice.

"Yes." She swallowed.

"You do realize that the student has just steadied the teacher."

She nodded and forced herself backward, putting distance between them. Out of his arms, she was free to catch her breath. "Thank you for catching me."

He bent for his hat, but she was quick and put her hand on his arm. "Leave it. You'll skate better not worrying about it being on."

"But—"

"But what? It won't help you and I am your teacher—you told me so yourself. You should take my advice."

He looked between the hat and her several times before nodding. With an air of reservation, he said, "Yes, ma'am."

"Rule one," she proclaimed with a laugh, doing her best to look only at his eyes despite wanting to look at the whole of him. "You must make sure that when you lose your balance, you are near either the wall or a person you wish to get to know better."

"Ah, so that is why you nearly stumbled. You were teaching by example. Or am I someone you want to know better?"

She pushed forward, skating at a slow pace in front of him. "I find you rather intriguing," she said, looking straight ahead. "But as your teacher, I must continue your lesson."

"What is rule two?" He approached on her right. The wooden floor was clear of furniture and the dust had been swept away, but years of use left it uneven and rough. His skate hit the raised edge of a floorboard, warped from time and moisture. His hands went up, his legs forward, and down he went.

Sadie reached for him, trying to grab his arm and slow his momentum as he had done for her, but she missed and lost her own balance. To the floor she went, hard on her backside. They lay side by side on their backs, staring up at the ceiling and rubbing at their aches.

"Were you setting an example for me then too?" he asked, rolling toward her.

"Rule two: don't try to help someone if you are not steady." She groaned when she pushed to sitting. "I suppose this is why the newspaper is riddled with reports of broken arms and twisted ankles."

"If I don't want my name in the paper, I need to stay upright. Is that what you are saying?"

"You may end up with your name in the paper whether you fall or not." She ran her hand along the wooden floor. "Rule three: look out for uneven floorboards."

"To think this is what people do for entertainment." He sat up beside her and absently rolled his foot back and forth, his wheel clicking as it went over a bump.

Sadie shook her skirt out, ensuring that her ankles were covered. She was all too aware that everything about their evening teetered near scandalous. The entirety of their acquaintance was something many would frown upon. "If I were to say that I am having fun, would you think my life very monotonous and dull?"

"No, it's perfectly normal to enjoy colliding with a wooden floor and bruising one's rump. But what do I know about normal?"

Sadie giggled. "I'm not sure I know much more than you. I'm the country girl, the one other women love to mock. My clothes aren't fashionable, and my hair isn't pinned up the same way as theirs."

He put the palms of his hands on the floor behind him and leaned back. "What is normal?" His tone grew more serious. "Why can't it be normal to be varied and different? In a world full of colors and shapes and backgrounds, who decided we were all supposed to be the same?"

"It does seem unrealistic, doesn't it?" She reached for the latches of her skates and began undoing them.

"You're done? You only gave me three rules."

"Mildred will be expecting my help inside. I may have skipped the linens, but I can't leave her with everything." She unlatched her second skate and stood. "Ten hours sorting feathers doesn't sound like hard work, but it is. I've got to get things done so I can sleep. But . . ." She looked around the factory, once again recognizing the amount of work it must have taken to clean the building, and sighed. "This was a truly kind gift. The nicest a man has ever given me."

He frowned and muttered, "How often do you receive gifts from men?"

"All the time," she quipped, unable to keep a lively smirk from her face.

"I didn't realize." He smiled, but she sensed something off in his tone. He couldn't possibly believe that she had received gifts in abundance, could he? Head down, he worked the latches of his own skates. "I had Leon send word to Mr. Hoag today asking if you could be spared there so you could be here to help me. Well, I didn't say me. The note said helping with extra work around the mansion."

A wave of fear swept over her. "You did?"

"He sent word back saying he looked forward to being re-acquainted with me when I returned and that he understood the need for extra help."

"But I never agreed to this." Her family needed her income. The doctor's bill could not be put aside, no matter how badly she wished to skate, play chess, and enjoy Otis Taylor's company. Fury, brought on by fear, raged through her. "I can't. And you shouldn't have."

The corners of Otis's mouth turned down. "I'm sorry. I didn't mean to overstep."

"I don't care whether you meant to or not. You might be my employer, but you don't get to control my life."

"Sadie, please. I'm sorry. I should have asked you before I asked Mr. Hoag. I did a lot of impulsive things today."

"My father, my family." Her voice cracked. "They depend on me."

He ran a hand across his bald head. "I wouldn't want you to neglect your family. If you work for me, you'll be paid for your time. I only thought that, with the masquerade coming up and so much of the house left to clean, and with your long days there, it would help everyone. I was wrong. Will you forgive me?"

"I'm still mad," she said like she would have if she'd been fighting with one of her sisters. "But I forgive you. You do realize you have hired the very worst skating instructor in Monticello."

"That may be. What can I say, I'm a very poor businessman. Will you take the job?"

"You are exposing all your flaws. Trouble apologizing, terrible skater, and horrible businessman. Skating does seem to be the ideal way to get to know someone."

He fiddled absently with his skate. "You missed one of my flaws. You failed to mention that I am scarred and entirely without hair."

"I don't see that as a flaw. It's simply a different kind of normal." She hugged her skates to her chest. "I forgive you for making assumptions, and I accept your offer to work at the mansion during the days. I'll do all I can to make you the finest skater that ever rolled through Iowa."

> . . . I received the most thoughtful gift, and for a moment I had no worries at all. This house is not only mysterious, it is magical. . . .

Chapter 15

Otis propped his legs on his desk and leaned back in his chair. He flipped the key he'd found in Reginald's room back and forth, still unsure what it belonged to. Wolf lay near him, head resting on his paws.

"Otis," Leon said as he stepped into the study with a stack of letters in his hand. "Sorry to interrupt. I went to the post office while I was out but forgot to give you the mail."

"I didn't have time to read it until now anyway."

"You've been busy." The wrinkles around Leon's eyes lifted. "It's quite a feat you accomplished getting that factory cleaned up so well."

Otis took the stack of letters and tossed them on the desk. Since returning home, the post had contained mainly letters from businessmen trying to reach him in hopes that he would throw some of the Taylor money into their schemes. Tonight thoughts of Elisabeth and of Sadie made business proposals and other such nonsense seem trite.

"You ought to read them," Leon said. "It's easier to keep the pile down if you tackle it daily."

Otis groaned, picked the letters back up, and thumbed through them. "How many letters do you think Mrs. James Bowers has mailed to me?"

"She's mailed them consistently since your brother's passing." Leon sat across the desk from him, watching as Otis casually perused the mail. "She has a daughter of marriageable age. It's no secret she wants to marry her off to a wealthy bachelor."

"I'll burn this one." He chuckled, setting it aside. "I can't imagine that a woman who is petitioning a man she has never met, based solely on what he owns, is a woman worth meeting."

"Very idealistic of you," Leon said nonchalantly, "but the daughter could be charming and unaware of the mother's conspiratorial plans."

"Unlikely." Otis picked up the next letter and stared, surprised to see that the return address was the orphanage in Des Moines. "Leon, this might be about Elisabeth."

He tore into it and read aloud.

Dear Mr. Taylor,

I regret to inform you that we have not received a child named Elisabeth at any time in the last year. We take in mainly infants. The few older children we have all have histories we know well. I am sorry to say that none of our new wards could be the child you are looking for. I regret that we cannot be of further assistance to you. Perhaps another institution will be able to aid you in your search.

I pray you are reunited with your kin.

Sincerely,
Deborah Griffin

Otis crumpled the paper in his hand. He'd been able to remain somewhat optimistic and hopeful while he waited for word from the orphanages. But now the largest had failed him. Where was she? Des Moines was the most probable orphanage. Clinging to hope that a small, obscure children's home knew Elisabeth's whereabouts was akin to fishing with no hook and hoping to secure a big fat catch.

"What can I do?" he said, not actually expecting a response. "Could Mildred go and talk with the mother and daughter? Surely they are back by now. She thought they might know something."

"It doesn't take much convincing to get her to go visiting. She could take Sadie with her. Word's spreading that she works here, so it would do no harm," Leon said. "And there are other orphanages—news could still come. Don't give up hope."

"There are others. Hundreds. Thousands. Elisabeth could be grown by the time I find her. An orphanage is no place for her. She is *my* responsibility. I need her here where I can assure myself of her safety. More than that, I want to know she is happy."

Otis pushed out of his chair. He left the office and walked the halls, cursing Reginald and his secretive ways.

⚜

Sadie slept ten minutes longer than normal the next day and enjoyed every second of it. The bed she now called her own was aged and saggy, but it felt luxurious to lie there awake and not be rushing to ready herself for a day of feather sorting.

When at last she pulled herself from bed, she went to the small armoire and looked at her modest selection of clothes. Each piece was home sewn and practical, nothing fashionable and certainly nothing store-bought. In the end she wore the nicer of her brown skirts and her best shirtwaist. Her mama had bought the entire bolt of dull brown fabric and made skirts for all her girls from it, exclaiming more than once that the quality and price could not be beat. And she'd been right. The skirt had worn very well, but it was drab, and on this day of possibilities, a dress with lace or ruffles would have been fitting. No matter her clothes, she was going to be happy today.

"Good morning," she said to Mildred upon entering the large kitchen. "It's a beautiful day, isn't it?"

Mildred looked out the window nearest her. "Looks like it might rain."

"Oh." Sadie glanced past Mildred out the window and realized she'd been overzealous in declaring it a beautiful day without having looked outside. The sky was an ominous gray, not the shade of blue one often stopped to admire. She shrugged. "The rain will water my family's crops."

"Indeed." Mildred went back to her dough, kneading it to a silent beat. "I'm sure you'll be missed at the duster factory."

"I imagine anyone could do my job." She leaned against the wall and watched Mildred pull the dough closer to her and then fold it onto itself. "Some of the people at the factory have been there for years."

"My brother worked there when it was still making brooms, long before Hoag made a real name for himself. There weren't nearly as many employees back then." She lifted her dough and put it into a large bowl to rise. "The factory has been good for this town. During the hard winter, Hoag hired as many men as he could. I credit him with keeping bellies full that season. He used to buy broom corn from all the local farmers. Now he takes local feathers whenever anyone has them."

"Some of our neighbors used to sell their crops to him. My father even thought of growing broom corn. Now that they make dusters, he's glad he didn't switch crops." She ran her finger along the windowsill. "There are some sorters who hope to leave one day, but that's because they aim to marry and start families."

"Raising a family is a worthy ambition." Mildred brushed the flour off the counter to her hand and disposed of it. She kept her kitchen neat and tidy, often tasking Sadie with cleaning along the floorboards, above the cabinets, and along the back of the sink. "When your Marvin comes you might be bidding the factory goodbye as well."

"I wonder sometimes if that will ever happen. It's been such a long time since I've seen him." For years she'd imagined her life with Marvin, and she still did. But where once she'd believed she knew exactly how the future would look, it now felt fuzzy. "It's more likely that I will go back to my parents' farm and . . . I don't know what I'll do. We're so busy making ends meet, we haven't made plans past that."

"Plans are a good thing if they're held lightly. Some folks hold on too tight, and they can't let go when life changes."

Sadie turned from the window. Had she held on to her dream of Marvin too tightly? If he never declared affection for her, what would she do? She flinched, uncomfortable at the thought of letting him go.

"I suppose I need only worry about today," she said, leaving her spot by the window and moving closer to Mildred. "Do you think Otis will want to practice all day?"

Mildred's busy hands stopped moving. "I don't know what he'll want to do. Leon said he had news last night that may have changed his plans."

"Has something happened?"

She wiped at her brow, leaving a streak of flour across her forehead. "When you see him, ask him if all is well. Maybe scoot up close and bat those long eyelashes of yours at him. That might get him talking."

"I will ask him, but I will not scoot close to him," she said with an incredulous laugh. "You and Leon are as bad as Alta, always scheming. I'll go and find him, unless you think I should wait to be beckoned."

"Leon saw him wandering around the study." Mildred wrapped two hot biscuits in a napkin. "He told Leon he wasn't hungry, but see if you can get him to eat. We all know that a man thinks better on a full stomach."

"I believe women do as well." Sadie took the offering and went in search of Otis. She found him just where Mildred had told her he would be, clearly visible from the hallway, thanks to a partially opened door. He wore a hat, like always, but she could still see a crease low on his forehead. His arms were crossed and his shoulders tense. Something worried him.

"Mildred sent a biscuit up for you," Sadie said from the doorway. She held her hearty gift higher for him to see. "She thinks it will help you handle your troubles."

He let his arms fall to his sides.

"Can I come in and give this to you?"

"Yes, yes, of course." He pulled two chairs near the desk, motioning for her to take a seat in one of them. He took the other. His left leg immediately began tapping the floor. *Tap. Tap. Tap.* His restlessness also caused her to feel jittery for no explainable reason.

Sadie handed him the napkin filled with biscuits and waited. He opened it and offered her one, then silently picked at his breakfast. "Mildred's cooking . . . it's good."

"Yes." Sadie took a bite. "Don't you ever tell my mama, but Mildred's biscuits are lighter than hers."

"I won't tell." He wiped at a crumb on his face. "I'm one of the best secret keepers around."

"I'm not sure whether that is a trait to admire or not."

"Are you a good secret keeper?" His foot stopped tapping.

"No," she whispered. "I told you I have three sisters. We not only bicker but also tell one another everything. I haven't kept many things from them."

"Hmm."

"Once when I was small, my sister Molly asked me to sneak out to the barn with her. It was dark and we were supposed to be sleeping, but we knew our favorite cow was going to have her calf soon. We wanted to watch. We stayed out two hours before going back inside. We agreed to keep our escapade a secret from our other sisters."

"See, you *are* an experienced secret keeper."

"But I'm not. We made it two days before we confessed to not only our sisters but our parents too." She bit her lip, remembering the way her father had fought a smile as he scolded them. "The only other secrets I've had have been secret hopes or dreams and"—she looked at his head—"the secret about your presence in town and your condition."

"That's a prickly secret that follows me wherever I go. I didn't think about it nearly as much when I lived outside Boston."

"What was it like there? I want to picture it."

"It was quiet. I lived with an old man, a musician who took me in only because my father paid him handsomely. He let me stay there after I was grown because I was composing pieces he could sell. He took a cut and we both won. He had a cook and a couple other household employees who all kept quiet about my presence. I lived with them for years and never left their property. I never went to town, not to church or even to a store. He tutored me, so I was not uneducated. And I also had my music and a Bible and access to the house's library, which is why I've read *Jane Eyre* and know all about your secretive Mr. Rochester."

"An excellent but troubling book, but you should have been out playing your music and socializing."

"I was young when I arrived, at the mercy of the adults in my life. Eventually I got used to staying away from everyone. When I turned twenty my music was making enough money to support me, but where was I to go? I wanted a life of my own, but in the end, I stayed. I played the piano and I watched the road, always wondering if my father would return."

"Because you missed him?"

Otis paused. He wet his lips and looked away from her. "I missed the father of my childhood and the one I built up in my mind. I didn't know who he had become, but I couldn't stop watching for him. I suppose it was his permission to keep living that I waited for."

"But you never got it?"

"Never."

"You've no other family," she whispered, unable to hide the pain she felt on his behalf. Sadie stared at the half-eaten biscuit in her hand. "Why do you ask me about secrets?"

He wrung his hands together in his lap, his leg resuming its gentle tapping. "I have another secret and I don't know what to do about it."

"Don't tell me." She sat up straight, setting the biscuit on the desk. "I want to know. I really do, but what if I can't keep it?"

"You're scared of my temper?"

"No, well, yes, but . . . well, I don't know what it is that makes me nervous. I haven't been trusted with many secrets before, but Mildred did say that she is worried and I should listen."

His face went dark. "Is that why you came? Because Mildred told you to? This is all just a job to you, isn't it?"

"Otis," she said, shaking her head. "This *is* my job. I work for you and that is how I send money to the bank, but when Mildred said you needed someone to listen to you, I *wanted* to come." She put a hand on his smooth arm, shocking even herself, but she left it there. "Secrets, living in town, working for you—it's all new to me, but friendship is not."

His eyes were on her hand. "I wish friendship were not so new to me."

"We all begin somewhere. Tell me more about your life in the woods. Did you yell at the trees when you were angry?"

"No, I pounded the keys and stormed about the land. I always wanted something else to do in those moments."

"My pa would have us pull garden weeds when we were having a bad day. He claimed working the land was the perfect way to sort through troubles. Next time you're troubled you could ride out to my parents' farm and help with the crops. You could work off a whole year's worth of angst in a matter of hours."

He nodded his head slowly. His gestures were starting to make sense to her, and she believed that at this very moment he was concocting a plan.

"What if you were to help me with something very . . . delicate. And I agreed to help your family."

"You need me for more than skating? Or is rolling across the rink your delicate endeavor?"

"This other secret is a private matter, a family matter, and I know that makes you nervous, but I assure you I would not be asking anything of you that is not perfectly moral. I am cantankerous, but I'm not a villain."

She nodded, hoping that this secret was a missing piece, that with it she would be able to further understand Otis Taylor. "I'll listen."

"You say I have no family, and that is what I have believed since Reginald died."

"So you *do* have family?"

"My brother left behind a child."

Sadie looked around her as though the little imp might walk through the door that very moment. "A child?"

"Our mother taught both my brother and I about living a virtuous life, but she died young, and then I was sent away. I don't know the extent of Reginald's recklessness or what transpired. I imagine like most things, it was more complicated than those on the outside can see, but what I do know is that he was supporting a child. We believe her to be three years old, perhaps four."

"Is she with her mother?"

"No." He explained the few details they had about Elisabeth and the attempts he'd made to find clues—searching the house, reaching out to Mary, and writing letters to orphanages. "I don't know what to do next."

"And you expect that I will? I have no experience tracking down missing children."

"I don't know what I expect. Mildred is going to visit some women she thinks may have an idea. I thought you could go with her."

Sadie stood, took a determined breath, and said, "I will, and I will try to think of other ways of finding her. I do want to help."

"Thank you, Sadie."

"Otis?"

"Yes."

"We talked of flaws last night. We listed them, but they pale in comparison to your strengths. Your desire to find your niece . . . many men would not share in it. It speaks highly of your character."

He blushed, giving his face a pink glow a shade lighter than the scars on his head. "I've never met Elisabeth. I have little experience with children, yet I feel compelled to find her. I worry that she'll be afraid of me, but I will show her . . ." His voice, thick with emotion, gave an extra level of importance to his words and tugged at Sadie's heart. "I have never felt so needed as I do right now. She's out there, and I will find her."

"*We* will find her." She paused, her words ringing through the room and settling in her heart as she made his mission her mission also. "When I get back from my outing with Mildred, we will work together to think of a way to find her." She smiled, grateful to know that his secret, though heavy, buoyed her belief that Otis Taylor was not a beast but a man with heart.

> . . . People are much like plants. There is so much more to them that cannot be seen. Ambitions and dreams. Fears and hopes. Buried beneath the soil, overlooked, but vital . . .

Chapter 16

Upon first meeting Mildred, it would have been easy to assume her a typical older woman, prone to sleep and consumed with her own quiet affairs. It had not taken long for Sadie to realize this was entirely inaccurate of Mildred, aside from her affinity for napping. Her motherly friend was quick-witted and never short of things to say.

The two women sat side by side in the modest home of the Ascot family, looking at Anne, the mother, and her daughter, Louisa. They'd been welcomed in with warm smiles and promptly offered coffee. Mildred led the conversation, informing the Ascots that she'd been eager to show Sadie around and introduce her to the locals. It was a guise but not wholly fictitious, since Sadie was in fact new to town and not well acquainted.

"I heard you were working at the feather duster factory," Louisa said, her voice touched with the slightest note of condescension. "My friend Bridget works on the binding machine. How do you have time to make calls?"

"Mr. Hoag has allowed Sadie extra hours at the mansion while we prepare things for Mr. Taylor. You have heard that he will be at the masquerade skate, haven't you?"

"Yes, of course. Everyone is talking about it," Louisa said.

Mildred set down her cup. "Today we intend to air out some of the unused rooms, but first I insisted we pay some calls."

"We're glad you've come," Anne said in a voice that seemed truly welcoming. "Tell us where you're from and about yourself."

Sadie kept her answers short, quickly talking about her father's health and her sisters' joint efforts to save their farm. They seemed satisfied with her answers, though far from impressed. "I'm enjoying my time in Monticello and am grateful to now be at the Taylor house."

"No doubt. You've the job every woman wants." Louisa's pinky stayed high in the air while she sipped her coffee. "You'll meet him first."

"I keep her busy," Mildred said, taking the conversation back by the reins. With great skill she brought the discussion from Sadie being new in town to the last quilting night. She journeyed through one connecting topic at a time until she was able to comment, "Children with no home could easily be lost. It's a shame, is it not?"

Anne and Louisa shared a glance—these women must know something! Sadie edged forward on her chair, doing her best to seem unaffected when, in fact, her senses were firing alarms in rapid succession.

"Louisa has a cousin," Anne said softly. "She found herself . . . I'm sorry, I should not be telling you."

"Go on," Mildred said. "We all have a plethora of cousins. Tell your tale—we won't spread it around. I've been feeling the call to educate myself about the foundling cause. Perhaps you can help me understand better."

"I know little of the foundling cause. I only know that . . . well, when someone finds themselves in such a condition, it complicates things."

Mildred spoke slowly. "You know this because of your niece?"

"Yes, it was over four years ago," Louisa said, then turned to her mother. "It doesn't matter now if we tell. It won't change anything."

Anne grimaced. "It's not our story."

"I'll tell it," Louisa said, ignoring her mother's resistance. "She was twenty and I was sixteen. When she first came here, I remember being jealous of all the attention she got."

"She was lovely," Anne said. "Such a beautiful girl."

"I believe I remember her," Mildred said. "She attended church with you while she was here. I'm sorry to hear that her life was burdened."

Anne pulled a handkerchief from her pocket and wiped at her tears. "I blame myself. She was here with us . . . I was supposed to be taking care of her."

"It wasn't your fault," Louisa said with a defensive air. "She should have been more careful."

"I can't change it now, but I shouldn't have let her go out whenever she wished. When she told me her troubles," Anne said, wiping at her tears again, "I asked if she could marry the father. She said no, and then the next day she left. She went back to Blackwell, to my sister's home. I wrote to her asking after her condition, but my sister wrote back, saying it was all lies and that my niece had only been trying to get attention. She claimed that her daughter was prone to deceits, but that was not our experience with her. I have always wondered . . . There's nothing I could have done anyway."

"They hid her condition?" Mildred tsked. "How heartbreaking."

"My sister refused to ever confirm what Katie had told us, but an old friend of mine lived not far from them in Blackwell. She told me that my niece was bedridden and very ill. No one saw her for a long time. When I finally went to visit, she did not have a child, and no one speaks of it. I don't know what happened."

"How is your niece now?" Mildred asked. "I don't believe anyone can truly care about foundlings and not care about their mothers."

"I'm told that an intense melancholy fell upon her." Anne stood and began walking the floor. "She died not long later. No one understands exactly what happened—an accident I'm told. I cannot make sense of the details. Please don't tell anyone about her. I don't wish to tarnish her memory. She was a sweet girl. And if she did have a baby and gave it up, it was for the best."

"We don't want to slander her name or yours," Mildred said.

Anne smiled her thanks, but a heaviness in the room blanketed the women in sadness.

"Perhaps she didn't have a child?" Sadie suggested, only to immediately wish she'd not said it and simply let the conversation lull.

"I'll never know for certain." Anne exhaled. "Mildred, you've got my tongue wagging. It was all years ago. I've put it away the best I can."

"It's all you can do. Give it to God to sort out. But there will be others who find themselves in the same situation, and your story makes me want to offer a hand," Mildred said. Then she directed the conversation away from tragedy and regret. "Tell me, have you finished your quilt?"

"Yes, only last night." Louisa brightened. "Mother says it's the finest pinwheel quilt she's seen."

"Your stitching is exceptional!" Mildred said. For twenty more minutes they talked about quilts, socials, and church meetings. By the time they left, the mood was light and cordial. The hurt and pain of the past tucked away but not forgotten.

"Do you think Katie was somehow connected to Elisabeth?" Sadie asked five minutes after they left the Ascot home.

"The timing would work, but Anne never saw a baby. I suppose it is possible she gave the baby to Reginald to care for, but I don't know how we'd prove it with both Katie and Reginald dead . . ."

"It's all so tragic. Perhaps it's my country upbringing, but I cannot imagine denying a baby."

"The world can be cruel to unwed mothers or anyone else it feels like turning its back on. It's not right, of course." Mildred clicked her tongue, dismayed by reality. "Even Otis felt it when he was young. He was the sweeter of the two boys, so tenderhearted. I'm still haunted by his cries of pain from those foolhardy cures. It's not too late though. I pray he finds the love he's been missing."

"I believe it could happen," Sadie said, leaning on her natural faith and her love of happy endings.

Mildred laced her arm through Sadie's. "Come on, let's go shopping."

An hour later they walked, with parcels in hand, back to the Taylor mansion.

Otis greeted them at the door like a puppy eager to see its master. "Tell me, are we any closer to finding her?"

"Sit down," Mildred said, leading the way to the chairs in the parlor.

Otis listened to the recounting given by both Mildred and Sadie. Important pieces were missing—concrete evidence that Katie was connected to Reginald and that Elisabeth was their child. He rubbed his forehead, silent a moment before saying, "If we were to go to Katie's parents, do you think they would tell us more?"

"Anne's sister denies it all," Sadie said. "We could write them, I suppose, but I don't believe it would help. If there was a baby, they've already turned their back on her."

"And they would know Anne spoke to us, and we assured her we would not spread gossip." Mildred looked toward the doorway that led from the hall to the parlor. Leon, with Wolf at his heels, made his way into the room. "Come and help us think."

Leon sat and the four of them put their heads together.

"We could post a query in the paper here and in the paper where Katie was from. Her parents might see it and come forward themselves. Worded right, they can ignore it if they wish," Sadie suggested. "We could ask after an orphan named Elisabeth and have all the information gathered sent to a lawyer. That way no one would have to connect the story to you if they wanted to remain anonymous, and you would not have to reveal Reginald's role in it until you were ready to."

"I'm not ashamed of Elisabeth." His spine bristled at the thought.

"I didn't think you were. But you have been cautious and thoughtful about when to go through the streets of Monticello, so I assumed you would want to be equally cautious about how you broach the subject of your connection to Elisabeth."

"She's right," Mildred said. "Best to continue with caution until we have all the answers. But don't you worry. None of us will shun the child or look at her different because she's an orphan or believe her marked by her birth."

"We never would," Sadie said with confidence. "I've known orphans and good families that took them in."

"Elisabeth has love waiting for her—we just have to find her." Leon pulled a hat from a peg and put it on his head. "Should I go inquire after a lawyer? I'll make sure our conversation stays confidential."

This new plan, hatched so quickly, was already springing to action. But it was solid and the only ploy they had. There was no reason to delay. "Yes, I'll trust you to find someone willing to accept any correspondence that comes because of the newspaper queries."

"Write up what you want in the paper," Leon said, and Otis obeyed. He scratched out three different attempts until he had a brief note ready for Leon. He left out most of the particulars but made sure to include the words *loving relative has been found.*

He read it aloud to the others, and when they gave their approval, he handed it off for delivery.

"Now we wait," he said to Leon's back when he stepped out the door.

"No," Mildred said. "Now you go and skate. Sitting around here fretting won't bring Elisabeth home any sooner. Makes my nerves jittery watching you fidget. Go get ready for the masquerade."

"If Otis doesn't want—"

"I want to." He surprised himself with his enthusiasm. Mildred was right. Elisabeth had consumed his mind—and she still did—but they had a plan, and until that failed, he had to carry on. "Mildred, do you want to join us?"

The older woman laughed. "You're sweet to ask, but I'd fall on my backside and never get back up. I'll come and watch though."

Both Otis and Sadie were surer footed as they skated today than they had been the day before. Their pace was slow but steady as they made large circles around the factory. Mildred sat on the side, resting comfortably in an old chair. Every time he made eye contact with her, she nodded her head and smiled at him.

"Do I get another rule today?" he asked Sadie ten minutes into their escapade.

"Of course. I simply have to think of it first." She pursed her lips, drawing his attention to them. Her lips were the first he'd ever truly noticed. They were expressive, rising and falling depending on her mood, and at the top they formed the upper half of a heart. "Rule four: at the masquerade, be wary."

"Wary? I expected a rule, not a riddle. You'll have to be more direct."

"There are women eager to ensnare you. They will skate beside you, fall at your feet, and you with your lack of experience will believe yourself smitten with whomever first catches your eye. But my mama says it is better to be a lonely heifer than in company with wolves."

"Your mother compared you to a cow?"

Sadie slowed to a stop, put her hands on the hips of her shapeless brown skirt, and pulled her perfectly pink lips into a thin line. "I never thought much of it. But it's not very flattering to be compared to a cow, is it?"

"No," he answered with a laugh. "She should have said, 'It is better to be a spring flower on a hill being thrashed by the breeze than to be plucked and thrown in a vase with other flowers only to wither and die.' No, I'm not sure that works either. Hmm."

"I believe the meaning is the same. It is better to be sovereign and alone than it is to be saddled with someone you do not care for. I boarded with a Mrs. Smith before she gave my room to someone else. Her husband is a difficult man to be married to." She covered her mouth. "I'm sorry. I did not mean to chin-wag. I was only trying to think of an example to help you be cautious about who you marry."

"You're worried I'll marry up with some conniving woman after the masquerade? All these years I believed courtship took longer than that."

"It can happen quickly. One moment you are rolling along beside an unsuspecting partner, and then you look at them and see them as something more."

He looked at his partner then. They were just skating partners, weren't they?

Her cheeks went pink. She looked away quickly. "You don't want to end up with a bride you regret."

"I'll remember to be wary, though I don't expect it to be a problem. Are there other rules?"

"There are, but you had best master these ones first."

"I will work on my first four rules as quickly as possible." He skated faster, with more confidence, gliding ahead of her. A few feet farther and he turned to face her. "Do you think I'm ready to be an exhibitionist?"

"No." She shook her head, smiling. "But with effort, you'll be able to roll onto the Big Rink floor and not make a fool of yourself."

"I'll have you to thank for it."

She threw her hands out to her sides and offered an exaggerated curtsy. "How gracious. Now tell me, what will you wear?"

"Mildred has agreed to help me alter some of Reginald's old clothes to fit me, and she will make me a mask. What will you wear?"

"I'm not going," she said, and her feet faltered. Onto her backside she went with a loud *thump*. "Oh!" She rubbed at the pain. "I could never go. I would fall there and die of embarrassment."

"I'm not ready to skate without my teacher." He sat beside her with their backs to Mildred, who now slept with her mouth slightly open, giving them a sense of privacy.

"Otis, I really am not going."

"I thought you wanted to go."

A small patch on the side of her skirt kept her right hand busy as she picked nervously at the edges. "A part of me does want to go, but it's best I don't."

"You lecture me on going and showing the town I'm more than my appearance. Why shouldn't you go and show them you are their equal, despite your ragged clothes? Besides, you look much better now that you have taken up bathing. At first I thought I'd taken in a stray turkey."

"Honestly! You're insufferable."

"You know I was only having fun. Besides, we are our own definitions of normal. Why can't homespun be normal too? Come with me and show them you are important and . . . and that you are beautiful."

Her hand stilled for a moment before moving from her patch to her skates. She worked the leather strap free with an almost frantic motion, her bottom lip sucked in. This new look was one he did not know. Unsure what to do, he watched and waited. Had he said too much?

"I went to school with a man named Marvin Bennett," she said quietly, with her head down. "We would walk the fields together and I'd gather armfuls of flowers. We sat by each other at the church socials, and one summer he worked on our farm."

"I didn't know." His forehead furrowed as he tried to imagine the man whose arm she'd been on. Was he her beau? For no justifiable reason, he decided he did not like Marvin Bennett.

"There's not much to know. He is a good man who went off to college. He's due back soon."

"Ah, so rule four was not as much for me as for you. You don't want to meet anyone at the masquerade because your heart is Marvin's?" He managed to keep his tone nonchalant. After all, he had no claim to Sadie. She was his employee, his teacher—that was all.

At last, her head came up. She looked at him the way she always did, like she could see past his outer shell and into his soul. "Rule five is be honest. I said no more rules, but number five is so important I couldn't keep it to myself. And like a good teacher, I have led by example."

"The truth is that someone has claim of your hand and heart," he said through gritted teeth. "Is that what you are saying?"

"I don't know." She stood with her skates dangling at her side and looked at the corner she once slept in. "I know I believed myself in love with him for a very long time, and it only seemed right to tell you."

A dry throat kept him from speaking. Instead, he nodded, stood, and skated over near Mildred, afraid to be alone with Sadie because his heart felt wildly free when she was near, and she'd just told him to keep it locked inside its cage.

⚜

> . . . I have spent a great deal of my life daydreaming about what my future would look like. The longer I am here in Monticello, the more muddled my dreams become. . . .

She finished her missive to her sisters, frustrated that the writing of it did not bring her more clarity.

Be honest. She'd told herself and Otis to follow the timeless counsel. *Be honest.*

She pulled out a new sheet of paper and began another letter.

> Dear Marvin . . .

Chapter 17

Peter!" Sadie shouted as she ran down the street the next morning with two letters in hand.

"Hello there, Sadie. Another letter?"

"Yes, two. Will you be seeing the Bennetts anytime soon? I have a letter to send there for Marvin."

Peter shifted the parcels he carried and reached for her letters. "You wrote to Marvin?"

"He's due home soon. I wanted him to know where to find me." She picked at the edge of her nail. In the past she'd sent her letters directly to Marvin at school through the postal service, but with him due home, she didn't know if he would get it there.

"I have to go past their house today or tomorrow to deliver canning jars to Teddy Norris and his wife. I'll take it for you." He held out two of his parcels to her. "These are from your family. A gift."

They'd sent letters with the ever-loyal Peter many times, and Violette had sent her embroidered handkerchiefs so Sadie could sell them to the store, but she could not imagine what was wrapped in the brown paper.

"Thank you." She took the packages and hugged them to her chest as though she held the family that sent them. "Tell them I'm grateful. Can I pay you for taking the letter to the Bennetts?"

"No, it's my pleasure."

"Thank you. How is Bessy?"

He grinned. "When I left this morning, I snuck out quiet as I could, but she must have been listening. She crept out of bed and came running for a hug. She wanted to come with me, but with all the afternoon storms we've been having, I thought it best she stayed home."

"She's such a dear girl. Tell her I missed seeing her today."

"I will. I best get going. I've got seeds to deliver and some of my own goods to sell."

Sadie said goodbye and hurried back toward the Taylor mansion with her unopened parcels tight against her chest.

"You off shopping?" Leon asked when he spotted her.

"Peter brought these to me." She loosened her grip on her packages. "They're from my family. It's so good of him, taking my letters to my family and"—she cleared her throat—"and to Marvin."

"You've written Marvin." Leon studied her. "Gettin' eager for him to come home?"

She exhaled. "Otis paid me a compliment yesterday. Nothing romantic, just a word of praise, but it was more than Marvin has ever said. I suppose I felt anxious to hear him say something as kind. I told him when he returned home, I wanted to see him. He doesn't write often and usually it's very formal. If he wants to come calling when he's home, now he knows I would welcome it. And if he doesn't . . ."

"Then good riddance." Leon straightened a painting on the wall. "Are you skating today?"

"I don't know. I haven't seen Otis yet."

"He's pacing the upstairs hall, talking to Wolf, waiting for word about Elisabeth, which won't come because his query is not even in the paper yet. You'd better go and distract him. It could be days or weeks before we hear anything, if we hear at all."

Sadie smiled. Surely Otis's query in the paper would bring Elisabeth's true whereabouts to the surface. "I'll go and ask him what he has planned for the day."

He waved her off in his fatherly way.

The stairway was wide, with finely carved balusters and freshly oiled handrails, which Sadie had seen to herself only two nights before. She closed her eyes, imagining herself the lady of the house, walking up the stairs in a finely stitched gown with dainty slippers on her feet.

"You could fall that way." Otis's voice startled her when she was still four stairs from the top.

She gripped her parcels in her left hand and the rail with her right to steady herself. "I was lost in thought."

When he smiled back at her, she relaxed. She'd been unsure what it would be like between them after she told him about Marvin. "Are they thoughts you are willing to share?"

"No." She continued her ascent up the stairs, eyes open now. "But only because you would think me very childish if I did. I was coming to find you. I wanted to see what you had planned for today."

His gaze lingered on the gifts in her arms. She could see questions dancing through his mind, but his mouth remained closed.

"My family sent these," she said, answering his unspoken question. "I don't know what they are."

"Don't delay opening them on my account. There is nothing I need that should take precedent over you enjoying a piece of home."

"Are you certain?"

"Nothing pressing. I plan to practice, but not now. I have too much weighing on my mind."

"You should play the piano," she said as she took three steps away from him before turning back. "It soothes you."

"It does," he said, a softness in his tone. "Meet me in the music room when you are ready?"

"I will." She lingered, looking up at Otis. His gift was not tangible like the ones in her arms, but the invitation to listen and be his audience was not lost on her. Many times now he'd let her listen as he played. She'd stand in the doorway, quietly absorbing the notes as they swelled in the air. But this was the first time he'd asked her to come rather than simply allowing her to stay. Perhaps it was merely a peace offering, or a means of showing her they could be friends even after her confession.

He nodded to her before she set off for the staff quarters, where she admired the simple brown paper and string. She wanted to enjoy the moment but also found herself eager to get back to Otis. She took the end of the string and pulled.

"Oh," she uttered aloud when the paper fell away. There in her lap was her mother's finest blue dress, only it was different now, updated with a fashionable flair. Her breath caught in her chest—the dress was beautiful. It was not a dress bought from a shop window, but it was finely stitched by expert hands.

She shook it out and held it against herself. "You are a frivolous girl," she told her reflection when she looked in the mirror. Not so unlike the many characters she had written, who all longed to feel attractive, at least for one night. Was it wrong to want to feel beautiful?

With extra care she hung the dress, smoothing the wrinkles with her hand, and then she stood, staring at it in awe. In the folds of the dress, she'd found a letter.

> . . . Every day you are away, we miss you more. Spending time on this dress has been a comfort to my heart, filling me with loving thoughts for my dear girl. A mother's heart is always full when thinking of a daughter who has grown into such a fine woman. Violette is sure you will be the belle of the ball or the rink or wherever you choose to wear this dress to, and I agree.
>
> You are doing a noble thing, going off and working so hard for our family. I pray you know how truly proud I am.

Her mother's approval sent her soul singing with happiness. The rest of the letter talked of their hard work on the farm and their father's attempts to regain his strength. At the end she read,

> We had a bit of blue cloth left from the dress and decided to make it into a tie for your generous employer. Tell him we are indebted to him for his kindness. We do hope to meet him one day so we might thank him in person.

She opened the second, smaller parcel containing the tie and held it next to her blue dress. It was a perfect match. Her mother's sweet gesture deserved applause, and yet it seemed presumptuous to give a man a gift that matched her new dress. She tucked the tie into her pocket, unsure what to do with it. Then rule number five popped in her head and she knew, on her honor, that she had to give the tie to Otis.

Just outside of the music room door she stopped and listened to the enchanting melody. Hopeful. Promising. Like an embrace, the sound encircled her, filling her heart with eagerness and an unexplainable feeling that only good things lay ahead. When the last note faded, she stepped inside.

"That was not a sad song," she said, standing at his side. "What were you feeling when you wrote that one?"

"I wrote that very early one morning." He shifted on the bench and looked at her. "The sun was rising brighter than I ever remembered seeing it. It illuminated everything, and for that moment my life did not seem so worthless. I felt remembered. Which makes little sense, but I felt it all the same."

"It makes sense to me. There were mornings on the farm when the sky looked like a painting. I felt especially close to God in those moments. Perhaps that morning he was telling you that he remembered you." She looked at the room with its closed drapes. His fear of passersby spotting him caused him to hide from the sun on a beautiful day, but people rarely came this way. "If you opened the drapes, you could see the sun today." He sat very quiet, and she feared she'd spoken out of turn. "Why did you choose to play that song today?"

"I don't know . . . I suppose I wanted to feel that same feeling again."

She left his side and stepped near a window, peering out through the crack. "Shall I toss them open and let the sun in? It might help you relive that moment."

"No," he said with laughter in his tone. "Not yet, but maybe someday."

She smiled toward the window, keeping her back to him. "Halfway?"

"No."

"Just a crack?"

"Not even a crack." When he laughed this time, it was louder, less reserved. He played a few notes to a rousing ditty. "Do you play?"

"No," she said, facing him again. "We didn't have a piano, but my father plays the fiddle, so we did have music in our home."

"The fiddle is an instrument I have not heard in a very long time."

"It feels like a very long time since I've heard it as well." She forced a smile, refusing to go down the path that led to an aching heart and heavy homesickness. "What can I do to help you?"

"I keep thinking about Elisabeth. I feel useless waiting."

"When you find her, you will not just be her uncle—you'll be filling the role of father. You could prepare yourself for her homecoming by readying to take on such a role."

Otis stood and, just as she expected, ran his hand along the rim of his hat. He was thinking of his father. She felt sure of it.

"How do I learn to be a good father?"

She sat in a chair opposite the piano and searched for an answer. Example had been her teacher in so much of who she'd become. Her parents were hardworking, kind, and believers in virtue and moral living, but he'd not had such an example since his mother's death. "Do you have someone you could emulate?"

"No. I have Leon, but he has no children. Mr. Crawford had grown children he never saw, and he was not a father to me. He kept me fed and taught me to play and compose, but even that was done for money, not out of affection."

"Hmm . . . then I will tell you about my own father, and that will be a start. But first," she said and paused, her hand fidgeting with the tie in her pocket, "I have a gift. It's not from me . . . it's from my mother. She sent it as a thank-you for all you've done for me. She's grateful I have a place to live . . . though she still doesn't know about my time in your factory."

"Your mother sent *me* a gift?"

She forced her hand to remove the tie from her pocket. "Here, she made it."

He took it, shaking it out in front of him.

"I know you have plenty. I'm sure they didn't mean to imply you didn't. And it's not from the store or fancy," she rambled nervously. "My mother is always trying to show her thanks."

"Sadie," he said when she paused, "tell them I love it."

Otis took the gifted tie to his room and hung it next to his modest array of clothing. It was the first gift he'd received since he was thirteen. He'd celebrated Christmas with Reginald and his father, who had picked a gift for each of his sons. A new sled for Reginald. A bat and glove for him. Were they still in the closet of his old room? Someday he would gather his courage and find out. For today he was content with his blue tie and his friend, who made his heart flutter in a way it should not.

Sadie insisted on being busy, so they met near the old dog run. It was tucked in a corner, out of sight of the road. A large branch had damaged the fencing, leaving it in need of repair.

"I hadn't meant for you to take on repairs like this. The duster factory is probably less strenuous," Otis said as he pried the boards away.

"We did this sort of work on the farm all the time." She had her hair swept up away from her face. Her cheeks were rosy from exertion as she used her small frame to clear out debris.

"Tell me more about your father. Someday, I want Elisabeth to talk about me how you talk about him."

She stumbled backward when one of the boards came loose but managed to catch herself. "He is the hardest-working man

I know. He never complains. He just does what has to be done. I've always loved that about him. Whenever something would happen on the farm, he'd just grab his coat and go to work."

"He didn't grumble at all?"

"Maybe internally, but we rarely saw it. He loved his land, so he took care of it."

Otis threw the loose boards out of the dog run and into a heap. "You said he plays the fiddle. What else does he do?"

"When my sisters and I were growing up, he liked to listen to the stories we wrote and watch the plays we put on. He also liked to ride his horse. He'd take my mama and they'd ride out to the edge of our land and back. I always liked the way they were together. They're a love match. So many of the farmers aren't like them. They are married so that there is someone to tend the fields and someone to tend the house. But not my parents. They love being together. My pa still looks at my mama like she is the sun and the moon."

Otis hung on her every word. She talked of a father who was gentle when she was hurt, who had patience when she was learning new things, and who seemed to abound in love.

"I understand now why you've sacrificed so much for them," he said after nailing a new rail onto the fence. "Your family is very different from how mine was."

"But your family going forward can be like that." She took the end of the next board and held it in place for him. "My father was raised by a harsh man. He wasn't wealthy like your father, but he had a temper."

Otis held the nail in place and then swung the hammer. "Was it hard for him to be different?"

"He didn't make it look hard. But he did say he had good friends he learned from, and my mother came from a kind family. Her relatives lived close, and they were good to my father. That might have helped." She put her hands on her hips and looked at their progress. "If we put a few more boards up, this should keep Wolf in."

"He'll like being able to come out whenever he wants."

Sadie picked up the hammer. "Want to see who can put in a nail in fewer swings?"

"All right." He let her go first. She was a small woman, but he knew better than to make assumptions about how she'd do. She swung once, and the nail went a third of the way in. He held the board still for her as she swung again, sinking it deep.

"Your turn," she said with an adorable smirk on her face. "My father taught me. You'll have to teach Elisabeth."

"I'll have to get better myself," he said as he set the next board in place. She stepped closer to hold it steady. Her hand brushed his when she came to help, and like before, her touch left him in an unfamiliar tizzy that was nearly impossible to ward off.

"Are you going to hammer it in?" she asked when he delayed.

Afraid she'd suspect what he was feeling, he put the nail in place and swung quickly, missing the board completely. Sadie laughed delightfully at his mishap.

"You win," he conceded in a raspy voice. "Do I owe you a prize?"

She shook her head, already picking up the last board. "No." And then she stared at him. His old instincts told him to shrink away from her perusing eyes. "You're going to be a good father," she said at last. "You lost with grace. That's what my father would have done too."

Otis didn't trust his voice, so he finished the repairs in silence, grateful she didn't press him to speak.

The day raced by in an unnatural hurry. They watched Wolf as he examined his newly repaired run. They ate together. They played chess three times and polished silverware together.

In the late afternoon they skated, their feet growing steadier as they went around in giant circles.

"What are you thinking?" he asked when her eyes took on that faraway look.

"That the next story I write needs to have roller-skating in it."

"What do you do with all your stories?"

She slowed. "We used to do readings from them. On long winter nights we would sit in a circle and read our parts. It was great fun. But mostly I just wrote them as a way of feeling things I hadn't ever felt and going places I had never been."

"Someday will you let me read them?"

She blushed. "I . . . I'm not sure. I've only ever shared them with my family."

"I played for you," he said. "Maybe someday . . ." He let his sentence trail off, sensing her unease. He'd pushed too hard, even after telling himself that he had to keep his distance. She was courting someone else—she'd as good as told him that her heart was not free. Still, he felt drawn to her. Grateful for the friend he'd found.

An idea popped into his head, something he hoped would ease them back to comfortable.

"Wait here," he said. And then, over his shoulder as he went to the bench, he added, "We could make this scene better."

⚜

> . . . We skated to the sound of a single harmonica player. . . .

Sadie stopped writing, unsure how to put into words how glorious the night had been. Otis had returned to the factory with Leon and Leon's harmonica.

"I wanted to bring a piano," Otis had said. He grinned and her heart melted. "A harmonica will have to do."

They floated as though they were on a cloud. Everything else faded away except the two of them.

"This would make a very fine scene," she said.

"Is there anything that would make it better?"

Answers filled her mind, but she couldn't say any of them, not when there were so many unsettled matters at play. "No," she finally said. "This is perfect."

And it was. But if she ever wrote the scene into a story, she would have her leading man pull his lady toward him, closing the distance between them so their lips could meet.

Leon left when he said his mouth could not play another note. They were alone then, and though she felt the pull to linger, she went to the bench and sat, readying herself to leave.

"Another rule," she said. "Always skate to music if you can."

Otis nodded, a solemn, thoughtful expression on his face. "Is that an official rule?"

"No," she said with a small smile. "But it is my favorite one."

Chapter 18

Wolf barked from his spot near the window, his tail wagging and eyes following something outside.

"What is it?" Otis asked before cautiously peering out. Sadie was crossing the lawn and heading away from the mansion. Wolf barked again, and she glanced over her shoulder and waved before ducking her head against the early morning rain and hurrying on her way.

Otis scowled as she disappeared from sight. Leaving his chair, he went to the vast wall of books, pulled down a volume, fingered through it, and replaced it. His mind was firing too rapidly for him to focus on the tiny print. Today the citizens of Monticello and Blackwell would read his words in the newspaper. His hopes rested on someone knowing about an orphan named Elisabeth. If the right person saw the query he'd written, he would be welcoming a niece into his home very soon.

Needing to busy himself, he walked the halls, stopping near the attic door. He'd gone up once since returning home but hadn't spent enough time in the rafters to know what all was there. With nothing better to do, he climbed the creaking stairs, shocked to realize the boards squawked in the same way they had when he was a boy. And further shocked that he remembered the pattern to walk if he wanted to go unnoticed. Wolf chose not to climb the steep stairs, leaving Otis to face the cobwebs and memories alone.

Dense dust covered the relics, giving everything a dull, muted look. A rocking horse with a small leather saddle sat against the wall nearest him. He ran his fingers across the place he'd once sat, leaving a trail in the blanket of dust. Dim memories of rocking back and forth as a boy floated to his recollection.

"What a fine rider you are." He heard his mother's voice in his mind. The same lilt and cadence he'd so often tried to recall. *"Ottie, my boy, you're getting so big."*

He pushed the horse head forward enough that it rocked back and forth as though it had a rider on its back. How small he'd been when he'd first ridden this horse. Using his handkerchief, he wiped the dust from the once beloved toy, hoping his mother's voice would again jump to his recollection.

The horse, now free of its dust, looked new again and ready for a rider. He moved it near the stairs. Elisabeth, he hoped, would fit in the saddle as he once had. While she rode, he would speak to her gently, like his mother had, and he would fall back on the lessons he'd learned from Sadie's stories of her father.

A traveling trunk he had no memory of, an abandoned broom most likely made at the Hoag factory years ago, and a chair with a broken spindle all got pushed aside—they meant nothing to him. A chest beneath several milk crates, however, caught his attention. He could not remember where it had been before coming to the attic, but something about it seemed familiar. The hinges creaked as he pried them open, awakening them from a long slumber.

"Mama," he whispered. Her old dresses, folded neatly, came into view. They'd sat forgotten for years, and still his heart leapt at the sight. He rifled through the contents, unsure what he hoped to find. Dresses and more dresses. Despite having no use for them, he knew he'd found a treasure. Each dress had once touched the skin of his mother. They were no substitute for her presence, but somehow, they made her seem closer.

"I saw the door open."

He whipped his head around at the sound of Sadie's voice and searched her face, but there was no way of knowing where she'd been by staring at the curve of her cheek and certainly no way of knowing what she'd been up to by admiring the pink of her lips.

"I can go," she said when he only gaped at her.

"No, stay. I would have asked you to join me, but I saw you head out this morning."

"Are we looking for something?"

"I found my mother's old dresses." He moved to his right so she could see into the old chest.

"They're so fine." She ran her fingers across the lace of the top dress. "My mother sent me a dress of hers. That was what was in my parcel . . . I haven't worn many pretty dresses. Never anything like these."

"Ah, we are the same."

"Are we?" she asked.

"I've not worn pretty dresses before either." He laughed at his own jest.

"I should hope not. Tell me, what was your mother like?"

Otis wiped the dust from a wobbly-legged chair. "Here." He offered it to her.

She sat and smoothed her brown skirt around her. Her clothes were dull, but it made no difference. He found her strikingly beautiful and sadly out of reach. No matter how often he reminded himself of Marvin, he couldn't seem to shake the way she made him feel. She'd never declared herself promised, and so telling her about his mother was hardly crossing a line.

"I came up here to pass the time, but when I touched that old horse, I could almost hear her voice. She was soft-spoken, but I always wanted to listen to her." Restless, he began sifting through belongings while talking. "I would hurry home from school each day and tell her everything that happened. I am sure what I told her was boring drivel, but she never let on."

"She sounds like a very good woman. Not enough people know how to really listen."

"She excelled at it." He moved a basket off an abandoned dresser and opened the top drawer. It was empty. "When she died, her belongings disappeared. Or I thought they had. There are a few things here, and my brother had a photograph of her in his bedroom. I could show you if you like."

"I'd love to see it."

From the corner of his eye, he saw her rise and walk across the room. She stopped in the crook of the steep roofed attic beside the family's once cherished cradle, now covered in years of cobwebs.

"When I meet someone as an adult, it's hard for me to imagine them small, but you must have fit in this cradle."

"I have no memory of it, but my mother told me I was a very round baby with a head full of hair."

She chuckled. "I would have liked to see that. I'm told I was bald until I was four."

"And now you've a head of hair and I've none. Things have certainly changed."

"Indeed." She sneezed twice, apologized, and then sneezed again. "I'm sorry. Dust often sends me into a fit of sneezing. You should have heard me when I was in the old factory. I sneezed all the time. I would much rather be laughing at our changes since infancy, but—" Her nose scrunched up and she sneezed again.

"We can go. There's nothing up here that needs my attention."

"No, I'll be fine." She sneezed, covering her nose. "What's that?"

He followed her pointing finger toward another large chest. To get to it he had to move a crate of old medicine bottles. It'd been years, and the sight of them shouldn't bother him, but it did. His hands shook as he placed them on the side of the crate. His mother's voice had come to him soft and gentle, reminding him of long-ago love. Touching the crate of glass bottles with labels full of lies had the opposite effect. His father's coarse voice, his demands, his anger . . . Otis tightened his grip on the box. He wanted to be done with it all. He wanted it out of his head. He wanted to be free.

"Are you all right?" Sadie asked.

He trembled. The past was too strong and powerful. The chains tightened. The memories grew louder.

As a boy he'd been helpless. He'd submitted, letting his father torture him under the guise of health. Like a dagger the memory cut into him, twisted and tore at him. And with it his pain shrieked, telling him to fight back. He growled, screaming like a wild animal, and threw the box as hard as he could against the wall. Glass shattered and scattered across the floor.

He reached for a large broken piece and threw it. Then he grabbed another and another, caring nothing for the sharp edges that cut his hands. All he felt was the long-ago hurt and the deep aching wound that had never fully healed.

When at last his rage died, he fell on his knees, weak and ashamed.

Somewhere behind him Sadie sneezed, and then her hand went to his back, slowly, tentatively, touching him.

"Just go," he growled, filled with embarrassment and hurt.

"It's all right," she said near his ear. Her voice was like honey, sweet and soothing. It seeped inside him, robbing the bitter anger of its potency. "No one can hurt you now. He's dead. You're safe."

"I'm sorry," he whispered. "I'm so sorry."

"You're on glass," she whispered back. Her hand moved under his arm. She pulled, urging him to his feet. "Let's go downstairs. I'll clean you up."

He stood, his gaze remaining on the broken glass. She gasped. "Your hands."

"It's nothing." He clenched his hands and winced. "None of this is your problem."

"Wait." She sneezed again, and despite his storming emotions he nearly laughed. Never had he heard someone sneeze so many times. "I believe, before we clean you up, we ought to celebrate."

"Celebrate?" He froze, confused. He'd made a fool of himself and exposed himself for the broken vessel he was. There was nothing to celebrate, only a new memory to commiserate. "What is it you want to celebrate? My bloody hands or my temper?"

"Not your hands. We'll bandage those and they'll be better soon." She picked up a large piece of glass. "You broke them. If these bottles were chains, then you are free. Otis, you're free."

Free. Could it be true?

"That's reason to celebrate." She brought her hand back and threw the piece of glass against the wall. It shattered into smaller bits. Glistening fragments of glass covered the entire corner of the attic, a minefield of sharp edges and danger. Could she be right? Could this carnage signify his freedom? Accepting it felt so sudden after so many years of carrying his pain and anger. Too easy.

"I don't know," he mumbled.

When she sneezed again, he took a step away from the glass. She needed to get away from the dust. "I'll clean this up later," he said.

"I can help you."

"I think you'd best stay clear of the attic until I have time to dust everything. Come on." By the stairs he paused and looked back at the mess he'd made. A ray of light from the small attic window caused the glass to sparkle like diamonds. He looked at his hands and said, "After I bandage my hands, I'll come back for the horse. I thought Elisabeth might like it."

"Excellent idea." She wiped at her nose with her handkerchief. "Let me help you with your hands."

"It's not a job requirement. I can take care of it myself."

"Not everyone—" She stopped walking and looked at him directly, waiting to say more until he met her gaze. "Not everyone will run. Your father was wrong, but you broke the bottles. Otis, *you* broke them. He sent you away, but you came back. You don't have to do everything by yourself just because he was embarrassed of you."

He closed his eyes, not to hide from her but because she was saying the words he'd wanted to hear for so long. Night after night as a youth and even as an adult, he'd imagined his father, his brother, anyone calling him home. And now here she stood, unaware of the power her words carried. Could he trust what she'd said? Could he go on, even without an official welcome home?

"Otis." Sadie's hand touched his arm, and he opened his eyes with a start.

"I'm sorry. This house . . . there are so many memories." He took a step down the hall, pretending composure as best he could. Love, acceptance, abandonment, trust. He wanted to run from it all and in the same breath to make sense of the scattered pieces and find peace.

They stopped at the end of the hall. He dared a look at her. "You're red all over."

"I should be offended." She smiled her beautiful, bright smile, lighting up her red face. "But I'm not."

He winced dramatically, still teetering between his many emotions, unsure which pull to follow and which to fight against. "Let's blame my years of isolation. I haven't spent much time around women—very little, in fact."

"And now you spend every day with me. It must be quite overwhelming." She put a hand on his arm. "Go sit in that chair and I'll fetch water and bandages."

He obeyed, sitting on a chair in the landing, waiting for her to return. Aware that, despite their short acquaintance, he dreaded her return to the factory and his return to solitude. There was one thought that made sense in his muddle of woes. Sadie West made his days better. His plans to escape to the woods held less appeal when he was around her.

She returned, set her supplies beside her, and took his hand. "Someday you'll be used to having friends in your life again to help you."

Friend. Impulsively he pulled his hand back. Her head popped up, questioning him. The title should have made his chest swell. He'd not had a friend since his boyhood chums, but hearing her say it now left him hungry for something more. She had just been beside him as he fought a vicious foe. Surely that linked their souls together beyond mere friendship. She'd seen his head, his scars, his pain.

She broke her gaze and sneezed again. "Don't worry, none of these wounds are very deep. I don't expect these cuts will set you back much. Come on, give me your hand."

Fine. He put his hand in hers. "What do you do to stop the sneezing?"

"A long walk in the fresh air or a bath. Something like that usually works."

He nodded. "I won't be joining you on account of my avoiding the public and, well . . . you understand . . ." He cleared his throat. "Why I can't, well, bathing is a private matter." If pointing out her red face was uncouth, then commenting on a woman bathing was surely against every rule of propriety. He looked away.

"Don't look so embarrassed. I find your unpolished ways charming." After cleaning his hands, she stood. "I'll freshen up and find you later."

She paused, and when he said nothing, she walked away.

Alone, he turned left and then right, unsure what to do while he waited for her return. Mildred saved him from himself when she insisted they work on his costume for the masquerade skate. It did not take long before he regretted her suggestion. Standing with his arms out and his back straight while she pinned and tucked was not a diverting activity but a rather torturous one. It left him counting the seconds in every minute.

"How many more hours must I stand here?"

"You've brought this misery upon yourself. There is a fine seamstress in town, but you insisted I not call for her. That leaves me to fumble my way through the making of your costume."

"I don't know why I agreed to go anyway," he said like a sulky child while keeping his arms stretched out for Mildred. She chuckled softly but didn't slow her work.

"You're going because Miss Sadie came up with the idea and because you know we might need help from the town with finding Elisabeth. Besides, you must be curious about everyone. It's only right you go."

He groaned.

"Stop your fussing. You can still run off and leave this all behind if you want when the time comes."

When at last she set him free, he found himself wandering the house, secretly searching for Sadie—though he'd deny it if confronted.

"Do I look less red?" Sadie asked when he stepped into the parlor, where she stood with a duster in one hand and a cloth held over her nose in the other hand.

"I've been told it is not polite to comment on the . . . er . . . redness of a woman's face." He looked her over. Her puffy eyes and red skin had returned to normal. "Or lack of redness."

"You can be taught—that's important. I have also learned that when dusting, it's best if I cover my nose. I really ought to sew a mask that covers my mouth and nose. It would not only be practical but may start a popular fashion. Can you imagine, everyone walking around with masks over their faces?" She twirled the duster in her hand. "I can tell you which part of the turkey each one of these feathers is from."

"No doubt a useful skill. Tell me, where did this feather come from?" He stepped closer and touched a shorter feather, brown with only a small band at the top.

"That's a body feather."

"And this one—"

A pounding on the door startled them. His hand flew to his head. He'd taken off his hat when he was with Mildred and not replaced it. How odd. He usually never forgot.

"Go—I'll answer it." Sadie shooed him away.

Like a coward he retreated, too timid to fight his own battle, but he did not go far, only to the hall where he could listen unseen.

"Peter," Sadie said as soon as she opened the door. "What are you doing here? You must have turned around as soon as you got to the country."

"My second stop was your parents' home," he said, heaving for breath like a panting dog. "I took your letter to your family. Your pa tried to get up when I knocked on the door. He fell. He was crying out in pain, and your mama decided he needed the doctor again. They haven't wanted me to tell you how much pain he's always in, but he's not doing well."

"Are you going back there now?"

"Yes, I only came to tell you."

"Can you wait? I'd like to go with you if I can."

Otis's stomach clenched. He didn't want her to go.

"I'll go and see if Tobias at the store has any new deliveries since I'm here. Then I'll come back. Pack quickly."

Otis could hear a shuffling sound. Then Peter's voice called out again. "I forgot. I went to the Bennett farm yesterday. Marvin is back and he's read your letter. He wrote you one in return."

"Thank you, Peter. I'll read this later."

Drat these shadows. Otis wanted to see her face. Was this fool Marvin bringing a blush? A sigh? Or had she come to her senses and realized what a clod Marvin was? Impatiently, he waited for the door to close and for her to reappear. The beast inside him wanted to bark and scream and tell her no, that if she worked here, she needed to be here. He was justified. After all, she'd agreed to work at the house, and he knew she needed money—

But then she stepped near him, and he saw her face. Her desire to go was written into her every feature.

"Otis—"

"Go. Go for as long as you need to." His words came out terse and strained, but he didn't take them back. "Be with your father."

She paused, stepped closer, and put a hand on his arm. "Thank you."

"He'll want you there."

She nodded. "You . . . you will tell me everything when I come back? I want to know about Elisabeth."

He nodded. "I'll tell you."

"And you'll practice? The masquerade is coming."

"I don't know." He shoved his hands in his pockets. "I'm not sure I even want to go."

"The whole town is expecting you." She tightened her grasp on his arm. "They want to meet you, and when they do, they'll see what I see."

Afraid that if she looked too closely, she would see his burning jealousy and hostile thoughts about Marvin, and his anguish over her leaving, he looked away. "You best pack your things."

"I won't be gone long," she said as she backed from the room, her hand wrapped tightly around Marvin's letter.

Like a statue, he stared as she walked away. He might have stood there, motionless and aghast, until she left if Mildred had not come looking for him.

"What do you know—Marvin is back," Mildred said, startling him.

"She told you?"

"I asked her what she was holding so tightly. Said she wasn't sure she could read it just yet but that Peter said it was a note from Marvin about his return. Two years away at school and not a single promise to her. Poor girl doesn't know a thing about the man's heart." She pointed an accusing finger at him. "Don't be like Marvin."

"I don't plan to attend college."

"That's not what I meant. You know that."

"I have written her," he said, puffing out his chest. But he hadn't ever written her as Otis Taylor. Would she want that?

"I'm talking about more than letters. Marvin left her wondering, and because of that he may lose her. I'm going to pack her a basket of food. You're a smart man—make use of your time." She left him as quickly as she'd come, mumbling to herself as she went about men being naïve to what was right in front of them. He went to his study and attempted to do as he was advised, though writing proved a difficult task to complete with bandaged hands. In the end he feared he had failed to say what he truly felt, but there was no time to dawdle or rewrite. He folded his note and rushed back to the parlor.

"Goodbye, Leon," he heard Sadie say as she exited the kitchen. He rubbed his clammy palm on his pants and sat, then stood, unsure how to look at ease when he felt nothing but nervous. She approached, carpetbag in one hand and a hat on her head. He took a large step in front of her and held his arm straight out, the letter dangling from his fingers.

"Here." He practically shoved the paper into her hand.

"Is this for me?" She took his folded note, the first he'd ever placed in her hand. "You wouldn't look at me before. I thought I might not get a glimpse of your blue eyes before I left."

"I was surprised, about your father, and . . . and I heard your friend say you had a letter from Marvin."

"It's an unusual day. News of my father and now two letters to read." She adjusted the bag on her arm. "I don't know what to make of it all."

"I've no advice, only to be careful and . . . if you want to come back, you can."

"I left the dress my mother sent. I'll have to come back for that." Her playful smile gave him pause. He stood unnaturally still, and then she stepped closer. So close he didn't know what to do. He wanted to cut the difference in half. He wanted to take her in his arms and hold her and beg her to stay, but he knew she needed to go. He cleared his throat. "Do you need money?"

"You've paid me all that you owe me." She stuck his note inside her bag without breaking her gaze from his. "We'll manage."

"You will tell me if you are in need?"

"I don't know." Her honesty endeared him further. So often he'd been lied to, but she spoke truth. "My family has always stood on our own feet. We work hard. And then we work harder."

"Admirable. But is it wise? You bandaged my hands. You said everything I needed to hear. Why are you permitted to help me but unable to accept help?"

"I hadn't thought of it that way."

"You called us allies. That means if one of us is in need, the other can be relied upon for aid. Don't forget that."

"I have never had an ally like that," she said in a gentle voice. Her hand, her soft, beautiful, perfect hand, left her side, and the tips of her fingers grazed his cheek. "Thank you."

No words would come. Nothing witty. Nothing wise or profound. Like a river in winter, he stood immovable, aware only of the warmth of her fingertips. If they'd lingered, perhaps he would have thawed completely.

"I have to go," she said, stepping away from him at last.

Chapter 19

Peter wasn't there when Sadie stepped outside. She kept her back to the house, not wanting Otis to see her pouring over his words like a greedy child going for penny candy.

Dear Miss Sadie West,

I have little experience with letters. I scratched a few words out once to a Jane Squatter. You may have heard of her. She took up residence in the factory you and I have skated in. She tried to convince my dog she was a more pleasant companion than me, and she had an uncanny ability to make me laugh. Now that I think about it, you and Jane seem to have a great deal in common.

Writing to you as Sadie feels more meaningful. And scarier.

You are leaving, and I don't want to live my life harboring words I never said. I must tell you that in the weeks you've lived here, you have changed this dark house from a prison to an oasis. You've changed more than this house—you've changed everything. I am not the same

> man who returned to Monti with nothing but anger and coldness in his heart. In your presence I feel hopeful. You remind me that I am not alone and that I never truly was. Thank you for looking me in the eyes and believing that I, Otis Taylor, am merely a different kind of normal.

Such lovely words. The kindest she'd ever read. At the bottom were several slashed-out words and then his name. She laughed, imagining the flustered look on his face while he wrote and the murmuring he must have done when he made a mistake and didn't have time to rewrite it.

Under his name were a few more words.

> Remember, dear friend, Marvin has had years to proclaim his feelings. A wise teacher once told me to be wary. I offer you the same advice.

Wary of Marvin? Soft-spoken, steady Marvin? She folded the paper back up and tucked it into her bag, unsure how Otis Taylor, Monticello's most anticipated bachelor, had written such flattering words to her. With her head spinning and her mind grappling with this unusual turn of events, she pulled her second letter from her bag.

> Dear Miss West,
>
> I am recently returned and have received your letter. When time permits, I will arrange to call on you in Monticello.
>
> Cordially,
> Marvin

Sadie frowned, turning the page over only to find it blank. She'd written a detailed letter to him, telling him about her job at the duster factory and her father's current health. She'd shared small but important pieces of her life and heart with him. Was he so busy that he could not write a line or two more?

Two vastly different letters—two vastly different men.

One the dream she'd cherished, the other unexpected.

Peter's return startled her back to reality. His complexion was paler than it had been before, and there was something alarming about the way he carried himself.

"Are you concerned for my pa?" she asked once the wagon pulled away from the mansion.

"I've a few worries." He grimaced. "Your pa is one of them. No one likes seeing their friend down."

Sadie wanted to ask more—she'd been friends with Peter for years—but their sharing the same circles and her bond with his wife did not warrant her prying after his woes. She'd been taught better, and so she simply said, "I hope whatever is troubling you can be fixed."

He nodded, head still facing the horses, brow furrowed. Peter's normally calm and easy disposition was now taut and tense. Her fear for her father grew tenfold just sitting beside him. Could things really be so dire?

She did her best to distract herself by studying Monticello as they rode away. She saw the diner. The skating rink. The church. And then the Hoag factory on Maple Street came into view, capturing her attention in ways the other brick buildings had not. She'd come to town willing to work anywhere she could, and it was there, sorting feathers for dusters, that she had found employment. The struggle to send money home had been harder and more winding than she had anticipated, resulting in cold nights in the factory, the pungent smell of turkey—and now the Taylor mansion. This entire endeavor had been for her father, and now a chill raced through her. She wasn't supposed to be returning until he was well. Her father was supposed to recover. He had to.

For two hours they rode in relative silence, until at last her beloved home came into view. The two-story farmhouse was surrounded by outbuildings, and unlike the Taylor mansion, it was no architectural masterpiece—but it was home, and she'd missed it. *Go faster*, she wanted to shout at Peter, but already he'd gone out of his way and pushed his horses to come and get her.

The last stretch of road felt the longest, each turn of the wheel taking twice as long as the revolution before. When at last he reined the horses to a stop, she jumped from the side of the wagon without waiting for help.

The weeds near the house were taller, the spring chicks bigger, and the barn leaned farther to the right. The changes were minor, but they were a reminder that she had been gone and that life had continued without her.

A blur of color raced toward her with a high, shrill cry. Skirts flew, and then arms were around her, embracing her.

"You're back!" her sister Molly shouted near her ear while still holding her tightly. Violette and Flora, mere steps behind her, joined the embrace. They lingered in one another's arms.

"Come in and see Pa," Flora said in her gentle way. "I know he'll feel better just having you home. We all will."

The small house felt welcoming and bright, with sunshine coming through the windows, covering everything in a gentle yellow hue. Her mother stepped from the back room, looking older than Sadie remembered. But those tired eyes came alive when she saw Sadie. Next Nina, Peter's wife, came and said hello, with little Bessy in her arms. They'd come to be with the family while Peter fetched Sadie. For a moment every worry, every bit of confusion she harbored vanished. She was home, and these were her people!

"We've missed you," her mother said and then kissed her cheek. "Come and see your pa."

Sadie nodded and stepped away from her mother and sisters and friends as she went to her father's side. Where was the sun-darkened man whose hardworking muscles filled his shirt? This couldn't be him, so frail and void of color.

"I heard you fell," she whispered as she took his hand. "I'm here now. I want to help take care of you."

"Ah, my little bird has returned." Though he sounded tired, he propped himself up a little higher in bed with a wince. "It's hard for an old man like me to be waited on. The doctor gave me something for the pain—makes me look braver than I am."

"You're the bravest man I know." She pressed her fingers tighter around his leathery hand, the rough texture a beautiful testament to the many sacrifices he'd made for their family. "What does the doctor say?"

"I'm to stay in bed and continue praying that time will heal me. But my hip and leg don't feel right. I tried staying in bed, but they're not getting better. I never meant for you to have to do so much."

"Don't be sorry. Please don't."

"It's good for my old heart to have my little brood back together." The quiver in his voice pricked her heart, and then his eyes brimmed with tears. She looked away, unable to bear it. "Tell me about Monticello."

In hushed tones they conversed, her hand never leaving his as she shared the highlights of her time in the city. By the time she was through, she had herself believing that she'd just returned from a grand adventure. And, in truth, it had been.

"I think we'd better let your father rest." Her mother stepped into the room and put a hand on Sadie's back.

"Come back and tell me more," her father said, patting her arm. "I want to hear about the hard times when you come back. Don't keep them from me."

She agreed and then reluctantly followed the others from the sickroom to where they all sat together and whispered about the farm and the new bills they expected the doctor to send. Any amount of money, they agreed, was worth spending if it helped their pa. Nina and Peter took their restless daughter outside, leaving the family alone to worry over the future.

"The doctor believes with time his leg and hip might recover. The wounds themselves look better on the outside, but your pa is not convinced. He's afraid he'll never be able to walk again. And lying in bed has left him weak," their mother said. "We need to talk about selling. I've thought about it, and I could move to town and take in washing and sewing . . . but I don't know if it'll be enough. Your father has always been a farmer, but there must be some work he could do. A factory job . . ."

"We won't give up," Molly said with a vigorous nod of her head, but even she looked doubtful. "We can't lose our home."

"All we can do is our best, and we're doing that." Their mother stood, brushing her hands over her skirts. "Look at you. My girls don't sit around and mope. It won't fix anything. It's been a long time since we've all been together. Let's set our troubles aside. Go and do what you always do when you're together."

"Mama's right." Violette stood first. "Let's go for a walk."

"I'll show you the fields." Molly stood, looked back once at the door to the sickroom, and said, "Pa would want to know we were enjoying this reunion."

Fear tempered the joy of being together but did not extinguish it. They walked through the fields, where green shoots in nearly straight lines reached for the sky, proud and true, declaring to the world that the Wests were fighters. The new plants bent and straightened with the ebb and flow of the gentle wind.

"I'm glad you're back," Flora said as a strand of hair whipped across her face. "I've loved your letters, but seeing you is so much better."

"It's good to be home, though I wish it were under different circumstances."

"Were you always homesick?" Violette asked. "It sounded like you were having some fun."

"There were good times mixed in with the hard." Finding a friend in Otis had been the best part of her adventure, but she did not have his permission to tell her sisters his name. "As of late, I have not been nearly as lonely. But still, it's good being home."

Molly picked up a clod of dirt and threw it at a fence post. Of all the sisters, she'd been the most inclined to act out her emotions rather than bottle them up. The dirt crumbled and fell to the ground, her frustrations there for all to see. "What if he's never his old self? You might like the city well enough, but I don't want to move there. I don't want to work at a factory or mend other people's clothes all day."

"Do you think a doctor from somewhere else might have other ideas?" Sadie asked. How quickly she fell back into her role as the leader of the brood.

"We don't have money for that and won't until after the harvest, assuming we make anything." Violette groaned. "It's all so wretched. We've tried so hard. My fingers are calloused from stitching so many handkerchiefs, and it'll never be enough."

"We should be proud. We've done a lot." Molly straightened her shoulders and stared out at the land she'd plowed. "But I don't feel proud, just sorry I can't do more."

Sadie put a hand on her forehead, blocking the sun. "What other options are there? There must be something."

"Marrying," Violette said with a shrug. "But there are no men with money here, so I don't think that will help. A poor husband might only make our situation worse."

"Besides," Flora said, "we all promised we would marry for love."

"Love of family isn't a horrible reason," Violette said.

"For now, we will pray we get a miracle. And if we don't, then Violette can put an advertisement in the paper for a wealthy husband." Molly laughed and linked her arm through Sadie's, leading the group on the familiar path to the barn. "Tell us about Monti."

"Yes, tell us about your mansion and about your mysterious employer." Violette put a hand to her chest and sighed. "I always feel as though you are leaving something out when you write. You tell us the tiniest bits and leave us guessing about the rest. But you're here now, so we must learn everything."

"Is he a kind man? You are safe, aren't you?" Flora asked before Sadie could answer Violette.

"He is a good man . . . but he's not typical." She bit her cheek, trying to find words to describe Otis Taylor. "He's not anything like the men we used to dream of. He isn't dashing, at least not in a conventional way, and he doesn't always have the right words to say. But he is—"

"Romantic," Violette interjected. "You do care for him, don't you? When I read your letters, I always imagine you do. Your journey sounds like something from one of your old stories."

Sadie grimaced. She should have known her sisters would be perceptive enough to sense her tumult of feelings. "Real life is not the same as those silly stories I used to write."

"They weren't silly," Violette said. "I've been rereading some of them. I've even made some of them more romantic. Someday I want to read the new versions together like we used to." Violette put her hand to her heart. "You're going to swoon when you read it."

"Oh my," Sadie said, knowing the last thing she needed to read was a work of fiction that left her swooning.

Violette went on, oblivious to Sadie's ambivalence. "I still can't believe you are living under the same roof as a man. Do you run into each other in the halls? Does your hand ever brush against—"

"You think everything is romantic." Molly laughed, earning her a glare from Violette. "Sadie hasn't said anything about a blooming romance. But you *are* friends, aren't you?"

"Yes. We are friends." She crossed and then uncrossed her arms. She should have known her sisters would force her to face what she'd been trying to ignore. "When Marvin left, I always imagined him coming home and . . ." Her words trailed off. "It sounds silly. But I thought he cared for me and that we'd have a future together. He's back and says he'll call when he has time, and I want him to—at least I think I want him to."

"Have his letters gotten more exciting?" Violette asked.

Six eyes turned on her. These were her sisters, her dearest friends in the whole world, and she was a grown woman, free to care for any man she wished without having to feel sheepish about it.

"His letters have never been anything more than cordial and direct. He takes life very seriously. There's nothing wrong with that."

"They're never romantic?" Flora frowned.

"He could be waiting for us to be together again. Maybe he feels more comfortable expressing himself in person." Sadie's heart lurched, calling her own bluff. Marvin had had many opportunities to tell her his feelings, and he'd never taken them. He'd held her hand, he'd taken her for long walks, and they had sat for hours on the front porch, but that was all. "Or maybe he doesn't really care for me. My trivial letters with 'Mr. Rochester' were more heartfelt than Marvin's letters. But I've been waiting for him for so long. Don't you think it's wrong for me to give up on him when he has just returned home?"

"Look at you, all red and confused. I didn't think the General ever got flustered," Violette teased. And then, proving a far more perceptive romantic than anyone expected, she added, "I think you're falling in love with your employer, and that's what has you finally seeing the truth about Marvin."

"I never said—"

"You didn't have to. We can see it, and you don't have to feel bad about it. You never promised Marvin anything," Molly affirmed with a nod. "You only felt like you did because you have a very loyal nature."

"Don't you like Marvin? I thought you all did."

"We did . . . we do like him well enough," Molly said. "But *you* have to like him—or, rather, love him—and I'm not sure you ever did. You followed him around and sat sedately on the porch beside him, but you were never really yourself when he was here."

"You never told me you felt that way when he was coming around." Sadie balked at their betrayal. If they'd spoken up before, perhaps she would not have pined after him for so long. "Even if I wouldn't have listened, you should have told me."

Molly shrugged. "It did seem exciting at the time. At least you had someone coming around. But your letters now seem different. I don't think you're sitting silently beside your employer, pretending to be prim and proper when really, you're just a West girl, a little headstrong and unruly from being raised on a farm like the rest of us."

"I'm prim and proper," Violette said, smiling slyly. "But the rest of you never are. Tell us more. We need to know all the details so we can decide if it's really love or not."

"Well, I have sat beside him, and sometimes we've been quiet. But other times we talk so fast the time races by. He's peculiar. I can't explain it. He's been thoughtful at times, and other times he seems ready to leave and never look back." Ready to turn the conversation from her, she said, "Tell me, what is troubling Nina and Peter? When they came back from outside, they seemed upset. I had hoped they'd stay longer."

"We don't know," Violette said. Though she had been standing the farthest away, she now took a step closer, quick as always to join in on gossip. "Nina did seem troubled after that, and they left earlier than I expected. They'd planned to stay and eat."

"They were holding hands, so at least it's not a tiff." Flora picked up a long piece of grass and ran it between her fingers. "They are always good to each other."

"Could be money," Molly said. "He's been working hard, but he's not the only person making deliveries, and I heard the McCall boy charges less than Peter. He doesn't have a family, so he can afford to. I heard Peter talk about trying to find another job." Molly frowned. "Seems like everything is always changing."

Sadie dug the toe of her shoe into the soft ground, making a hole in the brown earth. "We used to work and play and never think about money or changing times. Now it's always on our minds. It makes me want to throw a fit and kick and scream. I hate money."

"I think you *should* throw a fit," Violette said. "Go on, we could all use a good laugh."

Sadie stomped her foot and was about to indulge them in more theatrics, but she laughed instead, and soon her sisters were laughing too.

Chapter 20

"This was left for you." Leon handed Otis a neatly folded letter late in the morning the day after Sadie's departure. "The same man who took our Sadie back to her family delivered it. I insisted on paying him despite his protest."

"That was good of you," Otis said. He took the letter and immediately recognized the distinct slant of Sadie's penmanship. "I suppose . . . I could write her back, then we could pay him again. It would be the generous thing to do."

"Indeed," Leon said. "Go and read your note so I'll have time to find him before he leaves the city."

Otis nodded, excused himself, and went to the music room for privacy.

> Dear Mr. Otis Taylor, affectionately and formerly known as Mr. Edward Rochester,
>
> I must thank you again for allowing me a visit to my family. My father is not healing well. He tried to stand and took a fall that has set him back in his recovery. He's weak and discouraged. He is certain something is not

set right inside of him, but the doctor has no answers and only insists he lie in bed. I believe in miracles, and we all desperately hope God decides to grant us one.

Being home, no matter the circumstances, has been wonderful. My sisters want to hear every detail of my time in Monti. They call you my employer or my Mr. Rochester. I told you I would keep your secret about being back in Monticello, but it would be so much easier for me to talk of Monticello if I could use your name. Nevertheless, I have kept them entertained with stories of our lessons, and once or twice I have even reenacted one of my many skating falls.

I stayed up late with my sisters. We whispered and even laughed so loudly my mother finally came and told us she'd paddle all our backsides if we didn't quiet down. Don't you dare tell her, but that sent us into a fit of muffled giggles. For a few blissful moments it felt like we were children again, free of the heavy worries that come with adulthood.

I'm rambling. I do hope all is well and that you hear news of Elisabeth soon.

I am sorry I'm not there to help you prepare for the masquerade. But I will give you a rule. Rule number six: when you skate, you must have proper form. Lean forward a bit—it'll help with your balance. Practice on your own now, and when I return, we will master the skill together.

If you feel so inclined, please pray for my father.

Your teacher,
Sadie West

Give Blue-Wolf a good scratch behind the ears for me. I'm sure he misses his favorite friend.

"His name is Wolf," Otis muttered.

His dog lumbered over. He could be mistaken, but Otis thought he looked sad.

"You miss her," he said as he scratched behind the dog's ears. "Her father's not well . . . I'm not sure when she'll be back."

He straightened, picked up the letter, and read it again. She needed a miracle. How often had miracle cures been tried on his scalp? Too many.

Wolf lifted a hind leg and scratched an itch.

"We should do something." He stood. Wolf stood too, his head cocked to the side. Otis had the means to provide a miracle, or at least hire a very good doctor. Surely the God who worked in mysterious ways could use his family's fortune to help. After all, he'd come home at this exact moment when Sadie found herself in need. Miracle or not, he could try.

"Leon!" he shouted down the hall. "Come and give me some of that advice you are always offering."

"For once he asks for it." Leon's voice echoed through the walls. As he got closer, Otis could hear him whistling. "What can this wise old man do for you?"

"Tell me, would it be wrong for me to send a doctor to an injured man? And to cover the bill?"

"Is this a question in earnest or simply one to ponder for philosophical reasons?" Leon adjusted his tie, appearing obtuse.

"Blast it all. You know I'm talking about Sadie's father. The doctor does not know whether he will recover. They can't afford to get another opinion. She needs a miracle . . . and, well, what I'm saying is that I could pay for the best doctor." Otis folded his arms across his chest. "I could . . . but not if it will make her obligated to me or resentful."

"I believe, handled carefully, you could find a way to send aid without overstepping."

"How would I do that?"

"Well, you could confess your affections for the girl, and then as a promised man, it would be entirely proper for you to assist her family."

"That would require the girl to return my affections." Otis scowled. "What other options are there?"

"You could find a way to help them without helping them."

Cryptic words only further unnerved him. Otis moved for the door, wishing he were back at the Crawfords', hidden away from the rest of the world and its troubles.

"Wait." Leon stopped him. "I wasn't trying to get you irked."

"Tell me what you meant."

"Let's see." He walked across the room. "You could find a way to give them a good harvest, or you could open your factory and hire her sisters for generous pay."

"They need help now. It can't wait for crops to grow."

"You could offer aid anonymously—"

He snapped his fingers. "That's what I'll do. Telegraph the best doctor from Des Moines. I don't care what it costs, just get him to come. I know Sadie told you about her father's injuries, so tell the doctor what you know and get him here. Tell him to be quiet about who sent him and make sure he requests payment from me."

"She might be able to deduce that it was you."

"If she does, then I will tell her that . . . that . . . blast, these ludicrous rules. Can't I just tell her I felt concern for her father and that everything in me wanted to help? Why can't I say that?

Why can't I tell her I could not save my own father or brother, but I can help hers, and so I have?"

The room, full of long shadows, seemed to change with each word he spoke. Or was it Otis that was changing? Stepping out of the darkness, this time with his voice and his resolve.

Leon nodded, a proud smile on his face. "There is no reason you should not tell her such things."

"Do it then. Send for the doctor. And don't worry about anonymity. I will write her, and you can send my note with her friend. Pay him well for his service."

"You do know someday you will have to bring in more money. Philanthropy such as this is not free, and most who get a taste of putting good into the world can't stop with one deed."

"I will solve that problem later. Let me get through the masquerade, find Elisabeth, and then . . . I don't know. I'll do something with my life." Deep in the recesses of his mind, thoughts of staying had begun to creep in. Such thoughts scared him. The more he wished for it, the more it would hurt when it didn't happen. "For now we will worry about only the most pressing matters."

"Very well. I'll call the hospital and see if I can figure out who the best doctor is." Leon left with a pleased grin on his face. Doubt and worry crept into the room in his place, but Otis shrugged it off. There was no time for indecision—only for action. If Sadie chose to fault him for his gesture, so be it.

> . . . Do you recall the promise I made to help your family with their farm in exchange for your help preparing me for the masquerade? In place of my physical labor, I have sent for a well-known doctor. He will come directly to your home and do what he can to help with your

> father's recovery. If necessary, your father will be taken to a hospital, and all medical bills will be paid. A second opinion may not prove valuable other than to ease everyone's minds that all has been done, but perhaps he'll have knowledge and skills that will help your father make a full recovery and get on his feet again.
>
> Please accept my help. I assure you, there is no ill motive. I simply have the means to assist and wish to aid my favorite ally.

He thought of wadding up the paper and starting over with a letter that pled for her return, since nothing had felt right with her gone, but he restrained himself, picturing instead her face whenever she spoke of her family. She was with them, and that was where she needed to be.

He ended his letter with a short note about Elisabeth, then folded and sealed it, hoping no one misconstrued his good intentions.

Sadie sat in the main room of her family's home, rocking near the fireplace, watching the gentle way Nina stroked her daughter's hair. The little girl rested her head against her mother's chest, her breathing steady, her eyes closed. Peter and Nina had come over again to be with Sadie and with her injured father. Though flattered and grateful for the presence of friends, she still sensed an uneasiness from the couple.

Otis's letter, brought by Peter, promised a doctor. His offer had surprised them all, leaving them grateful and uncomfortable with the arrangement, but not so much that they would reject such a gift. Instead, they clung to the belief that his gesture was the miracle they had prayed for so fervently.

The section about her father's health was all she read aloud. To herself she read about Wolf missing her, about staying as long as she liked, and about his ongoing quest to find his niece.

> . . . We have not had much word about Elisabeth. One source wrote saying they knew of a child living in the country with a family named Raymond. We are told she arrived as a very small child, not as a baby, and that her history was full of inconsistencies. The family moved, so they cannot be easily questioned. The source says they believe the child may have been left behind, but they know nothing further. If the child they wrote of is Elisabeth and she was once again moved a year ago, then it could be because of Reginald's death and his inability to pay for her care. I believe it's a clue but don't know what to do with it.
>
> I had hoped Katie's parents in Blackwell would come forward. But perhaps they have washed their hands of the situation. For some, I suppose that is easier. But I am not like that. I will find her.

The sun moved behind a cloud, and instantly the room grew darker. Sadie shivered, despite the comfortable spring weather. She frowned, hating that Otis was no closer to finding Elisabeth. If the newspaper brought no real leads, what then?

"She's been waking up early so she can say goodbye to Peter before he begins his deliveries in the morning," Nina said, and Sadie looked up from her letter. "It's leaving her very tired by the evenings."

"She looks content in your arms." Bessy's features were relaxed and at peace. Her smooth skin and perfectly shaped chin gave her the look of a cherub. Nina pressed a kiss to the girl's forehead. Bessy squirmed and sighed.

"She wouldn't let me hold her like this at all when she first came. I wanted her to so badly, but she was nervous. I don't know what sort of cruelty she's seen. I wish I could kiss it all away." Bessy's dimpled hand reached up and rested against Nina's neck. She yawned, and then her eyes opened and met Sadie's.

Sadie stiffened. Bessy's eyes were so blue, so very blue, so perfectly blue, like the eyes of—her heart lurched. They were Taylor eyes. It couldn't be. It simply couldn't. But those eyes demanded a reckoning. She shook her head, trying to will the revelation away, but like a ferocious beast, it clawed at her. Panic and disbelief tore through her.

"Are you all right?" Nina asked.

"It's nothing," she managed to whisper. "The letter has me preoccupied." There was truth in that. Otis's words and his plight had her mind reeling, but her feelings were wound up in so much more. All this time she'd believed they sought a neglected child, unwanted and abandoned. What if Elisabeth was happy and thriving? What if Peter and Nina's Bessy was also Otis's Elisabeth? She didn't want to believe it possible.

"Do you fancy him?"

"What?"

"Your employer, do you fancy him?" Nina repeated.

"Oh . . . that is not what troubles me." She shifted uneasily, but no matter how she sat, she still felt ill.

"If it is his kindness that has you flushed, try to remember that it was generous. And if it helps your father . . ."

"He is a kind man." Would they think so when he took their daughter? They would hate him. If he took Bessy, they'd be left with empty arms and broken hearts. Where was the kindness in that?

They were alone. Everyone else had gone outside, but Nina hadn't wanted to move with Bessy asleep in her lap, and Sadie had stayed beside her. Now was the time to face the possibility and kill the very idea of it before it consumed her. She had to know. "May I ask you something?"

"Yes, of course." Nina nodded but kept her eyes on her child as though she were a finer view than the most colorful sunset.

"Is something troubling you and Peter?"

When Nina looked up there were tears in her eyes. "Everyone is so worried over your father. It's not fair for me to discuss my own troubles now."

"Nina, does it have to do with Bessy? Please tell me—I have to know."

She buried her head into the little girl's hair and let her lips linger there before rousing the girl fully awake and urging her to go outside and find her papa. Bessy yawned and, on wobbly legs, left the two women.

"We took Bessy in a year ago. You know that." Nina leaned closer as she spoke, her now-empty hands clasped together. "We were told she was an orphan."

"I remember. You got her from an orphanage. You did, I know you did." It was impossible to keep the desperation from her voice.

"We hadn't decided how to tell what we knew about her past. We didn't lie . . . Well, in a way we did. We let everyone believe she was from the orphanage."

"What really happened?"

"A man Peter had done deliveries for, a Ned Raymond, was going west. Their farm hadn't done well, and there was land out there. His wife used to care for foundlings. They ran a sort of home for . . . well, for unwanted children, which is why we didn't tell anyone. We didn't want Bessy to think she'd been abandoned. Ned told Peter he was leaving and they'd be sending the last child to the orphanage in Des Moines because her father had just died and her mama was already dead."

The room was spinning. It couldn't be true. It just couldn't be.

"Peter said the Raymonds beat the children. They shouldn't have ever taken them in. He saw Bessy and offered to bring her home and save Ned a trip to the big city. He was afraid Ned wouldn't actually go to the orphanage and that he'd pass her off to someone else. Someone even worse than Ned." Her voice quivered. "It was all handled quietly, but we had no reason to believe the story was false. He even wrote us up a paper that looked official, naming us as her parents. There were not many details about her past, but how could there be with her so small and her family dead?"

"Oh dear," Sadie said, covering her mouth with her hands. "I'm so glad Peter took her in. I hate the thought of what could have happened to her."

"But now, I think she may have family. Peter saw an inquiry in the paper. It was about a child who would be Bessy's age. The child mentioned was named Elisabeth. It could be a different child—Bessy has always been just Bessy—but it's got me worried." She wiped at her eyes, but the tears were coming freely now. "We should have gone to a judge the moment Peter took her, but we had no money for a lawyer, and we loved her right away. We didn't want to lose her or see her grow up in an orphanage." A sob, low and full of agony like nothing Sadie had ever heard, came from dear, sweet Nina. "I can't bear the thought of how it would hurt her. I promised her I would keep her safe. I looked her in the eyes and I told her she didn't have to be afraid. I told her she belonged. What do I do?"

Sadie went to her, unable to speak. She offered the only support she could—open arms. In this moment mourning with Nina was all that mattered. Nina shook as she sobbed into Sadie's shoulder.

"Mama." Bessy's voice startled the anguished women.

"I'm here," Nina said, releasing Sadie and holding her arms out for Bessy to run to. Over her child's head, she mouthed, *"Don't say anything."*

Sadie wiped at her face. "I would never want to hurt her . . . or you."

Then, quick as she could, she stepped out of the house.

Chapter 21

Otis's fingers moved with ardent fervor across the piano keys, pounding out a melody that filled the room for him alone. He tried to capture the feelings that had started out as a whisper but now shouted relentlessly. Sadie had changed him. He missed her, and not in the same way he had missed his father all those years ago. With Sadie there were no wounds to heal, no all-consuming regrets. What he felt when she was near was sweet and pure. She inspired him, and now with her gone, he longed for her return.

Her letters were a solace but no substitute for her presence.

With more urgency, he played, thinking of Elisabeth now and his protective need to find her. He must! He had to. He'd heard back from two other orphanages, both claiming they did not have his niece. The lawyer had no new information for him. And so he waited.

Let them come home, the notes sang, pleading for both Sadie and Elisabeth.

Otis stayed at the piano for hours. His house was too quiet, the rooms too empty, but here at his piano, with music filling the air, he felt a measure of hope.

"You've a letter," Leon said, appearing out of nowhere.

Otis flew from the piano bench and crossed the room in two long strides.

"Thank you," he said, reaching out like a starved man who'd been offered a loaf of bread.

"I expect the consulting doctor will be there today. Once Sadie knows the prognosis, she may decide to return."

"I told Sadie to stay as long as she needs to. If Marvin—or whatever his name is—seeks her out, she may never come back."

"She's a bright gal. She'll do what's best." Leon moved to leave but stopped in front of a framed portrait on the wall of Otis's father as a boy. His grandparents and an uncle Otis had never met were all standing stiff and still beside him. "I don't know if it's important, but Peter seemed distraught today."

"Do you think Sadie is not telling us the extent of her troubles?"

"I think Peter may have troubles of his own." Leon turned away from the portrait. "Could be money troubles."

"You mentioned once my reopening the factory." Otis's grip on the letter tightened. "I had not planned to stay here . . . but if I did—" His voice stuck in his throat. "If I did, he could move to Monti and work here, at the old factory. It might help him make ends meet."

"It's a good option. A lot of people would benefit from your staying."

"I'm not promising it." His old stubbornness flared.

"A woman with sisters is likely going to want to be settled somewhere near her family." Leon pulled out his pocket watch and checked the time. "Hurry and read that. I know you'll be wanting me to catch Peter so you can send word back."

Otis shook his head but could not keep the smile from his face. "I'm going to read my letter now, but not because you told me to."

"Of course not." Leon smirked and then left the room, whistling as he went.

The letter began with words full of gratitude for Otis's kindness in sending the doctor. Sadie offered to repay him when she was able, which made him scowl. He would have to convince her that his gift came with no expectation and that repayment was not only unnecessary but unwanted.

> . . . When my father was last awake, he asked after you. And then he expressed his desire to thank you in person. You will forever be revered in the West home as the hero who came to our rescue in a moment of deepest despair.
>
> Being home has been lovely. Every moment I am here reminds me of what I have been working for. I will sort feathers until my last breath if my efforts will in any way aid those I love.
>
> There I go, rambling again. I apologize; you no doubt have enjoyed your quiet house, and now even in a letter, I go on and on. You seem to loosen my tongue and my pen.

He shook his head. She had no idea how much he missed everything about her presence, including the sound of her voice.

> . . . I'm grateful you have given me permission to use your name. Telling my sisters about our time together is much easier now. They find you very mysterious and exciting.

> I have something else I need to discuss with you. It cannot be written. I suppose it could, but I don't have the right words. It's a pressing matter that weighs heavy on my mind and heart. When I see you, I will tell all.

"Leon!" he shouted as he stormed down the hall.

"Did you need something?" Leon asked after Otis nearly collided with him near the back door where Leon was pulling a coat on, despite the warm weather. "Mildred's needing a few things."

"I don't mean to keep you. But if I wanted to go . . . if I had to go to the West farm . . . how would I do that?"

"Has Sadie's father worsened?" He froze with only one arm inside his woolen coat. "The doctor sent word saying he would be there today. I had hoped for good news."

"It's not about the doctor." How was he to explain that something deep in the pit of his stomach called him to leave his prisonlike mansion and go to Sadie? "There is something else worrying her. I don't know what it is, but I thought if I went there, I could assist."

"And you wish to travel unseen?"

Otis nodded and absently tugged at his hat. "I'd prefer to leave without causing a stir. The masquerade will be here soon enough—everyone can gawk then." His neck went rigid as he realized going to the West farm would mean seeing not only Sadie but also the rest of her family. In person, would they still believe him mysterious and exciting? "It was a foolish idea, forget I asked," he muttered. "She has her family. They can help her with whatever it is that's troubling her."

Leon abandoned his coat, pulling it off and putting it back on its peg. He moved in front of Otis and looked him directly in the eyes. "My boy, you've got to trust yourself. If you feel that you should go, go."

"What if I'm not being compelled to go and I just want to go because I am tired of being a lonely hermit? It's not her job to fix that." He glanced away from the door and back toward the depth of his cell, ready to lose himself in tedious accounts. "She'll come when she's ready. If she chooses to."

"She writes to you," Leon said softly. "Not to me or to Mildred, but to you. And from the sounds of it she's also shared important things with you."

"Yes, well, she wrote to Marvin too."

"That man practically ignored her for two years. And now her family is struggling, and where is he? Why isn't he helping? He's not deserving of her."

"On that we can agree."

"Can we also agree that neither Mildred nor I have taken a drive into the country for a very long time?"

"I don't know when you ventured out last. I will have to default to your answer on that."

"It's been a long time. With your permission I will go and ready the horses, and whoever wants to go for a jaunt into the country may come along. We will keep the shades closed so no one can look in on us. Now if you'll excuse me, I'm going to go and tell my wife." Leon turned and walked away from Otis, leaving him with his mouth open, staring at the older man's back.

Everything that came after happened quickly. Otis managed a muttered, "I'll go." Mildred bustled about, insisting on packing a meal for the Wests, and Leon made sure the house was in order before they left. Otis scowled as he readied himself but still managed to be the first one waiting by the door.

The Wests' rooster was large and red with a green sheen to his neck and tail feathers. When he crowed, he sounded like an old man with a chest cold. He was mild tempered, and that fact alone had earned him a long-standing place of honor on the farm. Sadie stood just outside the coop, listening to the bird bellow at the sun that had been up for well over half the day. Her heart was heavy. Her home had once been a respite from the troubles of the world, but now there were troubles at their threshold.

"I think you may miss Old Red more than us. You've left us all for the rooster," Molly said as she stepped beside her. "He's looking old, don't you think?"

"I feel older today too."

"There's something wrong. Are you missing Otis?"

Sadie turned away from the chickens and faced Molly. Molly's hair was pulled back in a loose braid that ran halfway down her back. She wore a pair of Pa's trousers with her shirt tucked in. Her skin was suntanned from her many hours working the fields, which she'd done for the very same reasons Sadie sorted feathers.

"There are things about the Taylor mansion I miss," Sadie said, choosing her words carefully.

"You heard the new doctor. He's going to take Pa to Des Moines for surgery. You don't have to stay here. You can go back to Monticello."

"I *am* grateful for the doctor and his news." She sighed, unable to fully hide the tumult of feelings she harbored inside.

"If it's not Pa and it's not Otis, then what has you so distracted?"

She couldn't fully confide in Molly. Otis deserved to know about Bessy first. So instead she said, "You know how Violette always wants to know all the gossip?"

"She's a regular busybody."

"I have never wanted all the gossip, except at the duster factory, but that was just because sorting feathers is so dull. But now I know something, and I don't know what to do with it." Sadie grabbed her sister's calloused hand and squeezed it. "I wonder if we'll ever find our footing again. Lately life feels like one storm after another."

Molly's brows creased together. "I can't make sense of you. Does this have something to do with the way Otis looks? You said he looks different."

"No, I don't care about his looks. People can gossip all they want about that. Who decided all handsome men must look the same?" She smiled, thinking of her similar conversation with Otis only days before. Her smile vanished the moment she saw Otis's face in her mind. His blue eyes . . . Bessy's eyes. "I can't tell you what it is, but will you promise to believe that I don't want to hurt anyone?"

"I could never believe ill of you."

The sound of company coming pulled them apart and ended their conversation before it had concluded naturally. Dust plumed behind an incoming carriage, rising high like a cloud as it bumped along the ruts of the old road.

"Who do you suppose . . ." Molly muttered. "Come on."

Leon's wrinkled, friendly face became clear as the incoming carriage rolled closer. His grin as he pulled back on the horses was a welcome sight.

"Hello there," Leon called from up high on his seat. "Mildred insisted on bringing a meal to the family, and Wolf was missing you."

Sadie's heart soared high the moment she saw Leon's mischievous smile.

"That was kind." She introduced Molly to Leon and welcomed him to her family's land. Mildred stepped out of the carriage, a basket hanging over one arm, while she rubbed at her back with her free hand. Molly immediately greeted her and then took her offering and led her toward the house, leaving Sadie to stare at the closed door of the carriage. Her shoulders drooped.

The door squeaked, opening again as Wolf bounded out and a man's boot appeared.

"Otis!" Sadie gasped as the door swung fully open. She couldn't take her eyes off him. He was here. On her land. Like a dream, her worlds were colliding.

"Sadie." He took long strides until he stuttered to a stop directly in front of her. He didn't look at her beautiful land or her humble home. He didn't look at her family's animals or the crops. His gaze was focused only on her. She could feel the weight of it as he searched her face, and in that moment she wished for more than his eyes grazing her cheek. She longed for his arms to take her in an embrace that would fully close the distance between them.

"You're here." She could only hope that just as she felt the significance of his gaze, he would feel through her words how much she'd missed him.

"I'm here," he whispered back in a husky voice. "Mildred likes feeding people."

"Indeed."

A horse whinnied, interrupting their reunion. Sadie took a half step backward and clasped her hands together. It was time to play hostess, and that could not be done on the dusty driveway, daydreaming about her employer and wrestling her fickle emotions. She cleared her throat. "You've got to meet my family."

Something shifted. Otis's features, which had been so soft and inviting, went tight with fear. She touched his arm. "They are safe—all of them. They will see you as I do."

"You must think me a weak man." He looked at his feet.

"No. You are at the edge of your fear. That makes you strong, not weak." He looked up, and unspoken words passed between them. He wasn't ready, but she would help him. "Come and see the farm first, and then we'll go inside. It will mean so much to my father to meet you and thank you."

"You've very few trees," Otis said, steering the conversation away from his generosity. He straightened, looking less fearful as they began to walk together with the dog they were both so fond of beside them.

"My sisters must have taken Mildred and Leon into the house." She looked around for them, not wanting to neglect her other guests. "Should I go and check on them?"

"Go look for them if you want. I'll have the chickens give me a tour of your land."

"Nonsense. If you let the chickens out, we'll have to spend all our time chasing them. I'll stay by you, and my sisters can look after Mildred and Leon." She patted his arm before pointing. "Over there are the wheat fields. I think they look like a sea when the wind blows."

"And those?" he asked, pointing to a nearby stretch of land.

"Those are the fields Molly could not get to this year. We didn't have money to hire someone to plant, so she's done it mostly on her own." She led him away from the carriage and farther into the fields. "Have you skated since I left?"

"No. I read your rule but could not decide what proper skating form was. Do you think you could show me?"

"All right. Watch carefully. If a skater is fully upright, they are prone to falling." She bent forward slightly and moved as though she were skating. "See how being bent like this helps with stability? Give me a nudge if you don't believe me." His face screwed up skeptically, but when she nodded, he pushed on her shoulder. She flinched but didn't fall.

He bent forward, much farther than necessary. His backside and head were on nearly the same plane. "Like this?"

"No." She laughed. "But that stance will draw a lot of attention. When I return, we will practice together. We're almost out of time."

"We could wait until the next masquerade and pretend we mixed up the dates."

"No, that would cause an uproar."

"Unfortunately, I think you're right. I've been receiving countless letters from people letting me know how they anticipate my return. If I don't show up, they'll come knocking on my door."

"I'm surprised Alta has not been waiting by the gate to catch the first glimpse of your return."

"If she shows up unannounced, I'll send Wolf to scare her off. He's been rather grouchy since you left and would probably enjoy growling at someone."

She stopped walking and turned to the blue dog. "You haven't been grouchy, have you?"

He, of course, made no coherent response, but he did step close and lean his head against her skirt. She scratched his ears, earning a contented whimper from the animal.

"He doesn't seem grouchy to me."

"His spirits improved the moment we turned toward your farm."

"It's hard to be unhappy on West land. Even with everything we've gone through, it still feels good here." They continued their tour, making their way to the old barn. "My sisters and I spent half our childhood in this old barn. The loft was our kingdom. We played pretend up there, and I used to write my stories in the loft while looking out the big front window. And now, as adults, we often go up there when we need to console one another."

"Is there a strict female-only policy?"

She pulled her mouth to one side. "We've never had someone of your sex ask to see our realm. As the eldest, I will have to consider this."

"Take your time, General." He waited while she tapped her lip in thought.

"I believe we will make a rule that says men willing to enter and abide by our rules may come up. You will be the first."

"Your Marvin never asked to see it?"

"No. I don't think I ever told him about it, and I'm not so sure he is *my* Marvin. Though I imagine I'll know soon enough."

She pulled the giant door on the front of the barn open for him, refusing to spend her time with Otis worrying over Marvin and his lackluster letters or the fact that he'd not come calling.

"Hmm," was all the response Otis made.

"Follow me—I want to show you." She led him up the ladder to the loft. Where hay should have been, there were four chairs, a table, and shelves covered with corncob dolls, jacks, and other remnants of a happy childhood. She ought to feel vulnerable, sharing something so dear with him, but she did not. Instead, her feelings were the opposite. An eagerness to build an image of what had transpired over the years in this very spot prodded her along, making her grin and point and tell him in a hurried voice about her happy memories.

As the last story hung in the air, a feeling of magic filled the fantasy world. For a few contented moments, they were both captured by it. But silence was not good. It let other thoughts in. All this talk of childhood led her mind to Bessy. Her conscience spoke up in the quiet, refusing to let her lose herself in the enchanting moment. It whispered, soft and then louder, and reminded her of the secret she knew.

"I need to talk to you . . ."

Chapter 22

A wave of apprehension sent a chill racing up his spine. For a moment they'd been so close. He'd almost believed he'd seen something more than friendship in her eyes, and it had given him hope that her feelings could one day match his own. But the moment was gone now. There was no longing in her gaze—only fear.

She picked up an old corncob doll and fiddled with the dry husk dress. "What if Elisabeth is with a good family? What if she loves them and they love her?"

"I am her father's brother. I *am* her family."

"Yes, I know that. But what if during this time when you did not know she existed, she found another family. What if she has a mama and a papa?"

"Sadie, you know I can't abandon her. I can't give up. I am going to find her. More than that, I am going to love her." She'd been his supporter. His ally. Why was she deserting their cause now? Had she given up? He stood, leaving his small chair behind, and slowly moved about the loft. "I want to give her this." He motioned toward the homemade toys and miniature chairs. "I want to give her a kingdom of her own. I want to give her memories worth cherishing." His voice faltered. "I have my flaws—you know that—but for her I will soften. I will treat her well."

Sadie nodded. "I believe you. I don't doubt your love for her or the father you would be."

"Then what is it?"

"It's . . . it's nothing. Just a thought that's been nagging." She smiled, but it didn't light up her face like it so often did. "Come, let me show you more of my farm. We can talk of Elisabeth later."

"Was that your pressing matter?"

"Yes . . . well, and about my father, of course. The doctor you sent is going to have him moved to Des Moines. He believes a different surgery will help him. He was professional, but I could tell he was unimpressed with the way the local doctor set my father's bones."

Otis asked more questions about her father's health as they walked the fields with Wolf beside them. He could tell her father's health was a worry for her. But there was something she was keeping from him. He wanted to call her out and tell her he'd come all this way to support her, and there was no reason for secrets between them. But then he thought of his scars and how he'd needed time before he was ready to show them to her. If she was harboring a secret, he would have to trust that when she was ready, she would share.

They talked about her sisters' efforts on the farm, about the cows and calves, and about her childhood memories. The heaviness he'd felt in her absence vanished.

"There I go, talking up a storm again. I'm sorry," Sadie said.

"When you were away"—he stopped walking and put a hand on her upper arm—"I missed our conversations. Life is not the same with you gone. I can't explain it, but the house is darker now."

"You do know you could open the drapes and the sun would come in?"

"You know how I feel about drapes and people looking in."

"I do. And I still hope one day you'll throw them open." She turned toward the sun and let it shine on her face. "I love this place." She inhaled deeply, as if breathing in the scent of the land itself, before facing him. "Is it strange that I have missed the Taylor mansion even while being here?"

"I believe it is possible to love more than one place at the same time. My mother loved Monticello and still talked with fondness of her childhood home."

They continued their meandering about the property. Her arms swung easily at her sides, drawing his attention from the waving fields to her inviting hand. Mr. Crawford and his hired tutors had never taught him about courtship. Never once had they spoken about the desire to reach out and take a woman's hand.

"Is something wrong?" Sadie stopped near one of the few trees. Its low-hanging branches created an arbor above them.

"Why?" he snapped, embarrassed that somehow she'd read his mind.

She grinned, and his eyes moved from her once swaying arms to her lips. He jerked his head away. What was wrong with him?

"Why are you smiling?" he snarled, but it didn't sound as unaffected as he wished.

"Because it is so good to have you here. Even if you are a bit ornery." Her airy laughter made it impossible for him to do anything but smile in return. "I think beneath your rough exterior, you are a gentleman."

"Tell me, what would a gentleman do in this moment?"

The wind picked up, sending the crops dancing first to the west and then east. Her loose hair joined in, blowing at will. The strands of auburn reached for the sky and then brushed across her face, skimming the skin he longed to touch.

"A gentleman would agree to come in and see my father." His hand went to his hat. She put her hand on his arm. "Don't worry."

He let go of his hat and put his hand on top of hers. "You are the only person who makes me forget my scars."

"You don't have to forget them," she whispered, their hands still touching. "Just remember there is more to you than what happened in the past. I've seen pieces of your heart—others will too. Come and meet my family and you can see pieces of mine."

Otis didn't want to move. Her hand, he feared, would be taken away, and the warmth that crept from her touch to his heart would go with no promise of ever returning.

"Otis?"

"Sadie," he said, so softly his voice was almost lost to the wind, "say no if you wish, but . . ." He tried to slow his heart. "Could I hold your hand?"

Long seconds passed in silent agony.

"If my hand," she said at last, "will help you, then take it."

Instantly he berated himself for not speaking clearer. Meeting her family scared him, but it was not the reason he longed to take her hand and hold it in his own. Something else, not fear, compelled him to seek her touch.

"I'll meet them." He tugged at his hat and started toward the farmhouse with Sadie struggling to keep up.

"What is it?" she hollered against the wind. "Don't walk away from me."

"You work for me," he said without turning toward her. "You don't have to hold my hand. That's not your job. I . . . I forgot that for a moment. Let's go meet your parents and sisters and be done with it."

"No," she snarled back at him. Like a fierce animal protecting its territory, she stood her ground. "Stop right there and tell me what I've done. You have no right to be angry with me, at least not until you give an explanation."

He stopped walking, turned toward her, and with arms thrown to his sides, said, "You broke into my factory, and then ever since, you've been there, smiling and making me believe . . . giving me hope that I could have a life. I was just waiting for every day to go by, and then you came and . . ."

"And what?"

He couldn't say it. Once he confessed and told her of his growing affection, he could never take it back, and he could lose her completely. Too much was at stake. He backed away from the fight.

"And . . ." He faltered. "You have changed things. I suppose I am worried your family will not like me."

"You can be contrary, but so can they. Trust me, you'll get on splendidly."

He nodded and made for the house, ready to be done with this conversation and this foolhardy trip to the country. What a fickle, spineless man he'd become. Too afraid to bare his heart.

He left his hat on as he stepped into the small farmhouse. Simple furniture, floral wallpaper, and framed stitchery gave it a homey feel. One moment was all he had to take in the sight of Sadie's family home and the scent of stew bubbling on the stove before a flock of women with singsong voices and sparkling eyes that matched Sadie's came at him.

Sadie's sisters introduced themselves, and then like a gaggle of geese, they clustered around him and asked one question after another, barely giving him time to breathe between answers. His palms were sweaty, and his heart raced as he stood amid what felt like a hundred women.

"Is it wonderful being back in Monticello?" Violette asked. "Someday I plan to move to a city. Do you love it there?"

"I'm still deciding," he fired back, taking one breath between this answer and the next.

"Do you plan to reopen your factory?" Molly was next to ask him. "Bicycles are still in demand. I've always wanted one."

"I haven't made a decision yet." This response led to further questioning that challenged his ability to keep his personal plans to himself. He did his best though, answering every question in brief, short replies, all the while watching the women's faces. They held no malice, at least not blatant malice, but they were bursting with curiosity.

"You don't talk easily," Violette said, interrupting their interrogation.

"Violette!" Sadie snapped back. "Watch your mouth."

"It's only that from your letters, I expected someone different."

Sadie glared at her sister, then turned and offered an apologetic smile in his direction.

"Otis is our new friend. He has only just arrived," Flora spoke up. "Perhaps we should not ask so many questions. He may not be used to our prying ways. Not everyone was raised in a family of sisters."

Otis only half heard the second part of her statement. Her reference to him as a friend echoed through his mind, and instantly he felt a kinship with Flora, the quiet sister.

"The questions are good for him," Leon said from the doorway that connected the kitchen and front room. It was Otis's turn to glare. "Relax, boy, I don't think they'll bite. This is what friends do. They converse, they laugh, they ask questions."

Leon's *help* had Otis feeling sheepish. The conversation hit a lull, leaving everyone unsure how to proceed. It may have gone on in awkward silence if Sadie's mother hadn't entered the room with Mildred at her heels. Something about the tears glistening in the family matron's eyes nudged him to action. He left his spot beside the sisters and went to her.

"It's a pleasure to meet you," he said and moved his hat slightly up and down on his head.

"It is our honor." She put a hand on her heart. "When our girl left home, we were so worried. You were there when she was in need, and now you've sent a doctor. I'm so grateful."

Forgetting the others in the room, he stepped closer and said, "It has all been my pleasure. Your daughter was there for me when I needed her."

"God is good." She patted his cheek. "Come and meet my husband."

Ten minutes beside Sadie's father, and he understood the role of a father in a way he'd not before. His tired eyes were full of warmth, care, and gratitude, despite the persistent pain. His words were gentle and kind.

"Take off your hat," the man said from his bed.

When Otis sat, unmoving, Sadie's father said, "Son, I don't care a thing about how a man looks on the outside. I just want to see the face of the man who came to my family's rescue."

Otis sat silently another moment before removing his hat and putting it in his lap. "I haven't made peace with it yet. Though I've had years to try."

"I've seen far uglier men."

The tension eased, and they talked like two friends. They spoke about Iowa, factories, and Otis's exile. His guard down, he told the man about his struggles. And then they spoke of Sadie.

"You care for my daughter, don't you?" Sadie's father asked.

"She's a hardworking woman."

"Better come up with a better line if you ever expect to woo her."

"I never said I wanted to woo her."

"You should want to. She's a treasure, but living out here so far from the town, she hasn't had much chance at being noticed."

"She said something about a man named Marvin." Otis hoped he wasn't breaching her trust. "She must have done enough to catch his eye."

"I guess we'll know the answer soon enough." He sank deeper into his pillow. "But she never spoke about him like she speaks about you. Better go and spend time with the others and be good to my girl."

"You have my word."

"And you have my blessing."

Sadie did her best to join in the conversation and even steer it if it went in a dangerous direction, but her heart was not in it. She was too distracted, too busy thinking about Otis's request to hold her hand. What had it meant? Again and again she rebuked herself for not telling him Elisabeth's whereabouts. She'd justified her omission by telling herself that Otis could not bear such news and enjoy his time with her family. She would tell him soon, when the timing was better. Her resolution didn't sit well, but she stomached her discomfort, burying it as deep as she could.

"We best be heading back," Mildred said, looking out at the darkening sky. "We don't have much daylight left, and with those clouds rolling in . . ."

"Oh dear." Sadie's mother shuddered. "Do you think you ought to wait and go in the morning? When the storms come, the ruts in the road fill with water. It can flood clear over. I would hate for you to get stuck."

Mildred looked at Otis and Leon. Sadie gripped the edge of her seat with white-knuckled hands, anxious to hear what they would decide. In truth, she did not know what to hope for. Of course she wanted them safe, but to have them sleep under her family's roof...

"If the Wests are certain we are not imposing, then I think it wise we wait," Leon said. "Traveling a rough road would be easier in daylight."

Her sisters clapped their hands and squealed.

"If only Papa could play his fiddle," Flora said when the sisters' excitement died down. "That would make a jolly evening."

"He will again someday, thanks to Mr. Taylor," Violette said. "We will just have to find other ways to pass the evening."

Oh dear. Otis would surely think them an odd bunch if her sisters decided to plan the night's entertainment.

"What shall we do?" Violette asked.

Molly stepped away from the parlor and returned with a broom. "We could stick pull, entertain Mr. Taylor by showing him how we kept ourselves occupied when we were younger."

"You just like pulling sticks because you always win," Violette said.

Sadie gaped. This could not be happening. There was nothing ladylike about stick pulling. It was a game played by little boys and, on occasion, men who wanted to boast about their strength.

"Let's think of something else," she suggested. "Something everyone can participate in if they wish, even Leon and Mildred."

Leon sat near the sisters and Otis, a jolly smile on his face. Mildred rocked quietly in the corner, talking to Sadie's mother, unaware of the decision-making.

"A dramatic reading," Violette suggested, already moving to the bookshelf. "It's always entertained us before, and tonight we will have men to read."

"Yes!" Flora clapped her hands. "It'd be good fun."

"If that is what everyone wishes, I'm willing," Otis said, already showing loyalty to the family's quiet sister. "I can't promise to be very good."

"None of us are." Molly leaned back in her chair and crossed her legs. "Mother says we are all overly dramatic, and if anyone ever saw us, they would hightail it out of here."

"It's a good thing the weather gives us no option of hightailing anywhere," Otis said, appearing more at ease with every passing minute. "I'm not opposed to pretending to be someone I'm not."

"It'll do an old man like me a world of good, watching young people enjoying life. Even if they are overdramatic." Leon settled deeper into his chair. "I'm happy to read whatever part you wish."

Sadie kept her eyes and attention on Violette, silently pleading that she pick a safe reading, one with no romance or silly lines. Something sedate and serene, boring even.

"Our nights have been dull since Sadie left. I read some of her old stories and decided to fix them up a bit." Violette stood in front of the group, playing the part of leader.

"You put so much work into it. We should do it," Flora said. "Daphne was always one of my favorite characters."

"Daphne?" Otis asked.

"You don't need to know," Sadie said.

"I do." Otis leaned forward in his seat. "Tell me everything."

Violette ignored Sadie. "She started writing stories about a character named Daphne when she was thirteen or fourteen. Little adventures, and when she got a little older, she added in romance."

Sadie groaned. It was all so childish and embarrassing.

"I used my nights to edit and embellish them a bit," Violette said with a grin. "They're so much more romantic now. And I have made sets of them so we can do a reading. Molly thought it was a waste of time"—she shot an accusing look at her sister—"but it wasn't. It's going to be so much fun."

"I think we should pick something else," Sadie said, a weak attempt to deter the already enthusiastic crowd. "We should do one we are more familiar with."

"I haven't read any of them," Otis said. "I think Daphne's story, with Violette's edits, sounds intriguing."

Violette giggled as she handed the copies to everyone, all painstakingly written by hand. "You'll be Alexander Darling." She smiled at Otis. "When Sadie first wrote him, she said that Alexander Darling was the most romantic name there was."

"I was much younger when I said that!" She held the copy she'd been handed high enough that it hid her face.

Otis cleared his throat. "Alexander Darling? It'll be my first time playing the hero."

Sadie lowered her copy, and if they'd been alone, she might have told him that he'd been a hero before. For their family and for her.

Violette looked at Sadie. "You're blushing. It's like you're in character already. You'll be a perfect Daphne."

"No, it should be you—you always begged to be Daphne. You love being the lead."

"Nonsense. You're the oldest and you know Daphne best."

Sadie acquiesced, not wanting to cause a scene, but later Violette would be getting an earful. Reading Daphne with Otis reading Mr. Darling, even if everyone knew it was only a dramatic reading, would surely become a memory forever accompanied by a blush.

"Let's begin," Violette said as though she were the train conductor and everyone was dallying on the platform.

They all scooted their chairs closer together, except Sadie, who received a glare from Violette that brought forth a huff as she, too, scooted closer. Violette and Molly began by reading their lines, each with an exaggerated delivery as they took on the roles of the imaginary maids. Flora entered the story as the horse trainer, and even Leon participated, becoming the gardener at the fictional Roseland Hall.

Daphne's Destiny opened with the two maids gossiping about the woman who had just been hired to muck the stalls. They saw her as a threat to their grand schemes to fall in love with the mysterious owner themselves. Then poor Daphne entered, a woman who'd taken the job simply to provide for herself and escape her tyrannical uncle.

Sadie read her first page of lines using a steady monotone voice. "'You weren't supposed to see me like this,'" she read aloud. Poor Daphne was seen by the mysterious Mr. Darling with tears streaming down her face, but Sadie didn't even attempt to cry.

"'Those women thrive on gossip.'" Otis surprised her by using a voice that was different from his own. "'Tell them to go away and to leave you in peace.'" He snickered before reading his next line. "'And tell them you hope they walk through cow dung as they go.'"

The whole room snorted with laughter, even Sadie, who had been determined to remain stoic.

"I added a lot of my own lines," Violette said over the laughter. "I'm not as good at this as Sadie."

"It's delightful," Leon said. And they went back to the story.

"'I do hope they step in dung and then track it all through their fine houses. But they won't go away. Every day they talk of my leaving. They tried to convince me to marry the old preacher. He's old enough to be my father, and I always hoped for a love match.'" She nearly choked on the word *love*. This script was only a shadow of what she'd once written, leaving her unsure what she'd be reading next. From the corner of her eye, she saw Otis move his chair a little closer. "'But I am desperate and poor and that is enough for them to believe me unworthy of true love. They want to run me off.'"

"'Everyone ought to have a love match. No circumstances should prevent it.'" Otis's character voice slipped to his own. "'They should . . . they should all marry the person who makes them smile and laugh and go weak in the knees.'"

"'Oh dear,'" Sadie read. "'Mrs. Smalls is coming. She's as bad as the gossips, except she wants me to become a governess and move to the big city. All I want is to be free to choose for myself. I'm tired of running.'"

"'There must be another way. Perhaps there's someone you love already. He could be right in front of you, and you've just never realized. There must be—'"

"'What are you two doing together?'" Mrs. Smalls, played by Flora, asked. "'You, Mr. Darling, surely have better things to do with your time than spend it with the likes of Daphne. You ought to go out and meet the fine women of the city.'"

Sadie rolled her eyes but played along, covering her face as she let out an exaggerated sob. The reading went on. The residents of Roseland Hall continued trying to marry Daphne off or belittle her, while Daphne tried her best to understand the reserved owner. Several lines brought laughter from the group. Before long Sadie found herself engrossed by not just the story, which felt only faintly familiar, but by Otis, who seemed to be enjoying the freedom he'd found as he took on the part of a different man.

As Mr. Darling, his guard was down, and a playfulness she'd not expected filled the room.

"'Ride horses with me,'" he said, and she felt tempted to saddle a horse right then and there and ride away from all her cares. "'Let them say what they wish. I see past it all.'"

"'You can't possibly see past my drab clothes and—'"

"'That's not what I see.'" The sincerity in his voice . . . It pierced her heart. "'I see a friend, and—dare I say it?'"

"'Say it.'" She held her breath.

"'I see kindness and loyalty. I see the most beautiful woman I have ever met.'"

The scene went on. The room was quiet, all except for the couple who teetered on the edge of reality and fiction. Who was talking? What was real?

Otis grabbed her hand near the end of the story. "'Don't go, Daphne. Stay here. I know you believe yourself desperate. Let me give you another option.'"

"'What might that be, Mr. Darling? I am a penniless soul. If there are no more horses, there is no more work for me here.'"

"'Me. I am your option—pick me. I've loved you since I first met you. Let me marry you, and I'll be your darling forever.'"

The laughter that followed instantly filled the farmhouse, but Sadie could not laugh. Her hand in his made it all feel more real than fictitious. "'Yes,'" she whispered, squeezing his hand. "'If I had every option in the entire world open to me, it is you I would pick.'"

He scooted to the edge of the chair, their knees touched, and then with his hand still holding hers, he brought her fingers to his lips and kissed them. A thousand sensations flew through her.

"Otis?" Sadie whispered, slipping out of character.

"It says here that Alexander Darling kisses Daphne."

"That was hardly a kiss," Leon said. "Do it right, boy."

Everyone watched Sadie and Otis. Or rather Daphne and Mr. Darling.

He looked at her with questioning eyes. "Daphne?"

"Mr. Darling," she managed to murmur.

He leaned in, and then she felt the gentle brush of his lips against her cheek. The room exploded in applause.

"Your evening readings are quite entertaining," Otis said with his head still near hers. His breath tickled her ear. "Is it my superb acting that has everyone so enthused?"

"We always applaud at the end. We pretend we've a grand audience." She swallowed, unsure how so gentle a touch could travel all the way to the tips of her toes. "Normally we just read the lines and do not act it out."

"Ah, someone should have told me." He kept his voice low enough that only she could hear him. "But I don't regret it. Poor Mr. Darling was so in love. I feel I've done him a service by allowing him to kiss his fair Daphne's cheek. Do you suppose a kiss on the lips would have been more appropriate?"

"I . . ." She swallowed, but the lump in her throat would not go away. "I don't know. Violette wrote that part."

"Do you not think they were in love?" he asked. "I think he wanted to take her in his arms and tell the whole world."

"I always imagined Daphne and her Mr. Darling living happily ever after. But I never finished the story," Sadie said, placing her hand on the cheek he'd kissed. Her lips burned, begging to know what it would feel like to have Alexander Darling kiss her in a more forward way.

Chapter 23

Otis slept in the loft of the barn that had once been the West sisters' imaginary kingdom. His bed of straw left much to be desired, but the setting kept his mind reeling for hours. What must it have been like to be poor by way of possessions but rich in a way most men yearned for? His one evening spent laughing with the West sisters had left him longing for more. When he'd taken Sadie's hand under the guise of Alexander Darling, he'd almost believed himself a man worthy of her. And when he'd pressed his lips to her fingers and then to her cheek, he'd wished he could make the moment last forever.

"Breakfast is ready," Sadie called, startling him. "My mama has prepared a feast for everyone. She's a wonderful cook but has no patience for stragglers."

"I think I can smell it from way out here." He stopped short after helping Wolf down the ladder and tried not to stare, but her loose hair made it nearly impossible. Thick and lush around her shoulders, her hair begged to be touched. A pleasant unrest grew in his chest.

"I haven't had time to do my hair." Her hand moved to her long locks, touching the strands he longed to run his fingers through.

He put his hand on hers. "It's beautiful." Closing his eyes, he asked himself what Alexander Darling would say in this moment. Alone with a woman who roused his spirits and awakened his desire to love and be loved.

Mr. Darling would speak his heart. He swallowed and added, "*You* are beautiful. Every part you."

"Truly?" She held his gaze, and the hand he touched trembled. "No one has ever—"

"They should have." He moved his hand to her face and, with his thumb, stroked her soft skin. "Sadie West, you're the most beautiful woman I've ever met."

Sadie smirked playfully. "It is my understanding that you have not met many women, at least not in recent years."

"Do I have to know a great many to notice what is right in front of me? You make me feel . . ." He wet his lips. "You know I'm not good with words, but you make me feel safe." His hand moved from her cheek to the thick tempting hair that hung long around her shoulders. "When I'm around you, everything is different."

"Otis." She sucked in her bottom lip. "When you wanted to hold my hand—"

"I wanted to hold it because when you were away, I missed you."

She took his hand in her own and brought it to her lips, kissing him the same way he had kissed her the night before. Except now they were not in character. She was not kissing Alexander Darling but Otis Taylor. If a heart could sing, his would have rung out with joyful noise. Emboldened, he lowered his head. He'd never kissed a woman, but in this moment with their hands clasped together, he could almost believe she felt the same desire that consumed him.

"Sadie," he whispered. She tilted her head back, her gaze traveling to his lips. The moment moved slowly, giving him time to take in every sensation. The look in her eyes, the smell of hay, and the sound of the rooster crowing.

Her breath touched his skin, caressing him before his lips ever met hers, sending waves of hope and anticipation through him. He closed the distance, pressing his mouth to hers. It was a dream—it had to be. A perfect, beautiful dream. She kissed him back, and then her hands moved up his neck, running over his many scars as they conversed with no words at all. Her touch was so soft, so gentle and accepting.

"Sadie," he murmured with his cheek pressed to the top of her head. "Sadie, I—"

She pulled back. Her hands still touched him, but now with lighter pressure. The dream began to fade. Her expression changed—a shadow creeping over where only light had been before.

"What is it?" he asked, unsure why the soft, willing woman in his arms was now tense and stiff.

"I'm sorry. It's not fair. I don't want to hurt you." She stepped out of his arms, then took another step backward. His insides went hollow. Where was she going? Another step put more distance between them, and she nearly toppled over her own feet. Her hand covered her mouth. "I have to go back to the house. Come for breakfast when you're ready."

"Sadie?" He took a step toward her, only to stop when she shook her head. "I don't understand."

From her spot near the barn door, she paused. "Otis Taylor, this"—she motioned between them—"can't be. Not now, at least."

All the air in him left. A blow to his chest would have hurt less. Winded and confused, he watched her go.

Sadie stopped by the side of the house and leaned against the wall for support. She'd just kissed a man, her first kiss. And it had exceeded every dream she'd ever had.

But it wasn't fair to kiss him or to toy with him and then tell him the secret she harbored about Elisabeth. She kicked at the mud, not caring about the state of her boots. She had to face her fear and tell him the truth. But then everything could change. He may not want to kiss her or look at her with tenderness. One kiss, cut short by her conscience, and already she knew she would spend the rest of her days wishing for another chance to be in his arms.

But kissing and romance would have to wait. Running back to Otis and his loving touch was not an option. The truth about Elisabeth was bigger than she knew how to navigate, and she couldn't avoid it forever. No matter what happened, someone would be hurt. Peter, Nina, Elisabeth, Otis. She cared about them all.

"There you are." Molly came around the corner. "Where's Otis? I thought Mama sent you to fetch him?"

"He's in the barn." She kicked again at the ground.

"Did you fight?"

"No, nothing like that."

Molly put a hand on her forehead. "Did you kiss him?"

"Molly," she groaned. "Don't tell anyone. It was impulsive—no, it was romantic. Molly, it was perfect, but it was all wrong."

"What did you do?"

"Stop looking at me like that. It was a little kiss, nothing to run and tattle to Mama about."

"If it was so terribly romantic, then what was wrong with it?"

"It just can't be. I can't court Otis Taylor."

"I saw the two of you last night. You were both stealing glances at each other and blushing. Don't tell me it was only acting—even Flora saw it. Why wouldn't you want to court a man who looks at you with so much love?"

"It's not so simple."

"I thought you weren't vain."

"What?"

Molly pursed her lips. "He looks different. And he wears his hat all the time, which is the oddest habit. I just . . . I thought you saw past all of that."

"You sound like Violette talking about looks. I don't care about his head or his hat. I work for him. I can't kiss him. I can't be romantic with him."

Molly grabbed Sadie's hands and forced her to still herself. "Sadie, you have spent your life looking after your sisters, and now you are working hard for our farm and for Pa." She gripped her hands tighter. "You are allowed to think of yourself from time to time. If you love him, it doesn't matter that he's your employer. People find each other in all sorts of ways."

"I wish it were so simple." Sadie pulled her hands away. "Don't worry about me—I'll manage. And whatever you do, don't tell Violette. I'm going to pack my bag and be ready to go with Leon and Mildred and Otis. I need to get back to work. He's paying for Pa's doctor." She put her hand on her forehead, still trying to steady herself. "I need to get back to work."

"You're going back today?"

"Pa will be leaving for the hospital later today. We can't expect Otis to pay for his care forever. Are you sure you'll be okay here without Mama and Pa?"

"You do know I am only a year younger than you? We'll be fine. Just promise to keep writing your letters and sending them with Peter."

Oh, Peter. She wanted to cry at the mention of his name.

Saying farewell to her family was difficult, especially bidding goodbye to her father, and the drive back to the Taylor mansion was painfully quiet. Leon drove, and Mildred nodded off as the carriage bumped along the muddy road. Otis spent most of the ride looking out the window. When their eyes did meet, they both quickly looked away.

Sadie spent most of the drive wondering how she was going to work for a man she could not look in the eye. How could she pretend not to care for him when her heart beat wildly in his presence and her thoughts were full of him? She fought with herself and her conflicting desires but to no avail. The war raged on.

In the safety of her small staff room, she tried to calm her worries. After all, she was not courting the man. He was not entitled to kisses and ardor. All she needed to worry about was how to accomplish whatever task she was assigned and prove to him that she was worth keeping employed, at least until her father recovered. And her secret . . . When the moment was right, she would tell him.

Mildred found her later, and like a mother hen, she pulled her close, pressed a kiss to her temple, and said, "Whatever it is that ails you, set it aside for now. Let's work together to get our Otis ready for the masquerade. Get your skates."

Sadie nodded. It was time to rise to the occasion and prove she could keep her emotions in line in his presence. On the way back from her family farm, she had decided that she would wait until after the masquerade to tell Otis about Elisabeth. She may regret her decision later—only time would tell. But the masquerade was days away, and Elisabeth was safe. For now, it was best if Otis focused on his grand return to Monticello. Then, after he'd faced his fear, she would give him the news.

Sadie entered their private skating hall, still nervous to be so near the man whose lips had touched hers. He was there already, in the corner adjusting the straps on his skates. She stared from the doorway. Keeping her budding feelings to herself was going to be very difficult indeed.

He looked up and caught her gawking but offered her nothing more than a stiff nod. No grin. No lingering gaze. No word of welcome.

Sadie walked to the bench with her head down. She put on her skates without looking up. And then she took to the floor alone. The room had never felt so intimidating as it did now.

Around once. Alone. Around again. Alone. And then his stride put him beside her. They'd come together despite where they'd begun. He didn't pass her. He slowed and stayed in line with her, their wheels whirring across the floor in unison.

"Do I get another rule?" Otis asked. Her jaw dropped. She didn't deserve his goodness. "You're here. You came back, so teach me."

"Otis, I . . ." She paused. He was offering a truce, and judging by the scowl he bore, it had required constraint. "Are we on rule seven?"

"I believe we are."

She looked up at the ceiling, trying to think of another rule. "Two nights from now you will be at the masquerade. Don't let your worries keep you from enjoying the event."

"So I am not to think of Elisabeth while I am there or the way you left me in the barn."

"Not during the masquerade." She took his hand, a daring move that had her wishing anew their circumstances were different. "Take your partner's hand, whoever that may be, and think only of them."

He did not let go.

"Let's practice," he said. "I will pretend you and I are skating circles at the Big Rink. I will be nothing more than a carefree gentleman who thinks only of you."

"Very good." She tightened her hand around his. Soon all of this would end—the skating, the conversations, the closeness—and she would be back to sorting feathers, wondering if there was a man out there who would ever look at her the way Otis had. Someone else would hold Otis's hand. Now that she knew him, she felt certain his big heart would be seen by any number of women.

"Tell me, Sadie, is it proper for me to compliment my partner while we skate?"

"I believe a carefully worded compliment would be appropriate."

"At the Crawfords' house, there was a pond back in the woods on the far side of the garden. I often walked around it when I was feeling bitter about life. I'd sit by its edge and watch the water ripple and glisten in the sun. I found solace there. I came here, and my pond was left behind. Not only was I back in this place full of memories that haunt me, but I had nowhere to run."

"It must have been difficult."

"I can't say I loved it at the Crawfords', but it was familiar." He paused. And then with what felt like genuine sincerity, he said, "So I must thank you."

"Me?"

"You have quickly become more comforting than any pond has ever been. You have helped me cushion the old memories with new, softer ones. I am a different man because of you. I will always be grateful."

She had no words, only a heart that swelled in her chest. Where once she had felt unimportant in Monticello, nothing but a dowdy feather sorter, his words had given her presence here a purpose. To him she was important, at least for a season.

"How was that for a well-delivered compliment?" Otis asked.

She snapped out of the daze his words had put her in. Pulling her hand away, she skated solo, no longer in unison with him. "If contrived flattery is what you are after, then you are well on your way. I imagine there will be many women lined up to partner with you. They'll swoon at your flattering words."

"If I give praise, I will stand by it. You, Sadie West, have been a comfort to me. An infuriating, confusing one, but a comfort nonetheless."

"Infuriating?"

"Yes! You don't know what you do to me. You write letters to another man, while at the same time making my heart beat like it has never beaten before. One minute you are in my arms kissing me, and the next you will hardly look at me."

"Otis." She forced calmness into her tone. "Let me give you another rule. Rule eight: if you feel infuriated at the masquerade, don't let it show. You feel everything. It's your curse and your gift. Too many men work hard but never slow down and feel anything."

"Are you saying there are times when it's good that I feel infuriated?"

"If our roles were reversed, I would feel infuriated as well," she said. "I only hope you can understand that I don't mean to rile you up. Someday I'll try to explain, but not tonight." She rolled closer to him. "Come, let's skate as fast as we can. I'll race you around the circle."

His lips twitched as though he wanted to say more. No doubt he wanted the explanation he was entitled to.

"Very well," he said through gritted teeth. "Ready—"

She flew by him, not waiting for a command to go. He laughed, and the magic of the rink once again pushed away reality. For an hour they skated—laughing, racing, and even trying to master tricks.

When at last they sat on the bench exhausted, Sadie asked, "Do you see now why some do this for entertainment?"

"I am now convinced that skating is not only diverting, but that one could even be in jeopardy of falling in love while skating."

The urge to wrap herself in his arms and lose herself in his touch was strong. She focused on the broken window. "I think anything is possible on the rink," she said, then stood and forced her legs to carry her away from him. "I'm going to go and see if Mildred needs me for anything."

Chapter 24

Leon gathered everyone together the next morning after his visit to the lawyer's office.

"A letter was slid under the lawyer's door. He found it when he arrived at his office this morning. He doesn't know who delivered it." Leon pulled a creased paper from his pocket and cleared his throat. "Do you want to read it?"

"You go ahead," Otis said.

Leon began reading to his captivated audience.

Dear Sir,

I don't know what to say or how to say it. I saw your request in the newspaper about the child Elisabeth. I believe the girl you seek is in my home. She calls me Papa and my wife Mama. She is happy here, and I beg you to tell whoever it is that seeks her that she is well.

I don't have a lawyer yet to help me understand what can be done. I will write again when I do. Until then, tell your client not to worry. She is safe and loved.

"There is no signature," Leon said. "Our lawyer said he will ask around and see if anyone saw who left the note, but so far there are no leads."

"She's close." Otis stood, unable to sit still. His niece was nearby, and soon they would be together. "Someone must know where she is. We could get the police to go door to door."

"Perhaps . . .," Mildred said. "They might be able to help."

"What kind of a man leaves a note like this and doesn't even sign his name? Why bother with a note at all?" Otis looked to Sadie, needing her support in this moment.

"Otis." Sadie looked up when she said his name, her eyes red rimmed. Her reaction made no sense. Where was her indignation? He needed her to come to his aid. "He may be a good man," she said in a voice that shook. "He might be trying to do the right thing."

"A good man would not keep her from me."

"I will go to the police if that is what you want. I can consult them and see what they advise." Leon, always ready to act, stood and moved to the door. "Mildred, will you walk with me?"

"Tell them it's important we discover her whereabouts," Otis said. "Tell them I am willing to do whatever it takes to have her brought home."

Leon nodded. "We will tell them you are devoted to your family."

Once they were alone, Sadie approached him. "You have known about Elisabeth for more than a month, but all these people know is that they've loved a little girl as if she were their own, and now someone wants to take her away. They may want to hire someone so they can be assured she is really your kin. Can you fault them for that?"

She reached out to touch his arm, but he brushed it away. Could her loyalty be so fickle? He knew she had worries, but he'd not believed they ran so deep. How could she stand there and say such things when he'd seen the bond of her own family? Was he not entitled to the same familial love?

"She was never theirs to have." He pressed a hand to his chest. "*I* am her blood. You and I . . . we were searching for her together. I'm sorry for the barn. If that is what this is about, forget it ever happened."

"Otis."

"What?" he snapped.

"I do care about Elisabeth. And about the barn . . . can we set it aside, like we did while we skated?"

"I don't know if we can," he muttered. It would be near impossible to put it from his mind. He'd thought of their shared embrace and the taste of her kiss countless times since the barn, and he'd questioned her fleeing with equal frequency. "I'll try if that's your wish."

"For now it is." She shifted, looked toward the door, and he felt certain she was about to leave. He wanted her to go, but he also wanted her to stay. A photograph of him as a boy, standing beside his brother and parents, all rigid but together, gave him an idea.

"I have not been to my childhood room since I returned." Did he truly wish to go there now? With her? It was too late to take back the words. "I have wondered whether it remains the same or if it was altered."

"Are you asking me to join you?"

"I'd rather not go in alone."

"I have been meaning to clean your old room. But Mildred said to wait until you were ready."

"I won't ever be ready. But I want it over with."

His room was on the second story, near the back of the house, overlooking the creek, all details he remembered. Many other details he could no longer remember. He could not recall the color of the quilt he'd once slept beneath, but he knew he had left clothes in the closet, waiting for his return, and that his collection of wooden animals had been lined up on the windowsill. He could not remember what portraits hung on his walls or how many cars were on his train set, but he knew his Christmas ball and bat were under his bed, tucked away in a safe spot because they'd at one time been treasured gifts.

She followed him to the door, quietly supporting him. An awkwardness existed between them, and he blamed himself for assuming her capable of caring about him as more than a mere friend or employer. It hurt to think about, but she was here, as a friend, and that was ever so much better than being alone.

At the door he hesitated. And then he handed her the key. She unlocked it and waited until he nodded to push it open. He stepped into the once familiar room, only to find himself in a foreign land. There were no remnants of his childhood left except for the view.

He'd expected it to hurt, to know that his belongings had been packed up or discarded. That at some prior date, his family had decided he would not be coming home for them. Instead, he simply looked around at the unfamiliar furniture and shrugged.

"It's not the same," he said, ready to back away. But she stepped deeper into the room, making her way to the window.

"I am very glad you did not sleep in this room when you first returned home." She winced and he chuckled. "If it's all right with you, I'll dust everything and mop the floors."

"I can help," he said, preferring their uneasy relationship to silence. They were still busily removing the layer of dust when Leon and Mildred returned.

"The police listened." Mildred was first to speak. "They were concerned and said they would have to speak to someone else before they set out looking for her. They said an abandoned child—"

"I did not abandon her."

"We made that known," Leon said. "However, if your brother abandoned her and the child's mother did as well, or if she died, like we believe, then someone may have already taken the legal recourse to adopt the child."

"So what do we do? There must be a way to get her back."

"They said they would ask questions so they understood the law better. And if it is within their power, they'll go searching. For now, we have no choice but to trust them to do their job. It's more important than ever that you get yourself ready for the masquerade. If this becomes a legal battle, then it will help for you to have a good reputation. Even the law can be influenced by rumors."

Everywhere Sadie went the next day and night, she listened for Otis. If she heard his tread on the stairs, she went the other way. If she heard him playing the piano, she paused and allowed only a note or two to touch her heart before returning to work, refusing to follow the music to him. It was better for him if she stayed away. After the masquerade tomorrow, she would tell him what she knew, and she would accept whatever reaction he had. She would have to.

Her efforts to avoid him, though mostly successful, were not foolproof. She managed to dodge his presence, but a note was slid under her door at night, accompanied by a sheet of music.

Dear Sadie,

When I could not find you, I went to the music room and wrote this piece. The notes flowed in the way a musician always hopes they will. Straight from my heart to the keys.

Find me, and I'll play it for you. Then we'll talk. Say you'll come.

O. T.

Oh, how she desired to rush through the house, find him, and then lose herself in his music. However, her desire to keep her distance won over impulse. Instead, she held his music close, hoping that she would someday have a chance to watch Otis's hands dance across the keys as they played her song.

"You've been polishing that silver for a mighty long time," Mildred said the next day as she leaned into the pantry. "Are you hiding?"

"I'm working."

"I'm not blind. You and Otis have been like sap on hands since meeting, and now you are avoiding him. Did you have a tiff?"

Sadie shook her head. "Mildred, can I trust you with a secret?"

"This house is full of secrets—what's one more? Come along, let's go to your room and we'll talk while you try on what I've made you for the masquerade."

"I'm not going." Sadie's voice squeaked. "I can't. I don't want to spend money, and, well, I'm not sure I want to watch him . . . I can't go."

"Nonsense." She pulled Sadie through the hall and down the stairs to her bedroom. "I saw your blue dress and thought it was perfect for going out. I made a mask that matches. You'll be beautiful." From within the depths of her apron, she pulled an exquisite blue mask, embroidered and edged with snowflake-like tatting. Delicate and angelic.

"You made this?" Sadie held it gingerly.

"I did, and I'd be heartbroken if you didn't wear it. You won't put me through that agony, will you?"

Sadie stared at the mask. It was like something from a fairy tale, fit for a princess. "I suppose I could put on my dress and this beautiful mask. I could sit in the back and watch the other skaters, but Otis can't know I'm there."

"That's a start. And then once you realize that you deserve to be there as much as anyone else, you can leave the corner and go to the floor. With the music playing and the crowd, it'll be a night you'll always remember." Mildred sat on the edge of Sadie's bed and patted the spot beside her. "Now, tell me what it is that's got you hiding in the pantry."

Her heavy secret, so tightly wrapped inside of faulty justification and endless worries, burst from its careful packaging. In a flurry of tears and words, she told Mildred about Bessy and Peter and Nina. She even showed her the sheet music from Otis and told her how badly she wanted to hear him play it. Putting words to her struggle was difficult, but having someone else privy to the details made the burden easier to carry.

"Peter and Nina prayed for a baby. They wanted a child so badly," she said with a sob. "They were so happy when Bessy came. They took her in and helped her when she was so thin and scared. She could hardly talk and was always hiding in the corner, but they were gentle, and with time she came around. Bessy loves them." She wiped at her face, trying to stop the tears. "They can't lose one another."

"But—"

"But Otis's intentions are pure. He wants to find her so he can give her a good life. He has money and a beautiful house, and he wants to share it all with her. He was abandoned, and it is right that he doesn't want the same pain to befall her." She groaned and fell back on the bed. "I plan to tell him after the masquerade. I thought it best that he not have the burden I do until after he has reconnected with the town. You and Leon both said it was important for him to make a good impression in case this becomes a legal battle." She couldn't meet Mildred's eyes. She had a list of excuses for not telling him, but that was all they were—excuses. "But I'm feeling crushed by the weight of it."

"You were trying to protect him?"

"Yes, in a way. And myself too." She rolled onto her side. "I have loved my time here. And you know I am fond of Otis. Everything will change once I tell him. He'll think I betrayed him for not telling him sooner. I've stalled, telling myself it was noble, only now I don't know. Maybe it was just selfish of me."

Mildred patted Sadie's knee. "With a secret like that I might want to hide in the pantry with the silver too. But you're a brave girl. Be brave again today. Get up and go to the masquerade. Otis will like knowing you're there, and when it's over, you'll tell him what you know and . . . well, no matter what happens, you will know that you said what needed saying."

"I have another secret."

"Oh dear."

Sadie walked to the closet and ran her hand over the blue dress. "I have dreamed of going to the masquerade since learning of it. At first I dreamed of skating with every man in town, but now I only want to skate with Otis. I think it'll hurt my heart to watch him with someone else."

"Once he sees you in this blue dress, I have a feeling he'll see only you."

"But the whole reason he is going is to make a good impression, not to start rumors. If he skates with me or arrives with me, I'll be in the way. Everyone in town believes he's returning now—they don't know that he's been here all this time. I can sit back and watch, but for his sake, that's all I can do."

"We will go late, after he's already shaken a few hands. When he asks you to skate, it won't shock anyone as long as he skates with others too. Besides, we will all be wearing masks."

She nodded slowly, considering the option. "I don't know about skating with him, but I would be willing to sneak in if you promise to stay by my side."

"We'll go together. I'll be back to fix your hair right after I shoo Otis off."

With Mildred gone, Sadie needed a distraction.

> . . . I have never felt so beautiful, nor have I ever felt so afraid. . . .

Chapter 25

Otis fought the urge to pout like a disgruntled child as he made his way to the masquerade alone. Where was Sadie? She'd gotten him into this fix. She should have joined him. But she hadn't, and she hadn't even said goodbye or thanked him for the music.

Now here he was, dressed in a dark suit jacket, complete with a cummerbund and the tie Sadie's family had gifted him, a sorry replacement for her presence. Covering the upper half of his face and his head, his mask looked like something a bandit turned dandy would wear. On top of that he wore a tall hat. The effect, Mildred said, was mysterious and surprisingly handsome. He wasn't sure he agreed but was grateful for the compliment and the shadows the costume created for him to hide in.

He stood with sweaty hands at the door of the large rink, peering in at the Monticello masses. Two women, perhaps twenty years old, walked by with skates in their hands.

The woman nearest him spoke first. "I saw you come from the road that leads to the Taylor mansion. Are you him?"

A lie formed on the tip of his tongue, but he swallowed it. "I'm Otis Taylor. It's a pleasure to meet you."

They turned toward each other and giggled. He touched his mask—it was intact and in place. There was nothing funny about him, was there?

"May we walk with you?" the second woman said, and he relaxed, realizing their laughter wasn't malicious. Women were a mystery. "We've no escort. So you can be ours."

He bowed slightly and offered himself. "I'd be honored."

The women introduced themselves as Nettie Plumb and Charlotte Bowers. He winced when he heard the second woman's name. She was most likely the daughter of the overzealous mother who had mailed so many letters, expressing her eagerness for him to return.

He darted glances at them out of the corner of his eye as they made their way into the Big Rink. They were attractive women, more fashionable than Sadie, and once they stopped tittering, they carried a conversation with ease. Both offered flattering compliments about his home and family. With the mask on, he could almost believe himself the social man he would have grown into had he not lost his hair and been sent away. A regular Alexander Darling.

Soon there were voices all around him. Some claimed to have known him before he left town, others exclaimed their excitement to now become acquainted. He did his best to shake hands, nod, and smile at everyone, but it did not take long for his newfound confidence to dwindle. These people were searching for a man who did not exist behind the mask. He'd proved himself a decent actor, but there were some things that could not be pretended away. If he could have shrunk back into hiding, he would have, but he was surrounded, everyone believing him the elusive bachelor, the handsome pianist returned to take over the family empire.

The noise increased, and his heart rate with it. Faster it beat, louder, harder. If only Sadie had given him a lesson in calming his nerves.

"I'm Dr. Henry, and this is my rink." A big man grabbed his arm and pulled him from the crowd. "Come with me, son."

Following blindly after the man was the only way to escape the throng of curious townsfolk. A band of ten played to his right, and the scents of popped corn and roasted nuts filled the air. Sadie would have loved the energy in the large room and the excitement of the crowd. *If only she were here.*

"Louie, John, and Harold have been playing in the band for years. All of 'em knew your father. The rest are younger, but they would know your family too," Dr. Henry said, absently gesturing toward the band as they walked away from the crowd. "Thought you might want to make a speech. Your father always knew how to work the crowd."

"A speech? I, um, hadn't thought of that."

"I'll give you some time to find your words. It doesn't have to be right now. Go and skate, and we'll gather everyone together later in the evening."

"I'll do my best," he said, at the same time wondering whether he could find a way to excuse himself early. The paper was full of stories of mishaps at the rink. A sprained ankle wouldn't be so bad.

"Go on, son—go mingle." Dr. Henry nudged him back toward the crowd. "I didn't mean to pull you away from all the fun."

They were standing at the far edge of the building, away from the rink and to the right of the seating. He couldn't just stand there, not when he'd been excused and told to enjoy himself. He turned back toward the crowd and found himself face-to-face with a woman whose eyes were hungry.

"I'm Alta. I've been so eager to meet you." She batted her large, fiery eyes at him. "Do you skate?"

Alta? He'd heard that name before. Sadie had mentioned her, but he could not recall any particulars. The low murmur of the crowd made thinking difficult.

"I do," he said, doing his best to appear at ease. "Let me put my skates on, and then I'd love to escort you around the rink."

She clapped her hands and squealed before casting a victorious smile at the women she'd pushed past. "I can hardly wait."

"My list of skating tricks is not long."

"I come every week at least once. I'll teach you." She smiled prettily. The moment his skates were latched, she grabbed his hand and pulled him onto the floor.

The floor of the great hall was like a busy street, but rather than wagons and carriages, skaters wove together. "Everyone is looking at us."

She looked over her shoulder, only to turn back with a pert smile. "I believe we are the couple that is making everyone envious. I told Sadie and Sylvia, two women from work, that I would be the one you would notice. And here I am the first to skate with you. It must mean we are meant for more than skating together."

Caught off guard, he nearly lost his footing. "I've skated before," he said.

"You have?"

"Yes, with Sadie." He winced, realizing his blunder. This town believed him only recently returned, and if that were true, he would not know Sadie well, if at all.

"Sadie!" Alta spat out her name. "She told us that she was working at the Taylor mansion, but I thought she was helping prepare it for your return. Not socializing. I can't believe she didn't tell us you were back in town."

"I asked her to keep my return a secret. Don't blame her. She's been nothing but a devoted employee who respected my desire for privacy."

"But you went skating together." She raised a skeptical brow. "Employers don't do that with their employees."

"When I decided to come to the masquerade skate, I convinced her to practice with me." Alta's face remained flushed, so he said, "It's been a long time since I've seen everyone here. Let's enjoy our time."

"Of course." She pulled her claws back in. "Now that you are settled back in your house, will we be seeing more of you?"

"Unfortunately, I still have many matters to resolve. I believe I'll be quite busy." A couple passed them on his right.

"You had best settle all those matters, because this town is in need of eligible bachelors."

He managed a weak smile, missing Sadie's less-predatorial ways. When Alta begged to skate the next number with him so they could become better acquainted, he offered a polite apology. "It's been so long since I've been in town. I need to go and visit with others. Please excuse me."

To his back she said, "Very well. I'll find you later in the evening."

He pulled his watch from his pocket. Would it be terribly impolite to leave after only fifteen minutes? Before deciding how to get through the crowd and out of the building, he felt a hand on his back. Turning, he noticed three faces that seemed faintly familiar, like ghosts from his past.

"Otis, you really are back," one man said before grinning. The gap between his front teeth was unforgettable. His mischief-making friends.

"Don't you recognize us?" the tallest of the three men asked, pulling his mask from his face. "It's Andrew, Dan, and Wilbur."

He pointed to each of them. These had been his chums. "It's good to see you."

"You all look so much older," he said, thinking of their last days together. They'd been in school talking about which girls they thought were pretty and who could hit a baseball the farthest one moment, and then the next he'd woken up with hair on his pillow and a patch of smooth skin on his scalp, and everything changed. His father sent him away without ever letting him say goodbye. So many years lost. "You've changed."

"Especially Andrew." Wilbur fisted his friend in the shoulder. "He's married, and his wife feeds him all day long."

Andrew patted his stomach. "A little extra girth is not worth complaining about when you have a wife like mine."

Dan laughed. "We can't tell what anyone looks like tonight. You're taller, but I'm guessing you still have the same baby face you always had."

"I suppose." Otis grinned, grateful for the masks. "Are you all married?"

"Andrew's been married two years. Wilbur will be married, once he gets brave enough to ask," Dan said with a laugh that made Otis feel young again. Memories of childhood bliss were louder than the band. Good times, long forgotten, felt like only yesterday.

"And you?" Otis asked Dan.

Dan puffed out his chest. "I don't need a woman in my life."

Andrew smirked. "Dan says that only because Sissy Walker just sent him on his way. She told him she hopes to find a more serious man."

"I was never going to marry her, anyhow." Dan's voice said otherwise.

"I'm sure you had women following you around. The famous musician, Otis Taylor." Dan whistled, then threw his arm around

Otis's shoulder and pulled him into a side hug. "My chances with a woman here just got slimmer. They'll all be chasing after you."

The men continued their teasing until the crowd moved toward them, enveloping them and encroaching on the men's reunion. With each song, each skate, Otis found himself inching closer toward comfort, the desire to flee losing its pull. The part of himself that had been starved for company was now overflowing.

An hour into the evening, Dr. Henry stepped onstage and quieted the crowd. "The Taylor family has been a pillar in this community ever since the late Mr. Taylor moved here. He was a hardworking man who left behind a legacy, and it is a pleasure to welcome back a part of that legacy. Welcome home, Otis Taylor."

The crowd roared. They clapped and cheered. Dr. Henry motioned for Otis to join him on the platform. Everyone's eyes were on him as he made his way through the crowd and carefully walked up the steps off the rink. Dr. Henry's arm went around his shoulder. "Time for a speech! Tell us where you've been and what kept you away."

Otis pinched the bridge of his nose. He should have left when he had the chance. The friendly faces he'd enjoyed and the comradery with old friends had done his heart good, but trying to explain where he'd been . . . He had no words. Was he to maintain his father's lies, claiming fame kept him away? Or did he break the Taylor mold and speak truth?

"Go on," Dr. Henry said again.

Otis searched the crowd. The band members held their instruments silent in their laps. The spectators sat without eating. The couples rolled closer and closer, crowding in, eager to hear and judge his words.

And then he saw Sadie. She sat beside Leon and Mildred in a back corner, her blue mask unable to fool him.

"It's been a long time since I've been in Monticello. A lot has changed. There are so many new buildings," he rambled. This wasn't what he needed to say. "My father," he tried again, keeping his eyes on Sadie. "He . . . he sent me away not only to learn music." She nodded, encouraging him. "He sent me away in hopes my health would improve."

A hum rose from the crowd as onlookers turned to one another, whispering.

"Your health?" Dr. Henry said, his face as confused as all the others. "Your father never mentioned an ailment. Are you well now?"

He faltered, his mouth too dry, his memories too raw for him to speak. Sadie stood, walking closer, but she couldn't reach him through the dense crowd. "I find," he managed to say, "it difficult to talk about."

"But you are back," Dr. Henry said, recovering his composure. "And we are glad to have you. Aren't we folks?"

The crowd cheered, but not as boisterously as before. They held back, unsure what to make of Otis and his cautious answers. Surely they expected a confident, boisterous Taylor like his father and brother had been. But he was his own man. For better or worse, he was a product of all he'd endured.

"To celebrate"—Dr. Henry slapped his back again—"you go and pick yourself a partner, anyone you want for the next number. Everyone be sure to visit the café. There's a feast in there tonight. Have fun, folks."

Any partner.

He didn't hesitate. He didn't look at anyone but her. The crowd parted for Otis as he stepped away from the platform. From the corner of his eye, he saw Alta flash a flirtatious smile, but he didn't turn or offer her one in return. It was Sadie he needed.

He bowed when he reached her and held out his hand. "Will you skate with me?"

"You're supposed to meet everyone else. You weren't even supposed to see me."

"I didn't hear Dr. Henry say that. I heard him say I got my choice of anyone in the room." He kept his hand outstretched. "I saw you in the crowd, in your stunning blue dress and mask, and I thought, *There is the woman I simply must have.*" She took his hand, and instantly he breathed easier. "You were going to hide in the shadows, but if I recall, we both agreed to do away with such nonsense."

It took her only a moment to fasten her latches, and then they began making their way around the circle, all eyes on them as they skated in their matching blue. Their movements were in perfect unison. Left, right, left.

"I didn't want to start rumors or be in the way," Sadie said.

"You heard me up there. Rumors are inevitable."

She squeezed his hand, leaned in, and whispered. "Once they really know you, they'll have only good things to say."

"Once I take this mask off, they may not care to really know me."

"Rule number nine." She kept her voice low, only for him. "Never care so much about the town that you are untrue to yourself. If they like you only with the mask, that's their fault. You must already know this, though, because you spoke truth up there with everyone watching. You did well."

"I was tempted to pull off my mask and be done with it all."

"You could have." She touched the edge of her own mask. "Do you suppose Mildred set out to make our costumes match?"

"I would not be surprised. It appears your family are also to blame. I do believe my tie and your dress are made of the same fabric."

"I didn't realize you were going to wear it tonight."

"I didn't realize you were going to come at all. I haven't seen you all day. I had hoped you would find me so I could play the song I wrote." He nodded his head at a couple who skated past them. "I want to be friends, and I'll be content with that. I'm glad you came tonight."

"I wasn't going to come, but I had to watch my favorite student. As for your gift, I intend to beg you to play it once the masquerade is over." She looked away and waved to Alta and the woman beside her, earning her a piercing glare. "Oh dear. Alta doesn't look pleased with me. I had hoped she would not recognize me."

He winced. "I may have mentioned that we'd skated before."

"Oh." Sadie's face went dark. "She will think I have been conspiring against her."

"Let's not worry over Alta right now. Look around." He let his gaze wander over the high ceiling, many windows, and rows of spectator seating. "We're at the Big Rink. Is it how you imagined?"

"The crowd, the music, my dress." She blushed. "It's all perfect. It's magical. I feel like a princess."

"A princess? No." He shook his head. "Remember, I've read every type of book. A princess leads a dull life, but you, you're an adventurer." He winked. "I don't think I've ever heard of a princess named Jane Squatter."

"I don't think I've ever heard of an adventurer named Jane Squatter." She laughed, and enchantment touched everything. He didn't need the rest of the world, only her, if she would have him. If she had not run from him in the barn, he would have been tempted to pull her close and kiss her rosy cheek with the entire crowd watching.

"When this song is over," Sadie said, "I'm going back to the mansion. Leon and Mildred did not want to stay long, and we will draw less attention to ourselves if I go. I'm afraid we look too comfortable together. Everyone will suspect that we are long acquainted."

"And if they do?"

"Otis, I work for you. This town has plenty of gossips. It won't do either of us any good if they think you've formed an attachment to your maid."

He nodded. He hadn't anticipated this moment when he'd asked her to keep his being in Monticello to herself, but he saw her reasoning, and he knew the importance of keeping appearances up as he readied for a legal battle over Elisabeth. "If you are going to leave, then let's at least enjoy this while we can."

They skated fast and to the rhythm of the music with smiles on their faces and their hands clasped together. He brought her in close before the song ended and whispered, "Thank you."

"For what?" she whispered back before stepping away.

"For choosing *my* factory."

She squeezed his hand, then rolled away from him without looking back.

With her gone he felt alone despite the crowd. The songs seemed longer and the minutes slower. His childhood friends asked after his health, as did his other skating partners, and though he did his best to give vague but honest answers, he could not shake the feeling of being a spectacle. One more song, and then he would leave.

"Are you looking at the door because you tire of our company?" Alta asked, skating toward him. His back was to the wall, making escape impossible. She rolled so close the toes of their shoes touched. "Won't you remove the mask before leaving so we can see your face and discover whether you resemble your father and brother?"

"It'll have to wait for another time."

She pursed her lips. A devilish twinkle in her eye sent warning alarms blaring, but he was too slow to heed it. Grabbing the corner of his mask, she tugged at it. His hat fell to the ground, and the mask came half off. She yanked harder.

"Stop!" he barked, drawing attention from the crowd. "You've no right."

"We only want to see you." One more tug and it was off.

The room fell silent. Frantically, he tried to cover his scarred scalp. He picked up his hat and put it on, but it was too late. Gasps from the audience told him they'd seen him. Wide-eyed, horrified, they stared at him, some with mouths agape, others murmuring. This was the moment he'd spent his life avoiding. A decade of hiding was not enough to keep it from happening.

"What's wrong with you?" Alta asked as she backed away from him.

"What's wrong with me?" He turned to the crowd, facing them fully. He was done hiding. *"Be honest,"* Sadie had told him. "Nothing is wrong. I have scars from life. Who doesn't?" His voice grew stronger and louder. "My father could not see past them. You may not be able to either. But here I am, Otis Taylor, returned."

He bowed, he turned, and he left.

Chapter 26

Otis slammed the door after entering the mansion, then leaned against it as he replayed the scene over and over in his mind. Sadie came rushing toward him.

"Otis—you're back." She skidded to a halt. "What happened? What did they do to you?"

He moved to the nearest chair, slumped into it, and buried his head in his hands. He'd faced the crowd, he'd seen their eyes, and he'd been honest. Now he felt weak. The moment he'd long feared had come and gone. There had been no stone throwing, no casting him out—he should feel relieved. Ten years in the making and it was over. Done.

She knelt in front of him and put her hands on his shoulders.

"Tell me," she said as her hand stroked his arm. "I want to hear. Share it with me."

He exhaled, regaining what composure he could. "Alta decided it was time for everyone to see my face." He ought to thank her. She'd forced the dreaded moment into existence. A cynical chuckle started in his tight chest and worked its way out. "She's a determined woman. When I refused, she tore off my mask."

"No." Sadie covered her mouth. Then, like a good doctor, aware of which medicine worked and which did not, she moved her hands from his shoulders to his scalp and gently ran her fingers across his ridged scars before leaning in and pressing her lips to his marked skin.

"I'm sorry," she whispered, and then she kissed his scalp again, letting her lips linger on the part of him he'd tried so hard to hide.

"Don't be." He kept his eyes closed, lost to her touch. "I wasn't brave enough, but now they know. They've seen me. It's over." He brought his head up and looked at her. "I gave up ten years because I was afraid. My father's voice . . ." He shook his head. "It was so strong for all those years, but now—"

She leaned her forehead against his. "Let go of his voice."

"I have. It's an echo of what it used to be. I wish I'd done it sooner." He put his hands on her face and ran his thumbs across her cheekbones. She didn't pull away or flinch at his touch. He brought her closer, searching for permission and finding acceptance in her eyes. He kissed her cheek, but he wanted to kiss her lips, to hold her and celebrate the demons he'd faced. "Sadie."

She pulled back, putting space between them. Not much, but enough that the intimacy of the moment faded. "Be brave, be honest—those were my rules."

"Yes, and they helped me. I heard your voice and your rules. Without you I'd still be hiding. The people of Monticello may not trust me, they may hate me and even cast me out, but I looked at them and knew I couldn't keep hiding. I don't want to hide ever again. Not when I've realized there is so much life I want to live."

"Otis, you followed the rules I made, but I have not."

"You don't love Marvin, if that's what this is about," he said, trying to keep the desperation from his voice. "You don't. He's a fantasy. A fairy tale that sounds romantic, but it's not what you really want."

"I know I don't. I don't love Marvin. I think I've known for a long time, but waiting for him was a habit. I clung to it because I was afraid of letting it go, but it was never real."

"If you don't love him, then—"

"Otis, Marvin is not the problem. If he ever finds time to see me"—she wiped at her eyes—"I'll ask after his schooling and then wish him well." Her laugh was a soft, breathless sound. "I have tasted something so much sweeter. I could never—he's not the one for me."

"Sadie." An urgency to speak the unspoken burned in his heart. "I have never cared for anyone the way I care for you." He reached for her hand. "I want to court you, and when you tell me it's been long enough, I want to marry you." He brought a knuckle to his mouth, stopping himself. "I shouldn't say it, I should wait, but it's true."

With tears glistening in her eyes, she shook her head back and forth. "I can't. You don't understand. I haven't been brave or honest."

"Tell me."

"I know something," she said at last. "I know where Elisabeth is."

Otis sat up straight and stiff, his arms and hands pulled far from her. She wanted them back, but the truth could no longer be hidden. He deserved to know, no matter the cost to her, and the knowledge could no longer be buried under the guise of compassion.

"What? Where is she?"

"Otis, it's not so simple—"

"How could you keep this from me?"

Because I care. Because I am falling in love with you, and I don't want to hurt you or anyone else. She kept her mouth closed, despite the many things she wanted him to understand. When she reached out to touch his arm, he pulled away.

"My friends Peter and Nina have a little girl named Bessy. I have known her since they took her in. She was so small when she arrived." Nothing but a frail bird. Skittish and dirty. "She was so afraid. But now . . ."

He said nothing, but he didn't have to for her to know that he hung on her words.

"A family was going west and decided to leave the orphan they took care of behind. I don't believe it was handled properly, but not because Peter or Nina wished harm on anyone. They'd never taken in an orphan before. They believed what they were told." She sucked in her bottom lip. "Otis—" She reached again for his arm. He didn't pull away this time, but he didn't meet her gaze. "Peter and Nina only ever knew her as Bessy. They knew nothing of her past, only that she needed a home. When they saw your post in the newspaper, they were distraught over it. They don't know that you are the man behind the query. I didn't tell them—"

"You didn't tell me either."

"I'm so sorry. I didn't know at first. But then when I saw Bessy's eyes, I knew." She'd wronged him. The realization hit her so hard the wind left her chest. This man she cared for so deeply was suffering because she'd believed him unable to choose what to do with the truth. He deserved to be trusted, and she'd let him down. "I was wrong to keep it from you. I made a mistake, but I hated hurting them. And I hated hurting you. I want to bury it and just go on as we were."

"Elisabeth is mine to care for. I am her rightful guardian. I can't bury that."

"I know." And she did. She'd seen him sand and oil the old rocking horse and listened to him beg for advice on being a good father. Obligation was not his motivation. Love and family were. "But Peter and Nina . . ."

"They will have to understand. I don't want to hurt them, but I won't turn my back on my kin."

"What of Elisabeth? All she knows is the love of Peter and Nina."

"She's a child. She's not old enough to understand how family works. When she is older, she will."

Sadie nodded. It was not her choice to make, and for that she was glad. Her whole life she'd been taught about right and wrong. Good and evil. But there had been no lectures, no sermons, on the conflict of good versus good. Peter versus Otis. They were not enemies, and yet in this moment they were pitted against each other. There could be no compromise. Someone would win and someone would lose.

"I should have told you." She backed toward the door, ready to retreat and escape the look of betrayal she saw in his eyes. "This town may not have seen past your scars tonight, but they will. You're a good man, Otis Taylor. A very good one."

Chapter 27

Otis watched her blue dress sway as she left. She'd known about Elisabeth and not told him. The revelation left him treading water, searching for land. He didn't know how to reconcile the woman he'd come to care for and the one who'd kept the truth from him. Was she a fraud? A turncoat?

When the restless rumbling of uncertainty and confusion persisted, he went to the music room, sat on the hard wooden bench, and played.

He played a triumphant song, declaring himself free of his father's chains.

He played a tumultuous song for himself, for Peter and Nina, and for Elisabeth.

And for Sadie, he played a song of ambiguity that soared and fell and soared again, not sure what it was or where it led.

There were no songs for Reginald. What he felt for Reginald could not be soothed by a song. Reginald's carelessness forced Otis into the villain role. Because of him, Otis would have to take Bessy from Peter and Nina. Because of his brother, Sadie was forced to have torn loyalties.

Reginald. Otis gritted his teeth, pushed away from the piano, and stormed to his brother's room. With each step he added wood to his already raging fire. Only moments before, when Sadie's hands had been on him, he'd felt free of his anger, soaring high above the past. But now it was there again, knocking at the door, begging to come in and take up residence and mark the future in the same way it had marked the past.

Ten years stolen from his life.

Wasted.

Otis yanked open the dresser drawers and rifled through them, throwing what was left of Reginald's belongings on the floor. Then he let the drawers themselves fall to the floor, caring little for the chaos he left in his wake. He needed to find something, anything, that explained why this was happening. His breath came fast and rapid. There had to be something he'd missed.

He turned the mattress over. Nothing was there save the driving force, the uncontrollable desire to understand why Reginald had left such a disaster for him to deal with.

Sweat beaded his forehead as he yelled, "You did this!"

A childish urge to throw something took over, and he gave in. What was there to lose? Reginald had already ruined everything. He grabbed the sides of the painting on the wall, ready to throw it on the ground, only to have it resist his pull.

Disarmed and confused, he stopped. He took a step back. What was he doing? There was no solace here. His brother would never again set foot in this room. No matter how much he wanted to retaliate, it was too late.

"Dear God," he whispered, standing in the sea of disarray, a desperate plea for calm amid the storm. In crept a stillness that slowly pushed at the pain. His mind began to clear. Soon his breath and pulse returned to their steady rhythm.

The painting that had stuck tight and defied him now beckoned him. He pulled it again, not in a violent rage but with intent. It held tight. He pulled from the left. Nothing. Then he pulled from the right and it creaked on stiff hinges, revealing a hidden compartment. He inhaled sharply, staring at the discovery.

This was monumental, and he wanted to share it. Foolish though it may be, after only just learning of her betrayal, he wanted Sadie beside him. Deep down he knew she was not a villain. She'd wronged him, it was true, but she'd also stood by him many times, and he wanted her beside him now.

Without investigating further, he raced for her room and pounded on her door.

She opened it wearing a thin dressing gown over her nightdress, her eyes swollen and glistening with tears. Her hair was long and loose.

"I'm sorry," he sputtered. "I didn't mean to disturb you."

"You banged on my door. I thought there was a fire."

"No fire." He looked away. "I'm sorry, I don't know what came over me. I wasn't thinking."

"You're here. What is it?"

"Well . . ." He grabbed her hand and pulled her down the hall. "I was in Reginald's room. I don't know what I was after. I was feeling angry that he left so many problems . . . I was out of my head, but . . . well, I found something."

"You did? What?"

"A hiding place. I don't know what's in it. I didn't want to look without you. I did everything by myself for so long." He stopped pulling her along, let go of her hand, and rubbed the back of his neck. "I don't like that you kept Elisabeth's whereabouts from me, but . . . I think I understand. I kept thinking about Peter and Nina—that's why I was so angry. I don't want to cause them pain." He rubbed his chest. It hurt. There was so much to feel. He couldn't keep up with it all. "Can we declare another truce? I want you to come with me, and later we can sort out who is at fault and who owes whom an apology. Will you come with me?"

"Yes." She wiped at the corner of her eye with the edge of her sleeve. "I want to come."

He held his hand out this time, letting her choose to take it. She didn't hesitate. Her small hand slid into his. With shoeless feet they were nearly silent on the wooden floors as they scurried toward his discovery. Did all friendships make you feel this way—vulnerable, infuriated, but drawn to each other in the very same instance? "We are a sorry pair, aren't we? Always apologizing."

"Always . . . forgiving?"

Rather than say something he might regret, he kept her hand in his and silently led her through the rest of the house to Reginald's room.

"You did this?" she asked after surveying the mess. He cringed, seeing the room through her eyes. Clothes spread about, limp and disheveled. Drawers on the floor and the mattress askew.

"You once told me it was good to feel things."

"Not like this." She picked up a pillow and tossed it on the bed.

"I'm not proud of it. I just wanted to find something that would make it all make sense. I wasn't thinking."

"Sometimes I want to throw all the feathers at the factory at Alta. She makes me so angry."

"I think you should."

"And I think it's okay that you've struggled to make peace with Reginald's death."

He stepped to the painting and pointed. "I tried to throw this."

"It's a terrible painting."

He looked closer at it, seeing for the first time the muted colors. It featured a woman with a broad face, small eyes, and a mouth too large to seem real. In her arms she held a baby in a most dangerous fashion. "It is quite awful. But look." He pulled on the side of the painting and the hinges creaked. "Come and see."

Inside the frame was a wooden box, ten inches tall with no remarkable markings. "It's locked," he said when the top would not open. "Wait here."

He left, returning in a hurry with the once hidden key in hand. "I found this but never knew what it went to."

"What do you suppose he was hiding?"

"Something that will right all his wrongs." Sarcasm laced his voice, but in his heart, he hoped.

"That won't be found in a box," she said.

"You're right. I know you are." He slid the key into the opening and twisted. "It fits."

Their heads came together above the box. Neither spoke as he lifted the lid, letting the contents see light for the first time in at least a year. There were letters, a jar of buttons, and a bag of marbles—trinkets.

"I didn't picture your brother as a sentimental man," Sadie said. "I imagined him as a cold businessman who did whatever pleased him."

He picked up the bag of marbles, loosened the string, and poured the colorful glass into his hand. Blue, red, green. They clanked together, playing the tune of childhood. "These were mine. Reginald and our school friends used to trade them. I couldn't find them the day I left. Reggie helped me look for them, but they weren't anywhere. He said he'd keep them for me when he found them. Playing marbles . . ." He choked on his words. "It was mindless—frivolous if you will—but I missed it when I was alone."

"And the buttons?"

"They were my mama's. She would accompany our father when he traveled for business. When she returned, she would show us the buttons she'd found. I never understood why she enjoyed them, but for her, finding buttons was like digging for gold. She was always looking for unusual ones."

Sadie took the jar of buttons and rolled it back and forth so she could look at the myriad colors. "These are beautiful. Look at this one." She held the jar toward him. "A hand-carved horse. It's a work of art."

"I didn't know you had an affinity for buttons."

"My time at the duster factory has made me more aware of how things are created. Take a duster, for example. It's made of feathers and wood, which seems simple enough, but effort is put into each one. The hub and the handle are lathed and sanded, and the feathers are sorted. Some feathers are dyed, and they're all wound with care. Someone made these buttons too."

"And now I will never look at a duster or button the same." He'd waited to examine the letters last. With Reginald dead, these letters may very well be the last clue he ever had to his brother's character. "Read these with me?"

"Yes."

He looked around the room. Sitting on the disheveled bed seemed wrong. "Let's go to the music room."

"It's my favorite room." She followed him away from the chaos he'd made of Reginald's room.

Once settled on the piano bench, he tore open the first letter, only to find his name written on the top. "It's to me."

"Does it have a date?"

He nodded his head. "He wrote this right after my father died."

"What does it say?"

Otis read aloud.

> Dear Otis,
>
> Father wouldn't let me write you. I should have written anyway, but you know how father was, always in command. He said my writing you would only make you want to come back, when what you needed was to focus on your music. I don't know whether that's true. I don't know what to think anymore. I don't even know how to go about my life without him. I have made a few decisions to spite him, to prove to myself that I am my own man, but even those have come back to torment me.
>
> We were brothers once. We still are, but I don't know you anymore. It doesn't seem right, our being apart for so many years. The factory is still making wheels and bicycles. I'm running it now. And managing all of father's investments. It's what I've always known I would do, but it feels hollow now. I'm like a puppet, but now I have no puppeteer.

"That's all." He stared at the blank bottom of the paper. "He didn't finish it."

"His words make him sound lonely and full of regret." Sadie took the letter from him. "He missed you. He kept the marbles, and he wanted to write you."

"I only knew of my father's death because Leon wrote. If only Reginald had mailed his letter . . ."

"It might have all been different." Sadie finished his thought. "But he wrote this much of a letter, and even though he never sent it, you can choose to accept it as an offering of reconciliation." She scooted closer. "He made mistakes—Lord knows he made a great many. But look," she said, touching the marbles. "He was not all bad. Your brother thought of you. That means something."

"It does mean something," he said softly. "And now it is up to me to take care of his daughter and settle what he left unfinished."

He looked at the other letters in his hand, torn between wanting more and wanting to sit with Reginald's words.

"Another?" he asked, wanting her to carry the burden of choice.

"Do *you* want to read another?" she asked, giving the decision back to him.

"I'm not sure. These letters are the last of Reginald's words. Once I read the contents . . . that will be all."

She pulled something from her pocket. Paper. The moment she unfolded it, he knew it was the song he'd composed. "Save the letters," she said. "Take your time with them. Play this instead."

He didn't want to play it. It'd been composed when everything felt simpler and blossoming feelings of love blinded him. But he nodded, and soon the air rang with hopeful, joyous notes. A melody that so perfectly captured the feelings of affection grown during their time together. He closed his eyes. As he played, he saw their first encounter in the old factory, them skating arm in arm, exploring the attic, walking her family's land. A bouquet of little moments. With the last note still hanging in the air, he turned to see her, but she'd gone.

Silence and emptiness filled the place she'd been.

> . . . I have never witnessed so much in one night. I heard tales of bravery in the form of a man telling the crowd the truth, knowing they might cast him out. I saw tears of loss and pain. I saw love played into the notes of a song. My heart is full, and yet I wonder if this could ever be mine or if it will all be something to remember as what might have been. . . .

Chapter 28

Sadie walked through the Hoag factory doors five minutes before her assigned shift began, head low, doing her best to go unseen. Otis hadn't told her to go, but he hadn't told her to stay either, and so she'd quietly walked to the factory without so much as a hello to anyone at the mansion. She was prepared to work but not ready for small talk or gossip.

Otis's song had stirred her very soul. It had been beautiful beyond words. Even now, if she was still, she could hear it. She'd walked away, too overcome by it, too aware that if he did not forgive her for keeping a secret—if she was not able to watch him and Elisabeth without forever feeling Nina and Peter's pain—it could all be lost.

"She's here," she heard Sylvia whisper to Alta. "Sadie!"

She took a deep breath before saying, "Hello, Sylvia."

"Why didn't you tell us he was bald and mutilated?" Alta joined them like a panther ready to pounce. "Did you think it was funny, keeping a secret like that from me? I've never been so embarrassed in my entire life. It was a cruel joke."

Such meaningless pettiness. "It wasn't a joke."

"If you were our friend, you would have told us." Alta made a face of disgust. "I was horrified."

Sadie's mouth fell open. How dare she. "You should not have pulled his mask off. How dare you."

Alta straightened. "You need to go back to the country, and he should go back to wherever he came from. You're both frauds, and this town doesn't need you."

"This town is as much his as it is yours."

"No." Alta gritted her teeth. "You're wrong and you both should be ashamed of yourselves for your embarrassing display. Your matching outfits—he didn't just arrive for the masquerade; you know him. You act innocent, but you've been there living with him. It's wrong and you know it."

"I work there." She stood her ground. "You should stop judging everyone else and look at your own flaws. A man with scars . . . how could you be so harsh?"

Alta smirked. "Have you fallen in love with that monster?"

"Don't say that." She was a lion ready to fight. "Don't ever say that again."

Alta's nose wrinkled up. "We all saw him."

"You've never really seen him," she growled, not caring about the onlookers. The well-oiled gears of the factory stopped turning. They were the break in the cogs. She'd not been there to stand beside Otis the night before, when his mask came off. But in front of these forty people she could and she would speak up. "If you laughed at him last night, then you ought to question your character, not his, because—"

She stopped herself. Sylvia and Alta wore smug expressions, as though they'd won. She couldn't spend another moment sorting beside Alta. She needed to leave. "Excuse me," she said and stepped away, heading for the door.

"You can't just leave," Alta said to her back. "What about your father? Or did you lie about him too?"

She stopped. She couldn't leave. Her father was on the road to recovery, but he wasn't there yet.

"Go." Mr. Hoag's voice filled the air.

Her stomach dropped. The loss of her job could prove devastating.

"That's what you get." Alta's snide, triumphant voice added injury to her already wounded spirit.

"No," Mr. Hoag said. "You go."

Sadie gasped. Mr. Hoag was pointing at Alta and then the door. Alta's face grew red and blotchy. "But I—"

"I've had enough complaints about you. After last night I've seen for myself what your behavior is like. Gather your things and go."

The factory workers watched in silence as Alta balked and then did as she'd been told, cursing as she went. The glare she directed at Sadie was piercing, but Sadie's conscience was clear. She'd done the right thing, and it was time to do the right thing again.

"Mr. Hoag," she said.

"Yes."

"I have to go. I need to set some things right. I understand if I can't keep my job . . . but I'd like to come back when I can."

"You've worked hard." He looked tired but smiled. "I can't save your position. But when you return, come and talk to me, and I'll let you know if there's an opening. If there's not, I'll be happy to give you a recommendation."

Sadie thanked him. And though it was hard to walk away knowing that her job might not be there, she knew she had to leave. Thankfully, Otis had paid the doctor's bills, and the harvest was well on its way. Above all else, she was thankful that her father was finally on the mend. Still, a surge of fear threatened her resolve. But nothing could be set right if she did not tell the truth.

She reentered the mansion through the back door, careful not to be seen. Wolf liked to lie in the parlor, where the warm sun first came through the windows, and she hoped he was there now, far enough away that she could come and go unnoticed.

In her room she paused long enough to scrawl a letter to Otis and pack her few belongings. Then, with soft feet, she crept to the music room, leaving her note where she knew Otis would find it.

⚜

Feather dusters, no doubt, were important. No one wanted a layer of dirt on their mantel or window frames, but he still hated them. If not for the duster factory, Sadie would be here, and they could sit across from each other and discuss her secret keeping, as well as the letters he'd found and not yet read. After enough talking, surely they would close whatever distance remained between them. After all, they were allies fighting on the same side. What good would it do to hold a grudge longer than necessary? To hate Sadie was to punish himself.

He'd not seen her since she left him in the music room the night before. He needed to know why, but she'd gone to the blasted feather duster factory, leaving him to watch the clock as he waited for her to return. What was he to do for the next nine hours?

The nursery was set up for Elisabeth's arrival, Reginald's accounts were at last sorted, and Wolf had followed Leon outside to trim the shrubbery. He looked at the marbles he'd found in Reginald's room. Soon enough he would play them with Elisabeth.

Elisabeth. He smiled. She would be his family, even if Sadie could not accept his decision to step in and do his duty. He would not be alone. He would be needed and important in the eyes of a child, and if he had to, he would be content with that. They would be inseparable as he raised and doted on her, giving her the care she required and the love she needed to thrive.

On his desk sat the other letters he'd found. If he read very slowly, he could pass at least half an hour reading letters and be that much closer to Sadie's return.

The first he tore open was a letter to Reginald from a businessman. Without knowing more about Reginald and his past, it meant little to Otis, and though he was willing to go slow and ponder on it, there was nothing to be gleaned from it.

His hand shook with the opening of the next letter. It was not written in Reginald's hand, but instead it was addressed to him, from Katie.

Dear Reginald,

Our love was a spring flower that didn't last long enough. I don't know if you even think of it as love, but I always have. It must have been at least a type of love, because this beautiful girl, our daughter, came of it. I tried to tell you when we were last together, and I began many letters once I left, but I was so afraid. You have so much ambition, I could not bear the thought of slowing you down or burdening you with shame.

My circumstances have changed. I can only pray that you will not see Elisabeth as a burden but as a gift. Look at her dimpled cheek and her eyes. I believe they are Taylor eyes. I have stared at them every second I can, but now I must make the hardest decision I have ever made.

My parents have forced me to keep the baby a secret. They've told everyone I am ill. Now that she is born, they are busy making plans to send her to a foundling home. If she goes, I will never know what has become of her, and I will have no way of ensuring she is safe. I cannot bear the thought of never seeing her again. My parents refuse to help me raise her. I have no means to care for her and nowhere to go or man to call upon to provide a name and home for us.

I looked at her this morning and my heart felt full, ready to burst with love. I ran my fingers over her soft skin, and then I told her that I would do everything I could to give her a beautiful life, even if it shattered my heart to do so. I want her to be loved.

I have convinced our maid to take Elisabeth to you. I don't want to ask anything of you, and I would not for myself, but for Elisabeth I will swallow what little pride I have left, and I will beg.

Reginald, I beg you to give her love. I beg of you to tell her that I love her. Tell her that I did not kiss her cheek and watch her ride from my life for any reason except that I had to try to give her something better. Tell her that what I have done is an act of love—the hardest, most painful act of love, but that for her I would do anything. Keep her safe and cherished.

Forgive me,
Katie

Such bravery. Such love. Otis sat back in his seat, tipped his head back, and stared at the ceiling. Reginald, Katie, Elisabeth . . . there were pieces of their puzzle he would never know. What had Reginald done when he'd found himself the father of an infant daughter? Had his father ever known? He wanted answers, but they were not to be had. His actions alone were all he had power over.

I'll bring her home, he vowed, wishing he could look Katie in the eyes and tell her that he would honor her request to speak of her with kindness and to tell Elisabeth as she grew that love and selflessness often came at a grievous cost.

He shoved the faded letter into his pocket and went for a horse, stopping only to put the long-forgotten sack of marbles in his pocket—his first gift to his little girl. Then he stepped away from the house, bound for Peter and Nina's, emboldened by Katie's words. He would return with Elisabeth. It was time to bring her home.

Chapter 29

Otis shifted his weight, trying to find a comfortable way to sit in the saddle. He had enough riding experience to feel competent but not enough to feel completely at ease. The long ride to Peter and Nina's gave him ample time to think about what lay ahead. He could only hope Katie's letter would ease the pain that Peter and Nina were sure to feel. It was all he could offer, the mother's plea for her daughter and his promise to fulfill it. As for Sadie, surely she would understand that it was his responsibility to stand in Reginald's place and give Elisabeth a better life.

He urged the horse to go faster, grateful he'd paid attention to the landscape when he'd gone to visit Sadie, and that their many conversations had included talk of her closest neighbors. The nearer he got, the more aware he was of the magnitude of his mission. His stomach clenched, not with doubt but with pain for the soft-spoken Peter who had brought letters back and forth between Otis and Sadie, and for the good man's wife, who was a friend to Sadie. Tonight he would kiss his niece's cheek, and they would have an empty bed and a hole in their hearts.

He slowed his horse as he neared his destination. He slid off and tied the reins to a fence, deciding to take the rest of the journey on foot. The dusty road leading to the modest home was long and full of furrows. He ambled slowly, imagining what life at the Tippinses' home was like. Theirs was a small, humble farm, one that, according to Sadie, had always failed to thrive financially. But by all accounts, it was a happy home.

A lone tree waved in the breeze to the right of the house. Its leaves rustled in the wind, but it was the swing that drew his gaze. Someone had climbed the limbs of the mighty oak and hung a seat for a child.

"Papa," a small voice rang through the air. "Papa, I'll find you."

Otis stared. A girl, no higher than a half-grown cornstalk, stepped onto the yard, her flaxen hair braided and her face round and rosy. "One, two, three . . ."

Music. Her voice was music to his ears. A babyish inflection touched each word as she shouted out her numbers. "I'm going now!" She giggled as she ran across the yard with her arms pumping at her sides. She looked behind the tree and then pushed the swing as she ran past. The grin on her face never faltered as she ran to the porch and looked under it. "Where are you?"

She put her hands on her hips and looked around. Her hair whipped across her face only to be pushed behind her ear by plump little fingers. Each movement she made captivated him. She was beautiful. Breathtaking. She switched directions and ran again, her legs bringing her right to him.

Unsure what to do, he waited. She came so close he could see the blue of her eyes. "Taylor eyes," Katie had called them, and she'd been correct. Sadie had seen it too. He and this child were not strangers—they were family. Her pace slowed, and then she stopped. "I'm lookin' for my papa." She smiled. "He's hidin'."

He cleared his throat and bent down so he could look into the face of his family, embodied in one perfect child. Tears welled in his eyes, and happiness like nothing he had ever known overwhelmed him. He wasn't alone. Not anymore.

"Did you see 'im?"

Otis shook his head. His words, like so many times before, failed him. All he could do was stare and feel.

"I'll find him," she said, her mouth pulling into an impish grin, "or Mama will help."

When he still did not speak, she came closer and patted him on the arm. "I like your hat," she said, then turned around and ran back, shouting for her papa. Otis touched the brim of his hat. He'd been afraid she would fear him, but she'd touched his arm and smiled at him. They'd get on all right. How could they not, when he already felt taken with her?

"I found you." He saw Elisabeth point behind a wheelbarrow. Peter laughed as he stood. Then he picked up the little girl and tickled her, earning him a bout of giggles. A woman, Nina, stepped off the porch and walked to the man. Her shoulders looked heavy, but she smiled for the little girl.

"Come inside—I've made you cookies," she said.

"There's a man here." Elisabeth pointed toward him, and no matter how softly he planted his feet, he could no longer watch unnoticed. "He has a big hat."

Otis waved and walked toward them. The inevitable moment had come. "Hello, there."

Nina looked at her husband. He put a hand on her back. "Welcome, Otis." Elisabeth rested her head on Peter's shoulder. "Sadie came by earlier. She said you'd be coming sometime. She didn't know when."

"She was here?"

"About a half hour ago. You only just missed her. She went on to her house to see her sisters."

"Did she—"

"Yes." Peter patted Elisabeth's back, a gentle, reassuring tap. "Can we talk without Bessy here? We tried to explain, but—"

"I don't wanna go. I wanna stay with you." She wrapped her arms tighter around Peter's neck.

"Come here, dear. Let's go and have those cookies I made." Nina's voice trembled. She reached for Elisabeth, who looked at everyone before falling into Nina's arms and burying her head in Nina's shoulder.

Peter didn't speak, his attention fully on Elisabeth until she was in the house and out of earshot. When he turned back, the furrow of his brows was deeper.

Otis reached for Katie's letter, clinging in desperation to his resolve. Without even having to read it, he heard the words. *"Tell her that what I have done is an act of love—the hardest, most painful act of love, but that for her I would do anything."*

"We didn't know." Peter turned away from the house. "No one told us about Reginald or you. We were told she was an orphan who needed a home. I should have known it was all too simple. We didn't mean to do anything wrong."

"I know," Otis said. Katie's words continued to clamor in his thoughts. She'd wanted Reginald to give their daughter a loving home, acceptance, and a future. She'd let Elisabeth go and had done the most selfless thing she could, all for the love of the child. "Had I known sooner, I would have come. I never would have let her suffer, and I—"

He cut himself off and ran a hand over his jaw. It was true, he would have come. He would have faced any fear, any obstacle in his way, to get to her. But he hadn't known. Due to no fault of his own, he'd been oblivious to the fact that he was an uncle with a niece in need.

Peter looked back toward the house. "I'm real sorry," he said in a soft voice. "She was so scrawny, so scared, I didn't think to look for family. I just believed what Ned told me. When I saw her and the sorry state she was in, all I worried about was bringing her home and getting her settled and fed." His jaw flexed. "Now she calls us Papa and Mama."

"Tell her that what I have done is an act of love—the hardest, most painful act of love, but that for her I would do anything."

The words grew louder, like a firehouse bell, clanging until someone listened. His father left him, abandoned him, because it was the easiest thing for his father. It'd been selfish, not an act of love but of ease. The wound had been deep, leaving scars and remorse, nights of tears and regrets.

Elisabeth burst from the door, her short legs carrying her as she jumped over dirt mounds and ran full speed ahead. "No!" she shouted. "I don't wanna go. Papa, don't make me."

Peter scooped up the little girl in his arms and buried his face in her hair. "I'm sorry," he said, holding her the way Otis had yearned to be held as a boy and the way he'd imagined cradling his niece. Peter, lean and long, was a pillar of strength, reassuring Elisabeth with words of courage and comfort. "Don't be afraid."

Tears threatened to come. He knew what he had to do. His chest ached in anticipation of the words he was about to say and the dreams that would die because of them. He *would not* abandon Elisabeth like his father had abandoned him.

"Bessy," he said, using the name she was familiar with, "I can tell you love your mama and papa."

She nodded her small head, her blue eyes finding his. They were so like his own and like Reginald's had been. There was no denying the blood they shared.

"Good," he smiled, despite the ever-growing pain. "I rode out here to give you these." He pulled the marbles from his pocket. "They were mine when I was young, and they need someone to play with them now. Would you like that?"

She reached her hand out. "I'll play with 'em."

"Oh good," he said, wanting to touch the child's fair hair and wrap her in love. "There's a shooter in there that used to win me all sorts of marbles."

She pried the bag open and peered inside. "I like the red one."

"That was my favorite too." He tore his gaze from her, afraid his courage would fail him and he'd choose the self-serving route. Nothing had ever required as much courage as this moment, but for Katie and for Bessy he would say what needed saying. "I would . . . I would like to talk to a lawyer and see what needs to be done so that you can forever be Bessy's parents. I will cover any costs, and I want you to know that you have my blessing. She is where she needs to be."

Nina, who had been on the porch, fell to her knees and sobbed into her hands. Otis couldn't look. It hurt too much.

"Mama," Bessy said.

"Shhh," Peter cooed. "Mama's all right." Peter sucked in a rapid breath, tightened his arms around his daughter, and asked, "Are you sure?"

"I believe it's what her first mama wanted." He told them about the letter, using careful words so as not to confuse Bessy. Speaking was difficult. The words stuck in his throat, but he persevered, believing this course the hardest but most correct choice. "For Katie's sake, I ask that you tell her that her first mama loved her too."

"I will, and I'll never let her forget the love of her uncle," Peter said. They invited him to stay and dine with them, but he couldn't. The decision hurt too much, robbing him of his appetite and leaving him weak and eager to wrestle with the aftermath in private.

"I best be going," he said before walking back to his horse, the sun beating against his back and the road ahead a lonely one. The agony did not change his mind; it only confirmed that his choice, hard as it was, had come from a place of love.

⚜

Two days had passed since coming home, and Sadie still did not feel at peace. She sat beside the bed her father had so long convalesced in. He was still in Des Moines, recovering from his surgery, but here, where she'd seen him last, she felt closer to him. If only he were here now. She would take his hand and tell him all her troubles. Voicing her faults was never easy, but she knew he would listen and then give her advice. If he were here, she'd tell him how she kept Elisabeth's whereabouts to herself and how she'd hurt a man she deeply cared for.

It had been with a heavy heart that she'd told her neighbors about their daughter. They'd cried, and though she knew it was not a malicious act for Otis to take his niece, she'd come home to let Otis and Elisabeth settle into their life together without her in the way. Unsure where she would stay if she returned to Monti, she'd remained with her sisters, helping with the crops and stitching handkerchiefs to sell. Their funds were still tight, but hope was on the horizon, thanks to their father's recovery and their beautifully growing harvest.

"Sadie." Violette popped her head through the doorway. "I rode over to the Warners' to deliver eggs. She showed me the newspaper."

Sadie left the sickroom and hurried to Violette's side. "What is it?"

"There's a letter to the editor. Alta wrote it." Violette handed her the paper. "Mrs. Warner let me take it so I could show you."

Sadie searched the page, skimming over advertisements for miracle cures, job listings, a notice about an upcoming Independence Day celebration, and then, there it was.

> Dear Editor and Citizens of Monticello,
>
> As a lifelong resident of this prosperous town, I find it is my responsibility to speak up and help keep our community a wholesome place. It has come to my attention that a recently returned bachelor, one we all anticipated and revered as an upstanding citizen, is in fact of low moral character. He was seduced by the likes of a country lass who stayed under his roof for some time, and it is believed that they have been living a life of iniquity together. It is our responsibility to weed such refuse from our town.
>
> Sincerely,
> Alta Brewer

Sadie sank into the nearest chair. Alta had always been changeable and selfish, but Sadie had never imagined her to be so spiteful and mean-spirited as this.

"What do I do?"

"I may love gossip, but when it's nothing but lies, I say you just tear it to bits and throw it in the fire." Violette reached for the paper, ready to do the act herself, but Sadie pulled the paper away from her.

"That won't fix anything. Some people will always hate Otis. They'll never stop to see him, and I can't change that. But I have to do something. It's not right for her to damage his reputation or mine like this." She gritted her teeth, thinking of Katie and Elisabeth, of the judgments and fear that had shaped the course of so many lives. "This is wrong." She waved the paper in the air. "This could hurt people who need to be loved, not shunned." She stood, and as it had at the factory, her voice grew strong. "I will write the editor myself."

"I hope Otis reads it and knows you're sorry and that your heart is his." Violette sighed.

"I left him a letter explaining where I went and my feelings. He hasn't written back or come calling. I'm going to write the editor because it's the right thing to do, not because I expect anything else from him."

Violette humphed. "I still hope he sees it."

Chapter 30

Dear Citizens of Monticello,

I feel compelled to write a response to a letter that was published in the last paper by a Miss Alta Brewer. I am the country lass she referred to, who came to Monticello to find work. Upon arrival, I did find work at the Hoag factory, a job that kept my family fed and helped us endure a season of challenge. I also discovered a town with beautiful shops, churches, and skating rinks.

During my months in Monticello, I learned about the people, discovering both kind hearts and chin-wagging gossips. I learned that we can be too quick to judge someone's appearance or to shame someone because of a mistake. I saw the pain and fruits of such actions.

Most relevant to the previous letter is my relationship with Otis Taylor. I did indeed get to know him, though never in the way described by

Miss Brewer. What I discovered was a man whose history many of you are familiar with: the son of a wealthy businessman and the brother to Monticello's once favorite bachelor. He is those things, but he is more than his family name. He is a man with a big heart who carries scars from the cruel deeds of others, and a man who came home but was not welcomed how he ought to have been.

I have seen beneath the scars, and if you would but look, you would see that Otis Taylor is the finest Taylor ever to set foot in Monticello. If you drive him away, you will lose an asset and friend.

The last letter said this town needed to weed out refuse, but the author was wrong. We need to rally around one another. Never again should we fail when a son or daughter of Monticello comes home. If you were one who looked with distaste or who believed idle rumors, ask yourself why and then make amends. The Monticello that I want to believe in does better than that.

Yours truly,
Sadie West

It sounds very good, and it ought to make everyone who turned up their noses at Otis stop and think." Molly set the paper aside. "Why haven't you gone to see him? It's been days now."

"I would," Sadie said, picking at her fingernail, "but I left a letter. If he doesn't want to see me, then I have to respect his wishes."

Molly frowned. "He wrote plenty of letters to Jane Squatter. I would have expected him to write, even if only to say he was not interested in further . . . courting, or whatever it was the two of you were doing."

"I thought he would too." She sighed. "He might be too distraught over his decision to let Bessy stay."

"You said yourself that it was the right choice."

Peter and Nina had come over three nights ago with tears of gratitude running down their faces as they told of Otis's generous act. Bessy had even asked everyone to play marbles with her. Sadie had been relieved, but then she'd thought of Otis in his big house with the freshly sanded and oiled rocking horse, void of a rider, and she'd felt his loss.

"The right thing can still hurt," Sadie said. "He loved her before he ever met her. He would have been a good father to her. I hate thinking about what his choice must have done to him. He spent so much of his life alone, and now he's alone again."

"You're worried about him, aren't you?"

"I am." She paced the room. "I've given up my job at the feather duster factory. I can't show up at his house and beg to live under his roof when I have no reason to be in Monti. Besides, there isn't enough cleaning to justify my working all day at the mansion."

"And so you just wait? Like you did for Marvin? Are you going to waste two years on Otis too?"

She groaned. "Marvin was a fantasy. I built him up to be something more than he was, but Otis is real. I love him."

"Love?"

"Yes, I didn't see it at first, but it's love. I know it is."

Molly grabbed Sadie by the shoulders, making it impossible to do anything but look into each other's eyes. "Sadie West, follow me to the barn. I believe we need to get the rest of our little brood together. It's time for us to make a plan."

Chapter 31

Otis meandered through the bright mansion. Every curtain was open, letting the sunlight in and changing the ambience of the once gloomy prison. It'd been over a week since the masquerade, and he'd seen no sign of Sadie other than the letter to the editor. Her strong words moved him and left him completely unsure why she'd defended him and deserted him. But they'd been kind words that soothed his pain like ice on a bruise. Not curing it but easing it.

Once he put distance between himself and Monticello, he'd be able to start driving thoughts of Sadie from his mind and heart . . . somehow. It would take time, that much he knew.

"Is there anything else that you want to keep?" Leon closed the large trunk full of heirlooms Otis had decided were worth saving.

"No. Sell the rest with the house."

"Are you sure this is what you want?"

Otis shrugged. He wasn't thrilled about his plan, but it made sense. Sadie was gone, and Elisabeth didn't need him. "I came here with the intention of selling. It's time. I've handled Reginald's affairs. There's nothing left for me here."

"You've done well." Leon patted him on the shoulder. "I was proud of you as a boy, and I'm proud of you now." He pulled his handkerchief from his pocket and wiped his large nose. "Your mama would be proud too. She'd say that you know more about love than most of us."

"I couldn't take Elisabeth," he said, thinking of the way Elisabeth had looked at Peter. "I wanted to."

"You could have if you were a more selfish man. You had the right to." He wiped at the corner of his eye. "You're a good man."

"If you could see inside, you might not think so. I wanted her—I still do," he said. "I wanted her to be mine. I didn't want to be alone anymore. I wanted someone to love. It's all harder than I thought. I used to know how to be alone, but now . . ."

"Wanting someone in your life doesn't make you selfish." Leon ran a hand through his thinning hair. "You could start a family of your own. Elisabeth isn't the only one you came to love."

"Sadie didn't love me back. She left, and it was her choice." He turned toward the window and watched the creek ripple by. He'd first seen her there, a streak of white in the morning hours. Everything had started there. "I'm glad I came back."

Otis turned away—he'd made up his mind. He would sell up here, go farther west, and start over. Purchase a little piece of land in a part of the country full of men and women who worked hard to survive and didn't have time to care about the way a man looked. He had reservations, but it was time to begin again.

"We'll be sorry to see you go," Leon said.

"I'll write you." Otis couldn't look at his friend. There had been too much loss already. "I will. I'll write you."

Otis left Leon then. He had to. He called Wolf to his side and went outside, walking to the creek, where he sat at the edge of the water. Wolf ran past him and leaped from the bank into the creek. The dog splashed and barked, sending water high in the air and all over Otis, who watched without bothering to wipe the moisture from his brow. He was going to miss this place. He'd hated it for so long, but now he saw it all so differently. The emptiness that was coming already hurt and scared him. It hurt just thinking about this season of friendship and love ending. He wanted to hold on but didn't know how.

"Excuse me." Mildred's voice startled him. "Leon said you came out here."

"I needed some fresh air."

"Peter dropped off a letter for you," she said, handing it to him. "He said that he hoped you were doing well."

Otis's hand shook as he took the letter. For days now he'd wanted an explanation, or at the very least a goodbye from Sadie.

"Take your time," Mildred said. She patted his shoulder before walking away and leaving him with what could be the last words he ever read of Sadie's.

> Rule number ten: when a man is gone for a very long time, give him a proper welcome home.

He turned it over, but there was nothing else. A riddle, but what did it mean? "Leon!" he shouted, surprised by the intensity in his own voice. He left the calming waters and stormed through the house. "Leon!"

"Leon . . . had to . . . go to . . ." Mildred panted as she followed after him.

"Where is Leon?" he asked, hoping to speed up her thinking. "He was just here."

"Yes, he was . . . He went . . . he went to the see the lawyer." Mildred smiled as though it was a great victory to have remembered. "He'll be back soon."

"He went to see the lawyer?" Otis scratched his forehead. "Why?"

"Umm . . . he didn't say. Come on down to the kitchen. I've made you beef stew with no carrots because I know you don't like them. Let me feed you while I still can."

Something wasn't right, but he complied, following Mildred to the kitchen just like he had when he was a little boy.

"Rule number ten: when a man is gone for a very long time, give him a proper welcome home."

What did it mean? He stirred his stew without eating a single bite, too distracted to eat.

"I guess I'm not hungry," he said when she narrowed her eyes at him. He stood up, too restless to sit.

"Oh no you don't." She hurried over and gave his shoulder a nudge. "No skipping meals on my watch."

For two hours he sat at the table, barely eating but unable to leave. Mildred struck up conversation anytime he thought their kitchen rendezvous was coming to an end. He had nowhere to go, and so he stayed, doing his best to cherish this time with his beloved housekeeper.

Leon returned, interrupting Mildred's reminiscing about his mother's favorite recipes.

"What did the lawyer want?" Otis asked.

"Lawyer?"

Mildred gave him a look.

"Ah, the lawyer. Nothing to concern yourself with. But you best come with me. I've something else that needs your attention."

"I'm coming too. Wait for me." Mildred untied the knot in her apron.

The three of them, with Wolf at their sides, headed out the door. When he asked where they were going, they said it was easier to show him than to tell him, so he followed. They took the well-worn path from the house to the old factory.

He expected to walk by, but they stopped at the door. Leon pushed it open and motioned for him to follow. Otis stalled, unsure he wanted to enter the factory and its plethora of memories.

"Come on," Mildred said.

He nodded. He hadn't planned on saying goodbye to his homemade rink right now, but there was no reason to wait. Standing tall, he braced himself for memories of Sadie.

"I'm coming." One more deep breath, and then he stepped over the threshold.

"Welcome home!" Shouts from every direction stunned him. What was happening? A mob of people stood in his factory, smiling and shouting welcoming words. He looked behind him, but there was no one there. They were smiling and shouting at *him*. Their faces blurred together. He blinked, still trying to understand.

Finally, his vision cleared. He spied his old childhood chums with their families beside them; Violette, Molly, and Flora; Dr. Henry; Elmer Hoag; and a woman who, if memory served, had taught him in school. New faces, old faces. All smiling faces. Slowly he brought a hand to his forehead as he stared at the crowd.

This was for him. He took slow breaths, attempting to stay calm. He failed. The sight was so beautiful, it unnerved him. And then he saw her. There was Bessy. Beautiful, perfect Bessy.

She stood on the far side of the room with Peter and Nina, wearing a yellow dress. She waved at him. He grinned and waved back. A vise tightened around his heart, squeezing tighter and tighter. And then out of nowhere Sadie was there, and the vise constricted so much, he thought his heart might burst.

"Rule ten—"

"A proper welcome." He choked on his words. "I thought you were gone. I thought I would never see you again."

"Gone?" She tilted her head, questioning him. "I left you a note. You never came. I thought you—"

"What note?"

"I put it on the piano. I knew you'd find it there. I explained—"

"Gah!" He could kick himself. For the first time in his adult life, he'd avoided the music room, afraid to face the many memories he'd shared with her within its walls. "I should have known." Pivoting, he turned toward the door, ready to go and find it, but she stopped him.

"Look around," she said. "All these people want to be with you. Enjoy it."

"It's . . . it's remarkable," he said. And he meant it. No western sunset could ever trump this view.

She grabbed his hand and pulled him into the crowd. "Come with me. I want everyone to know you the way I do." She reached up and put her hand on the brim of his hat. "May I?"

"If I'm to settle back into Monticello, I'd best remember my manners." He nodded toward the crowd, then took off his hat. Some eyes lingered, but no one scowled, no one ran, and the smiles of homecoming did not leave their faces.

"Alta chose not to come," Sadie said with a wink.

"I read your letter to the editor. She is probably hiding under a rock somewhere." He laughed, the vise gone, replaced by an embrace. "I can't imagine a finer welcome home. Thank you, Jane Squatter, for coming into my life."

"Thank you, Mr. Rochester, for not sending me away."

Others came closer, and the private conversation became a shared one before it was complete. Guests began eating food off tables that lined the walls, and the band from Dr. Henry's began playing. Children and a few couples danced, and soon others joined in. The atmosphere was jovial. Otis partnered with Violette, Molly, and Flora, with Mildred and a woman named Catherine. He'd never felt so wanted. When at last his turn came to take Sadie in his arms, he bowed and held out his hand. "May I?"

She took his hand and let him pull her close.

"How did you do this?" he asked when she was close enough that he could smell the familiar scent of rose water.

"I have sisters." She melted into his arms, fitting beside him perfectly. "We put our heads together and came up with a plan. It's what West women do."

"There is nothing as fine as a West woman." His cheek brushed hers as he whispered into her ear. "Don't tell your sisters, but you're my favorite West woman."

"Ah." She tipped her head up and smiled. "That is fitting, because you are my favorite Taylor."

He tightened his arm around her as they swayed to the music. In low voices they shared what had transpired since they'd last seen each other. After telling her about his plan to move, he said, "I don't feel as keen on leaving as I did before."

"Monticello needs you," she said matter-of-factly. "What will you do with the factory?"

"Perhaps it should become a button factory. My mother would like that and"—he looked around until he spotted Peter—"I could see if Peter wanted a job here."

She pursed her lips. "It's perfect."

"Will you skate with me, at least once more, before then?"

"Only if you promise to follow all the rules."

"I promise."

She bit her lip. "I may think up a few more."

"Whatever they are, I'll follow them."

He may have promised a great many other things if Bessy hadn't come near them and tugged on his pant leg, interrupting their dance. He smiled down at her. A ripple of pain and sadness swept over him, but he didn't let it show, because stronger than the pain was his love for Bessy. It would take time to grieve what might have been, but beside the grief was happiness. Somehow, pain and joy were walking side by side. He did not understand it, but he felt it.

"Mama says you're my uncle." She fidgeted with the end of her golden braid.

"Yes, and do you know what that means?"

She nodded. "It means you can play marbles with me and that I can like you, and I do."

"It does mean that." He reached out his hands. "It also means that if you are willing, we can dance together."

She stepped into his arms and let him pick her up. More joy, more pain. He smiled at Bessy—she was worth every emotion. Sadie sniffled, her eyes filled with shining tears. He pulled her closer, too, and the three swayed to the music. Every time thoughts of what might have been tried to sneak in, he pushed them away and embraced what he held in his arms—a niece and the woman he loved. "Well Bessy-girl, it also means that if you come to see me, I can give you bags of penny candy and rides on my rocking horse. And we can go to the soda fountain anytime you like."

Bessy grinned, and then she surprised him by wrapping her arms tightly around his neck and declaring in a delightfully charming voice that she liked having an uncle.

Chapter 32

Mildred and Leon convinced the West sisters to stay the night after the welcome home party. Peter made it possible by promising to take care of their animals until they returned. With all the guests gone and the three younger Wests visiting with Mildred, Otis took Sadie's hand and led her to the music room.

"I have a note to read," he said. "Want to read it with me?"

"I'll blush." When she'd written it, she imagined him reading it to himself, not aloud in her presence. But she'd been away so many days that she wanted nothing more than to be by his side, so she followed.

"Ah, there it is." He picked it up and held it to his heart.

"It's right where I left it."

He made a great show of opening it, and then he read it aloud. First he read her words about needing to leave to tell Nina and Peter about Bessy. She apologized for her dishonesty and vowed to trust him and others with the truth from then on. Then she wrote of her decision to return home because she was not sure if it was best for her to be at the mansion while he got settled with Bessy, which of course was no longer relevant. She told him to send word if and when he was ready for her to return to the mansion.

> . . . When I first came to Monticello, I dreamed of my little farm and my family. I wanted to go home. I thought about it all the time. But now, though I will always have a fondness for the blowing wheat fields of my childhood, I feel at home here in your presence and in this house.
>
> Ours has been an unusual path riddled with ups and downs, turns and ruts. But it brought us together, and like a traveler on a long road, I opened my eyes and realized the view was worth it. If you can find it in your heart to forgive me for keeping Bessy's whereabouts to myself, come and tell me so. Take my hand and let us keep walking together. With you beside me I believe there is no mountain we cannot climb.
>
> I should wait and tell you in person, but I don't want to leave without you knowing how I feel. I care for you like I have never cared for anyone before.
>
> Yours,
> Sadie West

"You do know what this is, don't you?" Otis smirked playfully.

"It's a letter that you should have read days ago. You kept me waiting, looking at the horizon for you."

He winced. "I'm so sorry. But this letter is more than that."

She waited.

"This, Sadie West, is a love letter."

"Where does it say love?" She matched his playful tone.

"So you're saying it's not a love letter?" He frowned. "I had hoped . . ."

"You're a tease. And I suppose I am too. It is a love letter." She fell into his blue eyes. "It is the first love letter I have ever written."

He took her hand, his thumb crawling over the ridges of her knuckles. "If I had paper, I would write one in return."

"What would it say?" Her voice was airy and hopeful.

"Dear Sadie." He paused, and she swallowed. His lips brushed her cheek. "You fill my thoughts." He kissed her other cheek. "You fill my heart." He kissed the tip of her nose. "You make me believe in love." He kissed her forehead, and his lips lingered against her skin, sending warmth and happiness in every direction. "You remind me what goodness is." His lips grazed her jaw. "Sadie, there is nothing to forgive. I know your heart, and now I want to tell you what is in mine." He pulled back just enough so they could look in each other's eyes. "I love you."

"Rule number eleven: after confessing love, kiss."

He followed her command. His lips found hers. Their time apart, the questions between them, and the struggles they faced all came together in a great crescendo. When their lips parted, he mumbled, "Sincerely, Otis."

"Sincerely?" She raised a brow.

"That won't do, will it?" He paused. "How does 'Forever, Otis' suit you?"

"Do you mean it?"

"If you'll have me, I'll be yours this very day."

She grinned, tightening her arms around his shoulders, and let out a shriek of delight. "Yes, I'll have you."

He lifted her into the air and whooped. He was finally home.

Epilogue

SIX YEARS LATER

Otis sat on a narrow wood bench in the waiting room of the local hospital. His foot tapped impatiently as he awaited word that Sadie and his third child were safe and well. The doctor had declared Sadie built for childbirth upon the arrival of their first, a son, who had come screaming into the world after only two hours of pains. Their second child, a daughter, proved herself naturally competitive and entered the world only an hour after labor began.

This time was different. Mildred had fetched him from the button factory four hours ago, telling him that it was time. He'd rushed to his wife's side and hurried her to the hospital. With each tick of the clock, his fears grew.

"Don't fret," an older woman sitting in the same waiting room said, interrupting his worrying. "They all come in their own time. I had six myself. Most were fast, but I had one that wasn't quite ready to enter this big, scary world."

Otis nodded. He could understand a reluctance. His life since meeting Sadie had been mostly exquisite, the happiest he'd ever known or could even imagine. But there were still cruel looks and challenges. A newspaper from up north had even published a story, trying to sell papers by telling the world that the famed composer Otis Taylor was a ghastly sight. Sadie had torn it to bits. Her scrunched-up nose and furrowed brow, so full of indignation, softened the blow. She'd promised to stand by his side on their wedding day, and she'd never wavered.

He tipped his head back and closed his eyes. Was she in pain? *Dear God*, he pleaded, *be with her.* He rubbed his chest, but the tightness remained. Childbirth was miraculous, but he would never enjoy these long moments of fear. If only he could be by her side.

"First child?" the woman asked.

"No," he said. "Third. We've a little boy, Leon. And we have a girl. She's not yet two."

"What's her name?"

"Jane."

Mildred was watching the children. They'd been reading books together when he left, happy and carefree. Someday they'd love reading Sadie's stories about Daphne and Mr. Darling. He smiled. Sadie would have to weave children into Daphne's storyline.

"Lovely names."

"Thank you."

The door opened. Otis held his breath.

"Mr. Taylor." The man spoke slowly, and Otis's heart beat faster. "I'd like a private moment with you."

A private moment? Why?

He was supposed to follow. But he couldn't move. Every worry, every fear, every heartache—they assaulted him. He couldn't lose Sadie. The look in the doctor's eyes, his tense expression, told

Otis that something was wrong. Where was the smile? The congratulations?

The older woman stepped near him. She put a hand on his arm. "Go on. It's always better to know."

"Yes . . . yes." He staggered to his feet and followed the man into the hall. They were alone there. Whatever wretched news he had, it was in this barren hallway that Otis would hear it. His life would change in this sterile, sad place. "What happened? My wife . . . is she . . ."

"Your wife is tired, but she will be fine."

Otis's legs went wobbly. He braced himself with the wall. Sadie was fine, she was safe. Oh dear. It hit him. "And the baby?"

"The baby is healthy . . ."

"What aren't you telling me?"

"Your son has a birthmark. A large one that covers a fourth of his face—"

"But he's healthy? He's well?" The onslaught of feelings came too quickly. He couldn't keep up. Relief. Worry. Joy. Confusion. "A mark? I don't understand."

"These types of marks don't affect the child's intellect or physical growth. They do, however, cause eyebrows to raise. And there's folklore around them. Some believe they're a reflection of the mother's state of mind during her pregnancy. The medical field does not adhere to such a belief, but that does not negate the difficulties it could present for him." He paused, his eyes full of concern. "I wanted you to know before you saw him."

"May I see him now?"

"Yes, if you're ready. Follow me."

The doctor led him to the nursery, where four tiny babies were swaddled and sleeping in cradles.

Otis stepped away from the doctor, ready to meet his son. He glanced at each baby, and then he saw him at the end of the row, eyes closed, asleep. He moved closer, and for a long moment he simply watched as the new child's chest rose and fell. With the tips of his fingers, he brushed his hands across the discolored skin.

"Hello, there," he whispered, his first words to his son. "Don't be afraid." Tears of joy and remembrance and love raced down his cheeks. "Don't ever be afraid. I'll be with you."

The baby's eyes fluttered open. Taylor eyes. Love, as strong as it had been when his other children were born, filled him now. He took his son in his arms, cradled him against his chest, and then kissed the babe's button nose, his forehead, his cheek. Otis turned back toward the doctor. "Can I take him in to see my wife?"

"Son," the doctor said, "I've seen a lot of babies come into this world." The man's voice cracked. "Well done."

Sadie propped herself up in the hospital bed the moment the door opened. He studied her from the door, assuring himself that she was indeed well. Her hair glistened with sweat, and her eyes looked tired, but she was smiling at him.

"I was worried," he said.

"Don't be," she said and then held out her arms. "They took him so quickly that I haven't really seen him. Will you bring him to me?"

"Come on, little one. The General wants you," he said to the baby.

Three long strides later and he was on the edge of the bed beside her. Into her arms he put their son. She pushed the blanket back so she could see him. And then just like she'd done with their other babies, she touched his nose, his ears, his soft head.

She cooed at him as she stroked his tiny hands and counted his toes.

"He's so handsome," she said after becoming acquainted with him. "What do you think of the name Alexander?"

"He is a little darling." Otis put a hand on his son's back. "It'll be hard for him. You know that, don't you?"

"He'll have us, and you'll show him how to be his own kind of normal." She bent and kissed the baby's cheek. And then she reached for Otis's hand and held it. "You're not your father. I've always known it, but right now I can see it. You look at this baby with so much love. I am not worried about him, because he has you."

He leaned closer, his head touching hers, the baby between them. She kept talking, soothing old injuries he had believed long healed. "Otis Taylor, I've never loved you more."

Author's Note

I have yet to write a book that isn't at least a little bit personal. This book is fiction, but pieces of myself and my experience are woven into it.

Here are a couple of things from my life and experiences that made it into *Beyond Ivy Walls*:

One of my sons had a small patch of alopecia that, in his case, went away after a few months. It was there long enough that I read up on it, and along the way, I learned of old superstitions surrounding the condition and about some of the "cures" that were tried many years ago. I was able to pull from both fact and fiction as I wrote this part of the story.

Another personal tidbit is that I grew up with three sisters (and a brother too), so I loved the idea of Sadie having sisters to whisper with, rely on, and care about. I have always known my siblings would be there for me if I were in need, just like Sadie tries to be there for her family. I enjoyed writing about a loving, functional family that supported one another. That is what I grew up with and what I am doing my best to raise.

The most personal aspect of this story is the quest to find Elisabeth and Otis's decision at the end. I haven't experienced anything exactly like their situation, but having been a foster parent for several years, I have witnessed (and lived through) a lot of different scenarios involving children in need. I have seen beautiful reunifications, adoptions, and family members who have stepped up. I have seen and lived through some incredibly painful experiences as well, which have left permanent scars on my heart. And I have come to believe there is not one outcome that is right every time, for every case. However, no matter the case, I believe the child should always come first, even if that is painful for the adults. If you have read my other books, you know that some of them feature children who are taken in for different reasons, or "rescued," for lack of a better word, and I have loved writing those stories. In this book I chose to explore a different "right" way to love a child. I hope it touched your life as much as it did mine. There is something truly noble about sacrificial love, and I wanted to explore, showcase, and honor that.

Researching this book was a unique experience. I discovered Hoag Feather Duster Company while searching for a potential setting. I had written several books set in Iowa, but only in rural settings, so I was specifically researching cities and factories. A feather duster factory felt fresh and new. I had certainly never read a novel set in such a factory. But I didn't know enough about it. I went to the Monticello, Iowa, library website and found the old newspaper archives, where I read about skating rinks, miracle cures, and small-town trivia (much of this reading prepared me for the story that would come). It was delightful! But I still had questions, so I messaged the library. Rather than point me to a book, they connected me with descendants of the Hoag factory owners. Thank you, Cathy Hershberger and Jan Hoag, for answering my questions, reading an early draft, and sharing your family legacy with me. I hope this book brings a smile to your faces and helps you remember your ancestors.

I would also like to thank other early readers: Joanna, Heidi, Leah, Stephanie, Amy, Karen, and Janet. I could not have completed this one without you. You not only gave me thoughtful feedback but also made this isolated job a social event.

Another big thanks goes to Lesley Sabga, my agent, for believing in this story and in me. Your upbeat personality is encouraging. I am always excited to chat with you, and I consider you not just an agent but a friend.

Laura Wheeler, you took this raw manuscript and saw its potential. I love getting my editorial letter from you because I know it will contain the pieces I need to put a beautiful story out there. Plus, working together is fun!

Whitney Bak, you know I am grammatically challenged, but that doesn't stop you from taking on the challenge. I so appreciate you!

The team at HarperCollins, thank you for putting so much of yourself behind my books. I love knowing that I have a small army championing my books.

This note is getting long, so sorry, but real quick, I have to thank my family for putting up with me and loving me even when I am sleep-deprived. You're my favorite people in the entire world.

And of course, thank you, dear readers, for picking up this book. I fell in love with Otis and Sadie as I wrote this book, and I hope you did too. Thank you for joining me on their journey to each other, and for joining me on my writing journey. Please keep in touch on social media and through my newsletter, or even send a message. Stories connect us, and I love that!

Happy reading,
Rachel Fordham

Discussion Questions

1. Sadie chooses to live in the abandoned building rather than tell her family the truth about her circumstances. Is she justified in doing so? Have you ever made a drastic decision to protect someone else?

2. Dark memories surround Otis when he returns to Monticello. Would it have been better for him to stay away?

3. Otis discovers his brother left behind a child. What do you think drove his desire to find her?

4. Sadie loves to write and uses fiction to help her get through some of her difficult times. What outlets have you used to get through your struggles?

5. Leon and Mildred prove loyal throughout the story. What do you think causes them to see past Otis's exterior?

6. Alta is self-serving throughout the book. Why do you think she views herself as superior to others?

7. Otis and Sadie experience several ups and downs in their relationship but are always quick to come back together. What pulls them back and prompts them to forgive?

8. The motif of scars (both internal and external) frequents this book. How does Otis find healing and acceptance?

9. Sadie comments that Otis is a "different kind of normal." How did her words help him heal? Have you ever had to accept something different about yourself or others?

10. Otis makes a difficult choice regarding Elisabeth. Do you agree with his decision?

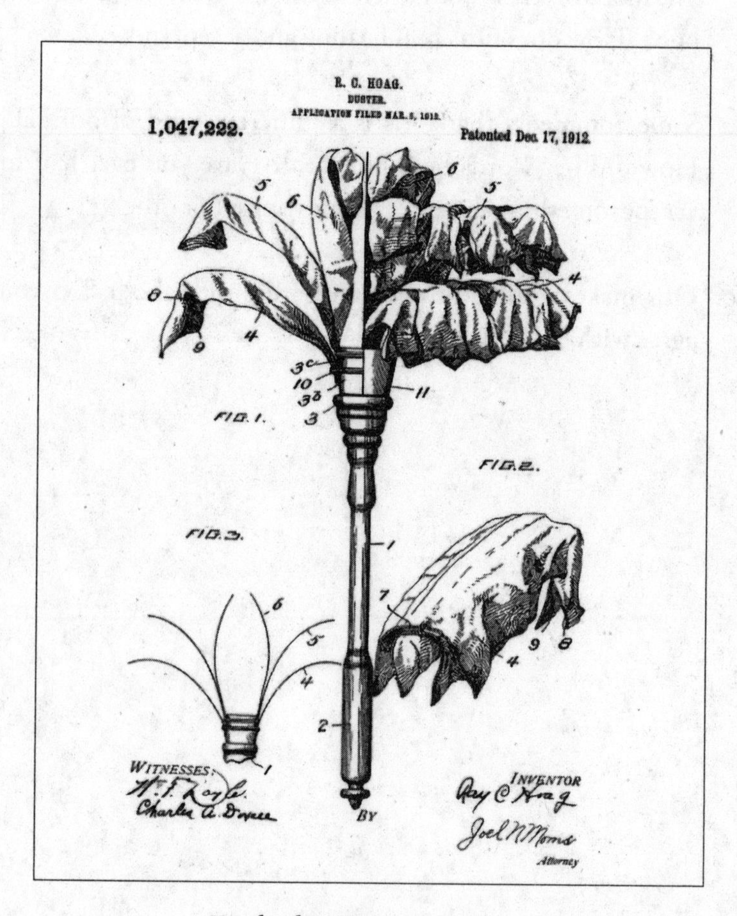

Featherless Duster, circa 1912

Hoag Duster Factory, circa 1917

About the Author

RACHEL FORDHAM is the author of *The Letter Tree*, *Where the Road Bends*, *A Lady in Attendance*, *A Life Once Dreamed*, *The Hope of Azure Springs*, and *Yours Truly, Thomas*. Fans expect stories with heart and she delivers, diving deep into the human experience and tugging at readers' emotions. She loves connecting with people, traveling to new places, and daydreaming about future projects that will have sigh-worthy endings and memorable characters. She is a busy mom, raising both biological and foster children (a cause she feels passionate about). She lives with her husband and children on an island in the state of Washington.

Learn more at rachelfordham.com
Instagram: @rachel_fordham
Facebook: @rachelfordhamfans